BAR   MAY 2 9 2014

Miss Chartley's Guided Tour

Marian's Christmas Wish

Mrs. McVinnie's London Season

Libby's London Merchant

Miss Grimsley's Oxford Career

Miss Billings Treads t⸍ Boards

Mrs. Drew Pla⸍   d

Reformir

Miss

⸍s Her Mind

⸍ood Turn

⸍₁⸍ Wedding Journey

Here's to the Ladies: Stories of the Frontier Army

Beau Crusoe

Marrying the Captain

The Surgeon's Lady

Marrying the Royal Marine

The Admiral's Penniless Bride

Safe

Passage

a novel

CARLA
KELLY

BONNEVILLE BOOKS
AN IMPRINT OF CEDAR FORT, INC.
SPRINGVILLE, UTAH

ISBN 13: 978-1-59955-896-7

Published by Bonneville Books, an imprint of Cedar Fort, Inc.
2373 W. 700 S., Springville, UT, 84663
Distributed by Cedar Fort, Inc., www.cedarfort.com

LIBRARY OF CONGRESS CATALOGING-IN-PUBLICATION DATA

Kelly, Carla.
Safe passage / Carla Kelly.
    pages cm
"Distributed by Cedar Fort, Inc."
ISBN 978-1-59955-896-7 (acid-free paper)
I. Title.
PS3561.E3928S24 2013
813'.54--dc23
                                    2013010599

Cover design by Angela D. Olsen
Cover design © 2013 by Lyle Mortimer
Edited and typeset by Melissa J. Caldwell

Printed in the United States of America

10   9   8   7   6   5   4   3   2   1

To Vondell Temple, my swimming buddy,
who doesn't mind listening to story ideas

If you want to go fast, go alone.
If you want to go far, go together.

African Proverb

PROLOGUE

ADDIE HANCOCK STOOD back from the lace curtains so no one could see her. Rain drizzled down the glass, obscuring her favorite view of the Sierra Madres. From habit, she touched the space on her ring finger where her wedding ring used to be, turning an imaginary ring around and around.

It would have been the work of a minute to go downstairs to the dining room, get on her hands and knees, and feel under the claw-foot china cabinet until she found the ring she had flung at her husband two years ago. She never was much good at throwing things and he knew it, so he hadn't even sidestepped when she yanked the ring off her finger and chucked it at him. He had just stared at her, stunned.

The ring had struck the lower drawer where Grandma Sada kept her tablecloths, bounced once, then rolled under the china cabinet because the floor tilted there. She knew the ring was still there, because they had both been too proud to retrieve it.

To put a finer point on the matter, Ammon couldn't have easily gone to his knees for the ring he had saved for months to buy in El Paso. She never asked him what

1

it cost, but she knew it was expensive. Papa said it was, and Papa had an eye for money.

Ammon was on crutches then, his leg broken in a logging accident that must have happened about the same time as her miscarriage. It had laid him up, and so he told her, when he finally found her at Grandma Sada's house in Colonia García. He had clumped into the house calling her name, relief on his face to see her mingled with his obvious pain.

"My leg's hurting so bad, Addie," he had said, leaning against the dining room table as she just stared at him, her own face tight and stony. "I went home first, hoping I'd find you there. Hungry too. I need something to eat."

Stung by that memory, Addie turned away from the window, but that only fixed her glance on the mirror, and she didn't like to look at herself. She faced the rain again, still twisting the imaginary ring. *Why was I so stupid?* she asked herself for the thousandth time. He truly hadn't known.

She closed her eyes, reliving the moment when she raged at him for not coming to her side at once when he learned about the miscarriage. She, ordinarily so quiet and calm—Thomas Finch's model daughter—had berated her husband for his absence, never once thinking that he hadn't heard the sad news. She had ripped him up one side and down the other while he stared at her, his mouth open, his tanned face going whiter and whiter. If she had slashed him open, peeled back his skin, and dumped salt under it, he couldn't have looked any worse.

Why couldn't she have accepted his astonishment for what it was? He had no idea what had happened to her during his three-week freighting trip to Pearson and the lumber camp. He had no knowledge of her pain.

Their pain. And when he just looked down at the floor, Addie had thought it was shame at his reprehensible behavior. She knew how much that lumber contract meant to him, to them, just starting out. It had never occurred to her until much, much later that he hurt too at the unexpected news flung at him.

"Am, I wish you had said something," she told the lace curtains. Even as she said it two years after the fact, she knew she had never given him a chance to speak. Her rage had overpowered her, she who never got angry or even raised her voice. She had never dealt with such loss before, and in her agony, she compounded it.

If only she had called him back or followed him out of Grandma's house. He had stumped away so awkwardly on his crutches, so it wouldn't have been difficult to stop him or just keep up with him. She had let him walk from her life, his head still down. She had flayed him alive. Barely breathing, she had watched him swing himself onto the wagon seat, scrabbling with his hands to keep his hold even as his crutches slipped out of his grasp.

A *paisano* hoeing weeds around Brother Thayn's corn had hurried across the lane to put her husband's crutches on the wagon seat. Addie still remembered the man's eyes so big with concern and his own darting, fearful glance at her house. Had she shouted loud enough for a common laborer to hear her?

Addie rubbed her arms and watched the rain fall, looking down that same lane her husband had traveled two years ago. She wanted to skip what happened next, gloss it over, and pretend Ammon Hancock hadn't really halted his team at the end of the lane, looked at the sky, and wailed.

The sound still rang in her ears. Once, she had heard Mexicans wail like that, when she was a little girl passing a graveyard. Mama called it keening and clapped her hands over Addie's ears against the awful sound, half-way between a murmur and a low note held too long. The Hancocks had always been closer to their Mexican neighbors than most of the colonists. Ammon said he had heard keening during that spring years ago when so many children died of diphtheria. He had talked about it once, and she had shushed him, saying something idi-otic about "Mexicans and their drama."

When he stared at the sky and keened his own sorrow, she had dropped to her knees in anguish. It had not occurred to her that he would feel as bad as she did about her terrible news. Maybe he really *hadn't* heard, even though Papa said he had sent a telegram to Pearson. Maybe she was wrong.

"If only I had gone to you," she whispered to the curtain. "If I had gone to you, you would have returned." She looked at the empty lane again. "Maybe you would have returned."

If. If. *If I had stayed here in García, maybe we could have patched it up*, she thought. *If Papa and Mama hadn't hurried me out of the colony and up to Provo, maybe we could have talked.*

With each day, week, and month that passed, reconciliation—always a shy guest at any gathering—had withdrawn, rebuffed. Papa had told her over and over that the Hancocks were a ramshackle bunch, and she had started to believe him. Reconciliation required a heart willing to listen and knees willing to bend and pull a ring out from under a china cabinet. Why was it that pride had no difficulty shouldering into that same gathering? One push and it sent reconciliation sprawling.

Why had she been so heartless to rip up every letter he sent her, stick it in an envelope, and mail it back to Pearson, where he had moved after his leg mended? She did that cruel thing every week for a year. Finally his letters dribbled down to every other week, then one a month, and then nothing.

Funny how even the revolution going on around them had not really penetrated until the letters stopped. *Was I that self-centered?* she asked herself and knew the answer.

Only last week, when Papa came to visit his ailing mother-in-law and complain about the rebel armies and the *federales* who looted the colonies with equal impunity, Papa had pounded his hand on the dining room table. His face red, he had declared to her mother, "I regret that we ever came to this horrible country. I've lost horses, cattle, hay, and everything except . . . except my suspenders! We're leaving."

And so they left, putting their ranch outside of Colonia Juárez in the hands of caretakers. Maybe life would get better, Papa reasoned, when one faction or the

5

other grew strong enough to hang onto power in Mexico City and leave the Mormons alone.

The only fly in Thomas Finch's ointment had been his mother-in-law's sudden turn for the worse (after years of turning for the worse, he had fumed to his wife), and her unwillingness to leave her home in Colonia García with its fine furniture.

The old lady had proved to be unusually insistent, and truth to tell, Papa had lost interest in her plight in his eagerness to get away. He was like that, Addie knew. She didn't doubt that he was already planning his next venture in a locale far removed from Mexico. She wasn't surprised when he approached her one night, turned on that charm he typically reserved for possible business partners, and wheedled her into staying with Grandmother Sada Storrs.

She saw through his unctuous sincerity this time, berating herself for not noticing it sooner. She listened to his blandishments, his assurance that she would be safe because the other colonists would watch out for her and Grandma, and wondered why she had ever believed a word he had said.

She agreed to stay behind, not so much because he convinced her that all was certainly well in Zion, but because she was suddenly ashamed of her father. All she wanted him to do was leave.

He did, along with Mama and her two little sisters. Mama had cried, but Papa hadn't looked back once. As she watched them go, Addie realized that everyone she had ever cared about had disappeared down that lane that she knew led eventually to Colonia Juárez, then to the Mexico North Western Railway in Pearson, and the border two hundred miles away.

The whole affair turned her even more quiet than usual, until Grandma Sada took her hand one night and held it tight, despite her growing frailty. "My dear Adaline, do you regret that you did not leave?" she asked, her voice so plaintive.

Addie shook her head, because she knew that was what Grandma needed. After her grandmother was asleep, she had gone to the window again.

"What I regret, Grandma, is that I did not stop my husband two years ago," she said softly. "Regret is the worst word I know, unless it's remorse."

ONE

THE MORMONS CROSSED the border at Dog Springs, in the brand-new state of New Mexico, the forty-seventh state in the union, which many of Ammon Hancock's *compadres* had left behind in 1885, before he was born.

If Pa had been there, he probably would have remarked that Ammon and his fellow priesthood bearers were a sorry lot, growling and snarling about leaving behind homes, crops, land, and cattle because they were good Mormons and listened to their leaders. Good thing Pa wasn't there, Am decided. He listened to his leaders better than Pa did.

As it was, their mile-long column of horses and wagons had to perform a little dance and wave their two white flags to avoid being shot by Negro troops stationed on the border to watch out for Mexican revolutionaries. There weren't any flies on the 9th Cavalry, though. As soon as the Buffalo Soldiers realized who they were looking at, their sergeant came out and waved them onto US soil.

Ammon grinned at the collective sigh that seemed to rise from the whole column of dusty, smelly, tired brethren. It had been a long two days, traveling across harsh country and avoiding all roads, because guerillas and *federales* alike were watching for fresh horses to steal, and the column had five hundred horses. It had been an even longer wait for the men from Colonia Dublán and Colonia Juárez, hiding out and waiting for the men from the mountain colonies to join them. Telephone lines and telegraph poles had been an early casualty of the revolution, working only now and then.

And here they were, back in the land of the brave and the home of the free. Ammon looked around, taking note of the riders like him who were born and raised in Mexico and maybe not even eligible for a welcome at all. *He* certainly didn't intend to call anyone's attention to his Mexican citizenship.

He had a larger concern; his backside ached from two days of sitting on the wagon seat of his freight wagon. The length of time was nothing new—his business was freighting—but he quickly noticed the difference between traveling so-so roads and no roads at all. He glanced behind at Blanco, tied to the back of his wagon and prancing along with lots of spirit left in his gait.

"What do you think, Ammon?" asked the man sitting on the seat beside him. The wagons had been reserved for provisions and men too old to fork a horse for the journey.

"Too hot to think, Brother Masters, but I guess I'm glad."

Hill Masters chuckled. "There's a bunch of men not so happy Bishop Bentley and President Romney said to bail out."

Ammon shrugged. "I follow my leaders. That's all. We'll go back when it's safe." He tried to straighten up and couldn't avoid a groan. "Looks like dinner off the mantelpiece for a couple of days."

"I think we left the mantelpiece behind, Am," the older man said. Then he turned away, as though the thought was too large to handle.

Ammon tugged his hat lower on his forehead. The mantelpiece and everything else. He couldn't help but think of Ma's piano. As they waited in line to file through the border crossing, Ammon remembered the look on his mother's face as she said good-bye to her piano. She ran her hand across the polished top. It was a real Steinway, freighted in from El Paso five years earlier with great difficulty—and considerable expense, Aunt Loisa delighted in chiding her. (Ammon had resisted the urge to remind his father's sister that he had freighted it for free.)

Pa was telling his mother to hurry up because they had miles of dangerous driving just to get down to the train at Pearson, if there even was a train that General Salazar's guerillas hadn't blown up or appropriated. Aunt Loisa was giving Ma that pinched look that usually moved things along, but darned if Ma didn't strip off her gloves, sit down, open the lid with a flourish, and play Beethoven's Sonatina in G. She took all the repeats, while Loisa fumed in the doorway and Ammon leaned against the piano, trying not to smile too big.

She played the last two chords louder than usual, raised her hands high off the keys like a concert pianist, and kept her foot on the pedal until the sound drifted away through the quiet rooms, empty of people now and already starting to look abandoned. He remembered it never took long. He knew that from closing up the little home he had built for Addie.

Ma closed the lid and locked it, wiping away imaginary dust with her handkerchief. She looked up at Ammon, her eyes liquid with unshed tears. "I've lived here twenty-seven years, son." She gave herself a little shake. "Stand up straight! Someone would think you'd never been taught!"

The rest of the Hancock children and cousins were in the wagon, and Pa had just settled his sister beside him on the seat. Loisa smoothed her skirts around her and smiled down at Ammon and his mother.

Ma smiled back and it was genuine. "It appears she left me the wagonbed with the kiddies," she whispered to him when Loisa looked away. "Good thing I like the kiddies."

Ammon followed his mother across the porch. He put his hand on her shoulder and felt her tremble. She pressed her lips tight together like she did in testimony meeting to keep from crying.

"You know where everything is. Better share that ham with the other García men before . . . before it disappears. You have clean socks in the laundry room. And if you have to leave . . ." She paused, unable to gulp back her tears, and Ammon tightened his grip on her shoulder. "Be sure to sweep out and lock the front door," she finished in a rush.

She bolted for the wagon, but Ammon grabbed her for a hug, lifting her off the ground. "Don't worry, Ma," he told her.

She clung to him. "If the house catches fire, don't forget to get the piano out."

It was a family joke, but no one laughed this time. His sisters and cousins in the wagon started to cry, from Junebug all the way up to Elise, who had put her hair up and her skirts down this year.

"Better go. You know how Aunt Loisa hates to wait."

She gave him another squeeze, straightened her hat, and let her son lift her into the back of the wagon. Ma took Junebug on her lap and whispered in her ear. Junebug waved to Ammon until they were out of sight down the road.

Nine days later, when the bishop got word for them to gather at the Stairs, a formation west of Colonia Juárez, Ammon swept out the rooms, locked the door, and pocketed the key.

Still waiting his turn to cross the border, he felt in his pocket for the key. Home was far away now, a too-small clapboard house that swayed in strong winds, crowded with Hancocks. Before he left Colonia García, he almost went into his own house but changed his mind. There was nothing in there he wanted to keep except a memory or two of Addie before things went so wrong, so fast. Maybe the rebels would make better use of the place.

One of the pleasures of his boyhood had been taking the train to the United States with Pa. Sometimes they bought cattle, or now and then there was a little Church business. As the years had passed and he became bilingual, the United States seemed more foreign to him. It had never been his home, so he had nothing to look forward to.

Once through the border crossing, Ammon looked around at his fellow travelers. Bishop Bentley was talking to a lieutenant who had ridden up, but everyone else looked glum and silent. Ammon sighed and faced south, wondering if the rebels had already rounded up and slaughtered the Hancock cattle, some of them his, some of them Pa's.

He had left them in a well-watered box canyon south of their land. The herd had been diminishing daily, the livestock roped and dragged away to slaughter. In the middle of night, he and Pa had trailed what remained of the herd ten miles south to that canyon, but it was probably just a matter of time before the guerillas or the *federales* found them.

The whole business was unfair, but that was revolution. The revolt against the increasingly oppressive regime of Porfirio Díaz had practically exploded in their laps. Chihuahua had been the first state to rise up and follow Francisco Madero in his bid to take over a tottering, corrupt government. Madero's control was not firm, and others rose against him as the revolutionaries did what factions tend to do and began devouring each other.

Advised from Church headquarters to maintain strict neutrality, the Mormons in the Mexican Colonies found themselves victimized by all sides. Cattle vanished to feed roving armies, and horses were fair game. There were days when everyone wondered just who the harvests of grain and fruit were feeding—their own families, the guerillas, or government troops.

The women and children were ordered out first,

packing what little they could and leaving the rest behind because there was neither room nor time. Pa had insisted on staying behind with the other García men in their mountain colony, but the bishop had insisted just as vigorously that he couldn't stay in the saddle long with his bad leg. Pa had protested all the way to the depot in Pearson, but he left on the train with his family, and then Ammon was all alone.

Ammon became expert at dodging roving bands of insurgents, traveling by night to Pearson to shut down his own freighting business and pack up ledgers and records. That was hard in a private way. Addie had kept his books, back when things were good between them. As he packed his ledgers, several notes fluttered out bearing the general theme of "I love you." He crumpled one and threw it away but saved the rest. He rode back to García in the dark, thoughtful.

He had maintained his philosophical frame of mind through the next week, when guerillas rode through García, taking potshots at chickens and looking around for horseflesh more lively than the worn-down animals they flogged. He held his breath when a few of the bolder rebels rode by the little house he had shared with Addie. To his relief, they didn't do more than glance at the half-burned house, unaware of the García horses tethered inside.

No more insurgents appeared after the latest bunch picked through a town already bare. One calm day followed another, which led to real anger when word came from Stake President Junius Romney for all the men in the colonies, from Díaz almost on the border to distant Chuichupa, to get out too. They obeyed their leaders.

So Ammon had saddled up Blanco and rode down the quiet main street with the other men. The quiet was so strange, so alien to the usual bustle of García. No smoke came from the chimneys. Family dogs moped about the gates and barnyards, sniffing for boys long gone. Ammon heard the Fowlers' canary trilling as they left García. The bird had been let out of its cage on the porch, and it sang from a tree.

He smiled at that, thinking of any number of sermons that could use that canary to symbolize the Colonies' Saints, singing a new song in another country, or maybe just Saints making the best out of what life dealt and singing anyway. Addie could have thought of other topics; she was good at that, he remembered.

Ammon had glanced down the tree-shaded side street to Grandma Sada's home before he turned toward the mountain road that would take longer than the usual road to Juárez but was safer. For the past two years, he had always looked down that street as he rode from García. Addie used to spend time at Grandma Sada's. She would watch for him and blow him a kiss as he let Blanco put on a little horse show for her benefit. It had been a long time since Addie Hancock had blown him a kiss.

Ammon thought about Addie that night at Alamo Seco, where the men had secured their horse herd, safe now from Mexican armies and under the watchful eye of the 9th Cavalry. The rain, long awaited in that dry land, had started before there was even time to cook dinner. Bishop Thurber blessed the cold bacon and hardtack, and they ate without much noticeable gratitude.

Hunched in a quilt someone had loaned him, Ammon gazed into the bare sticks of the washed-out campfire, wishing he hadn't left behind his little picture of his wife, taken in St. George on their wedding day four years ago. She wasn't the prettiest sister in the Finch family; that title went to Evangeline Finch, married now to a flabby banker in Logan, Utah. What had attracted him to Addie, back when he first saw her in Colonia Juárez at age fourteen, was her serenity and silence.

Although he loved his sisters and cousins, Ammon sometimes had found himself wanting peace and quiet, something in short supply in the Hancock house. It wasn't a longing he could put his finger on until he sat next to Adaline Finch during a youth meeting. A shy smile came first, followed by a brief introduction. After that, she had sat beside him in silence, a half-smile on her pleasant face, just *there*, which turned out to be enough, because he thought of her often after that. When she did speak, she made practical sense. Through the years, he admired her solicitude toward her Grandma Sada, who lived in García.

As the years passed, he even flattered himself that Addie—they had graduated from Adaline and Ammon to Addie and Am—seemed to spend most of the summer in García, staying with Grandma Sada. And Grandma never minded his presence on the porch swing when he was in town and not freighting lumber down to Pearson.

He couldn't have put a time or a date on the moment when he fell in love with Addie Finch. He knew Addie's parents weren't too pleased, but he also had noted that Thomas and Yvonne Finch focused more of their attention on their more beautiful daughter. After he passed his twenty-second birthday and his freighting business settled into respectable permanence, he took his courage in hand and drove the seven miles from Pearson to Juárez on a day when he knew Addie was in García.

His audience with Thomas Finch was brief. It worked in his favor that the Finches were just then in far headier negotiations with that banker in Logan, who had noticed Evangeline Finch at a cousin's house in Salt Lake City and decided only she would do. Ammon knew, even as he spoke, that his little business was just a cricket chirping on a hearth compared to the banker from Logan.

It was enough. Thomas grunted his consent, extracted a pledge from Ammon that he would take good care of his Adaline, and called it good.

Courage in hand, he had driven that night back to García and knocked on Grandma Sada's door after ten o'clock. A smile on her face, Sada had gestured for Addie to come to the parlor and left them alone. It was a moment's work to declare the love she already knew about and get a prompt yes. He was too practical to get an engagement ring, but she never mentioned it.

In November 1908, with other engaged couples and vigilant chaperones, they took the Honeymoon Trail from García, through Arizona to Washington County, Utah, where they were married in the St. George Temple for time and eternity. Loving Addie turned out to be even sweeter than he had imagined, and he had a good imagination.

Then it all fell apart through misunderstanding, and the wife he adored threw his wedding ring at him. Before he had turned awkwardly on his crutches and left Grandma Sada's dining room, he had watched her hands go to her empty belly in a futile gesture, because the child was gone. It broke his heart too.

I wish you had read even one of my letters, Addie, he thought now, as he knelt in the rain with the others for prayer. He prayed as he always did—silently, after other weightier issues had been broached before the Lord Almighty—for her heart to soften. He loved her still, but as he settled into an American mudhole and American rain poured down, he knew it was time to move on.

TWO

HE RAIN CONTINUED the next day as the men from the Colonies rode their horses toward Hachita, New Mexico. The rain still pelted them as they corralled their horses on a member's land and took the night train to El Paso, Texas, where their families waited.

Ammon was fifty cents shy for his ticket, so Bishop Thurber loaned it to him. He found a seat by the window and sat down with a flop that made the dust whoosh out of the cushion and rise in little clouds. He took his boots off, wishing again that he had brought along those extra socks Ma had mentioned three weeks ago.

The lady across the aisle looked at him with pointed disfavor, so he squished his feet back into his boots and just stared out the window until he fell asleep.

They arrived in El Paso just after sun-up. No one had any reason to hope that the families would be there to meet the train, but there they were, lined up on the platform, watching silently as the train pulled in before rushing forward.

Ammon craned his neck out the window, searching for his family. He couldn't help looking for Addie, but she wasn't there. He kept looking, and there were the

Hancocks. Relieved, he waved and was startled to see his father dabbing at his eyes. Eight-year-old Catherine was jumping up and down. His father carried Junebug, who clapped her hands when Catherine pointed him out. Elise and Joannie cried.

He waited his turn to get off, impatient, and then he was overwhelmed as he was engulfed by sisters and cousins.

Joannie hugged him and then backed off, wrinkling her nose. "Ammon, you're so dirty! What's Mother going to say?"

"It hardly matters," said Pa drily as he hugged Ammon, Junebug sandwiched between them. "She'll be too busy crying to notice how bad he stinks."

For all that she thought herself so grown up now, with longer skirts, Elise scrubbed at her eyes like a child, then hugged Ammon. "This is what happens when we leave him alone for a couple of weeks. He goes all to pieces. Ammon, I'm glad you're here."

"I am too," he told her, swallowing a boulder of homesickness for García and Mexico. He looked around, still hopeful for a glimpse of Addie. *At some point, I hope this stops hurting so bad*, he thought when she didn't materialize.

He smiled at his father, who had watched him look around.

"We haven't seen her," Pa said. He clapped his hand on Ammon's shoulder and gave him a little shake. He pointed to one of four US Army trucks, their engines idling. "Our chariot awaits."

Ammon helped his sisters into the truck, impressed

with their familiarity around engines and motors. The vehicle was a novelty to him. He clambered aboard, then took Junebug from his father while another man helped him in.

"Where're we going?" he asked, raising his voice to be heard above the engine. He grabbed for his Stetson when the truck started with a lurch.

"Just you wait, Ammon," was all his father said.

Only a few streets from the depot, the trucks stopped at Walter Long's lumberyard. Ammon jumped out to help his sisters. With a frown, he looked around. So this was home. His frown deepened to see families living in little stalls and cubicles where lumber had been removed. Washing was strung everywhere, and quilts were tacked up to offer some privacy.

"It's not so bad now, son. You should have seen things last week before some of the families left for Utah and Idaho." Pa chuckled. "We were all about as jam-packed in as those eccentric Hancocks back in García!"

His joke fell flat. Ammon stared at the laundry, the cooking fires, the lumber stalls, the blue-bottle flies already droning in the dusty air, which was starting to heat up. *These families own the nicest homes in Mexico and run the largest herds in Chihuahua*, he thought, shocked.

Ma stood in the entrance to one of the stalls, holding back a quilt with one hand and shading her eyes against the sunrise with the other. She spotted him and came across the yard toward him, walking at first and then running, her arms out.

Ammon picked her up and whirled her around. She hugged him and started to cry.

"Ma, I'm fine," he said softly.

"I'm just glad you're here," she replied, her voice just as soft. She nudged his arm with her head. "Even though you don't look so happy to be here."

"I'm not." He reached in his pocket and pulled out the front door key. "Here you are."

She took the key from him, turning it over and over in her hand as if she had never seen such a thing before. "Wasn't I the silly one? I'll probably never see that house again, and I worried so much about locking the front door."

Ammon laughed. "I did lock the front door, but we were almost down to Colonia Juárez before I remembered I left the back door unlocked."

His mother laughed too, and it was a genuine laugh. "For your information, I have no idea where that back door key is." She tucked her arm through his and pulled him toward the shade of the Hancock lumber stall. "It hardly matters, does it? You're here, and I'm content with that."

They ate breakfast together, all of them squashed tight. Ammon squatted Indian-style on the ground and his sisters perched on the lumber crowded into the back of the stall, which was arranged stair step fashion for seating. The food was army rations, the same as he had eaten yesterday when they crossed at Dog Springs, with the addition of canned salmon.

"Ammon, your mother and Aunt Loisa are so resourceful. We've only been here a few weeks and they've already devised umpteen ways to make salmon taste like . . . well, salmon."

Everyone laughed, including Junebug. After the silence of the ranch back in García, the sound of laughter made tears well up in Ammon's eyes. Ma must have noticed, so she passed around the salmon croquettes and fussed over her youngest daughter, who was scraping the mud off Ammon's pants with a table knife.

"I draw the line at salmon ice cream, however," she announced. "Wouldn't people wonder about us then?"

Ammon smiled at her, well aware of her effort to distract his sisters from their big brother's emotions, and he looked at his father. "You said something about people leaving. Where are they going?"

His father rubbed his chin. "Those that managed to get some money and valuables out have left for Utah, most of 'um to stay with relatives." He shrugged, and Ammon saw his embarrassment. "Our money's wrapped up in land and cattle, so we have to make do here, at least for a little while."

"Which reminds me," said Ma, her voice brisk now, as though she wanted to gloss over something else. "Father, you'd better hurry a bit or you'll be late for work."

"Dad, you got a job already?" Ammon asked. "Doing what?"

Pa's eyes were tired; maybe he knew better than to try to fool his son. "For the princely sum of five dollars a week, I clerk and box groceries in Medina's Mercado down the road. I get all the culled vegetables." He was silent a moment, then tentative. "It's a nice change from canned salmon, once you pick out the bad spots."

"Oh." Ammon couldn't think of anything to say.

He looked away, finding the quilt pattern hanging at the stall's entrance suddenly fascinating.

Elise cleared her throat. "Ma thinks I can find a job waiting tables in a café."

"And Bishop told me there's an opening for a maid in one of the downtown hotels," Joannie told him, also finding that quilt pattern fascinating.

Ammon looked from one sister to the other. His eyes filled up again, and he looked down at Junebug, leaning against him like she used to do at home.

"It's all right, Ammon," his mother said. "We're managing."

His father went outside to wash, and Ammon and his sisters were quiet, not looking at each other. His mother broke the silence.

"Ammon, I have a funny feeling that you didn't think to bring out another pair of jeans with you. All we have is your Sunday suit, and it's in the bottom of our one trunk now."

"I . . . I left my clothes in Pearson, because I'm planning to return soon," he said, which made his mother swallow and look away this time. "Ma, it's our country too."

"Is it?" she asked. "Then why are we here?"

He couldn't think of an answer, but he didn't think she expected one. He watched her a moment, relieved when she became the practical woman who had raised them all, maybe even Pa.

"Get him a quilt, Elise," she said, sounding like the sergeant at Dog Springs. "The rest of you, close your eyes. Drop 'um."

He did as he was told. He handed his grimy clothes to his mother and took the quilt that Elise offered to him, her eyes closed, but a grin on her face. He sat down cross-legged on someone's cot while Ma carried his clothes outside and dumped them in wash water.

The cot was too short to stretch out on, so he curled himself into a ball. His eyes grew heavy as he watched his sisters straighten up the stall. The flies droned as his eyes closed. Addie had told him once that he could sleep anywhere, and she was right. Before he slept, he did what he always did, and asked Heavenly Father to bless his wife. He decided he could be philosophical. If Addie had stayed with him, she'd be in a lumber stall right now. Maybe after a few months of more gentrified living in Utah, she would finally file for divorce.

"Time to move on," he muttered. He wasn't so sure he could provide anything fancier than a lumber stall, or at least that was how it looked to him as he drifted off.

"Wake up. I have to talk to you."

Ammon tensed. A man's hand on his shoulder brought him wide awake. He grabbed the hand that shook him and bent the fingers back until the man swore. Ammon opened his eyes, then sighed and closed them again, releasing his father-in-law's hand. *I can't do anything right with the Finches*, he thought, wondering if all husbands felt that way about in-laws.

Ammon opened his eyes again, hoping that Thomas Finch was a bad dream brought on by salmon croquettes. Nope. He was still there, rubbing his fingers.

"Sorry, Brother Finch. I'm not used to people grabbing me." He'd never tell a father-in-law how Addie used to grab him. The thought made Ammon smile a little. There was no returning smile. "What, uh, can I do for you?"

Ammon pointed toward the stacked lumber next to him as he swung himself into a sitting position and tried to keep the suddenly too-small quilt covering him. "Have a seat over there, sir."

Finch looked around with real distaste, sitting poker-stiff as always, but with his long legs stuck out at curious angles because he was too tall for the lumber seat. He looked like one of the blue herons that waded, stilt-like, on the pond behind the Hancock's house in García.

Finch was silent, staring at Ammon's bare feet sticking out from under the quilt, as if he had never seen toes before. Maybe he hadn't. Even Addie had joked about how formal her parents were.

They stared at each other. Ammon was reminded all over again how grateful he was that Addie didn't resemble her father. *Double dog dare you to look away first*, he thought.

To Ammon's satisfaction—he noticed his pleasures were getting smaller and smaller with each passing day—Thomas Finch looked away first.

"I don't know how to ask this."

"Then don't," Ammon said, ever practical. "We haven't really had much to say to each other."

"Where's Addie?"

"What do you mean?"

"I mean, where's Addie?" his father-in-law said again. "She was there in García, and she didn't come out with the women and children."

"You're serious?" Ammon said, fully awake now. "I never saw her there."

"Of course I'm serious! Who jokes about what I just asked? Maybe you don't know, but Yvonne and I were visiting in Logan when the order came to leave. Our other children were in Dublán, but Addie was keeping an eye on Grandma Sada." Finch stood up and walked the brief length of the lumber stall. "Where is she?"

"I have no idea," Ammon replied, keeping his voice neutral, even though goose bumps started to march up and down his back. "Addie and I haven't exchanged one word since she threw her wedding ring at me."

"She's your wife!"

"Not lately."

Finch shook his finger at Ammon, a gesture so impotent that Ammon wanted to laugh, even as his own uneasiness quickly crowded all humor out of his mind.

"You and your whole family are ramshackle ne'er-do-wells," Finch declared. "I don't know why we ever agreed to let you marry our little girl."

Maybe because you were so busy planning a better marriage for your show-pony daughter that you forgot the quiet one, Ammon thought but had the sense not to say it. "Well, you did agree, and it didn't work out, so what do you want from me now?"

Ammon winced inside after he said that, because it didn't seem much better. He hadn't meant to sound so hurt, but that whole dining room scene came back—Addie so pale and angry, him so stunned at her sad news. He wanted to get up and leave Finch standing there, but he couldn't think of a dignified exit from a lumber stall, wrapped in a quilt.

"I'm sorry you don't know where she is," Ammon said, his voice softer now, as he tried again to placate a man used to comfort, standing in a lumberyard. "My father said there are still a lot of refugees here and there in El Paso. I doubt Addie would stay in a lumberyard for long."

"She wouldn't have a choice, if you two were still together," Finch muttered.

I'll never be good enough, Ammon thought. He couldn't think of what to say. For all her quiet ways, Addie was much quicker with a comment, most of them funny. He remembered a few zingers, some of them at her own expense, because she didn't mind a joke. Too bad they couldn't weather a crisis.

Apparently Thomas Finch couldn't either, Ammon decided as he regarded his father-in-law. Funny what happens to some people, unused to difficulty, who find a problem they can't solve. He found himself looking at the other man with sympathy, something he wouldn't have thought possible two years ago.

"I'm sorry I didn't measure up," he said. "I'm sure you'll find Addie in a private room in El Paso, probably waiting for you. President Romney has a list—"

Finch grabbed Ammon by the quilt and gave it a shake, making Ammon grateful that his sisters and mother were in the next stall with Aunt Loisa. He struggled to hang onto the only thing between him and embarrassment. "Wait a minute, I'm—"

"You think I haven't already talked to Junius Romney and looked everywhere?" Finch raged. "I'd rather do almost anything than talk to you! I need your help!"

The words were nearly torn from his throat. He released his hold on the quilt and sat down. Mama came around the corner of the stall, her face stern.

"Brother Finch, my son still hurts over what happened. Maybe you'd better just state your business or go away."

Ammon stared at his mother, the anger leaving his heart as he watched her hands shake. She had never said boo to a goose in all the years he had known her, and here she was, standing up to one of the wealthiest men in the Colonies.

"It's all right, Ma."

"No, it isn't! Don't hurt my child, Brother Finch."

She said it quietly and simply. The angry lift to Finch's shoulders subsided. Suddenly he looked older.

"That's better," Mama said. "Let me get your clothes, Am. Brother Finch, you can stay here and watch him dress, or you can wait outside."

A muscle worked in Thomas Finch's cheek as he left the stall. He flung back the quilt that served as a door, almost as though he wanted to slam it hard. It was such a childish gesture that Mama couldn't help smiling. She left too, returning with Ammon's clothes folded neatly. "Here you go, son," she whispered.

Ammon took her by the arm. "Ma, I didn't know I needed a champion," he said. "I'm twenty-six."

"Everyone needs a champion, now and then," she said, then left him alone.

Ammon dressed quickly, tugging on his boots that someone had cleaned. He pulled back the quilt and gestured to his father-in-law. "We'll discuss whatever we have to discuss like civilized people. Come inside again, sir."

The fight had gone out of Thomas Finch. Ammon sat on the cot, waiting for him to speak. When he did, his voice was subdued.

"As you very well know, Yvonne's mother has been threatening to die for a few years."

Ammon knew *he* wouldn't have put it that way, but he also knew his father-in-law was not a subtle man. He just nodded.

"Addie has been in García all summer. You never saw her? Don't you go to church?"

Far from subtle, Ammon thought. *You're not going to rile me. Not this time.* "My freighting business is in Pearson," he explained, keeping his voice neutral. "I don't spend much time in García, and I go to church in Juárez." He looked his father-in-law in the eye. "I *know* you've seen me there."

While it could never be said that Thomas Finch wilted, the starch went out of his shoulders.

"All I can figure is that Grandma Sada actually took a turn for the worse, and Addie either couldn't move her or wouldn't leave her. She's still there; she has to be!"

"Heavens, I hope not," Ammon said. "I'm hoping you're really wrong and she's here in El Paso."

They were both silent.

30

"No one saw them in García?" Finch said, ending the long pause.

"No, or they would have come out with us, whether they wanted to or not. I never saw any smoke from Grandma Sada's chimney either." Ammon shook his head. "Maybe I never really thought about it."

That wasn't true. He thought about Addie all the time but assumed she was on the family ranch between Dublán and Juárez. He had almost gone over to Grandma Sada's house one evening after all the women and children left García, just to sit on the side porch, smell the honeysuckle, and remember better times with Addie. He had started down the side street, then changed his mind.

He looked up. Mama had come into the lumber stall, her eyes worried. She sat down on the lumber pile, Junebug on her lap, her arms tight around her youngest. Ammon knew just what she was thinking as she looked down at her own daughter, then at Thomas Finch. Then she looked at Ammon, and it was a look of calm resolve.

"Son?" was all she said.

He nodded, his mouth suddenly too dry for speech. The last thing in the world he wanted to do was return to García alone. On the train to El Paso, some of the García men had sat together and discussed how soon they could return, but even the most eager knew it depended on what their priesthood leaders told them.

"This can't wait until we get the go-ahead from President Romney," Ammon said.

"Of course it can't!" Finch snapped. "I'll pay you

one thousand dollars to find Addie and get her out of Mexico."

She's my wife. You don't owe me a penny, Ammon nearly said. He looked at his father-in-law, a man he didn't like and probably never would. He had discovered early in his marriage that people like Thomas Finch dealt in dollars and never in kindness. Thoughtfully, he appraised the man, knowing that Finch expected him to say, "You don't owe me a penny." *I believe I'll surprise you,* he thought. *Why not? It's been a pretty awful day so far.*

"Let's do this," Ammon said finally. "You pay my mother five hundred dollars in greenbacks before I even put my rump in the saddle and cross that border."

Ah, yes, Finch hadn't expected that, if the startled look on his face was any indication. He nodded, his eyes wary.

"If I die in Mexico, you pay my father another five hundred dollars."

Mama couldn't help her gasp. Ammon knew better than to look at her. It was one thing to think it, and another to say it.

"And if you get Adaline out and survive?" Finch asked.

"You pay that five hundred dollars to Addie. She can decide what to do with it," Ammon said. "If she wants to divorce me and start over somewhere else, that'll be enough money. If she has other plans . . ." He shrugged. "It'll be Addie's five hundred dollars, either way. Let's put it in writing."

"You don't trust my word?" Finch asked, the question a challenge.

"Nope."

"Oh, now, Ammon," Mama started.

He overrode his mother, not looking at her. "Brother Finch, tell me something: Did you *really* send a telegram to Pearson to tell me about Addie's miscarriage?"

Silence. Brother Finch looked away. "I think I forgot." He sounded sulky, like a boy caught at mischief.

"That's what I thought," Ammon said. He went to the quilt door. "Mama, get it in writing. I'm not coming back here until he's gone. I'm not even sure I ever want to see him again."

"It was just a miscar—" Finch began. He stopped when Ammon grabbed his chin and gave him a shake.

"Don't you even say anything like that to me, and for sure, not to your daughter," Ammon said, each word distinct. "I'll get her out of Mexico, but I'm not doing it for you. I'm probably not even doing it for Addie. This one's on me."

THREE

$\mathcal{A}$MMON LEFT THE lumberyard and walked toward the depot, needing to put distance between himself and Thomas Finch. He sat on a wooden bench inside the depot because it was cool there—at least, as cool as El Paso ever got in early September. With all his heart, he longed for the mountains they had left behind, where life had been hard, but peaceful, in those days before the long-overdue revolution began.

He thought of the time, years ago, that Mama had suffered a miscarriage. In that way of women, the Relief Society brought over casseroles and good cheer, comforting as best they could. Ammon remembered going to the barn where his father sat weeping. No one came to comfort him. Ammon remembered just sitting next to his father, their shoulders touching, because Pa never cried and Ammon was only twelve and didn't know what else to do.

Pa finally blew his nose and put his arm around him. "Son, for some reason, they don't think men need comfort."

Addie, that was my child too, he thought, leaning back. After Addie threw his ring at him, he had mourned by moving permanently to Pearson. He added a room onto his stable and cried there in peace and quiet when he felt like it, because only his team was around to listen. Mostly he just worked harder, wrote letters to Addie that were returned in pieces in another envelope, and watched the revolution unfold in front of him in that railroad and lumber town. He finally lost count how many times Pearson changed hands between the *federales* and the Red Flaggers. He freighted for both sides, kept his head down, and hid his earnings in the two-hole privy behind the stable.

He'd leave tonight on the westbound train to Hachita. The army had expressed some interest in hiring his team and wagon to haul rations to the Mormons now camped all along the border. Like every riding horse he had ever owned, Blanco would be happy to see him. He'd go overland, the same way they came out, avoiding major roads, heading into the protecting *sierra* as soon as he could. He knew every logging road and Indian trail in the mountain district, roads that armies never traveled. He could have Addie back to Dog Springs in a day or two.

It was a piece of cake, except that he wasn't sure he wanted to do that. There was his money in the privy in Pearson to retrieve, and he knew there would be other, hardier colonists sneaking back into Juárez and Dublán. Depending on who controlled the railroad, he could probably just put his wife on the train, bid her *adiós*, and stay behind. He thought about it in the dim quiet of the depot and asked the Holy Spirit what He thought. Nothing. Ammon decided to rethink the matter. He looked around; other men were sleeping there, so he knew he could close his eyes in prayer and no one would notice.

He received a different answer, one so bizarre that he almost laughed out loud. *That can't be right*, he told himself. *Maybe I'm rusty at this.* He closed his eyes again. Same impression. Maybe it was time to pay attention.

He didn't want to leave the quiet of the depot because it reminded him of the little home he had shared with Addie. He could count on quiet there, or near-quiet, because Addie liked to hum while she fixed dinner, and he enjoyed listening to her. And if he came into the kitchen and just put his arms around her, she never objected. She never even minded taking a pan off the hob, if she too had more on her mind than boiled potatoes.

Squinting against the brassy sun, Ammon left the depot. He reached in his pocket for his timepiece, then remembered that a guerilla had taken it from him on his last visit to Pearson. Well, it felt like an hour had passed.

Mama met him at the entrance to the lumberyard, where she must have been watching for him.

"Brother Finch gave me five hundred dollars," she told him, tucking her arm through his. "I'm so brazen. I asked him for another twenty-five for incidentals. Are you taking the train back to Hachita?"

He nodded.

"You'll need it for train fare and supplies. Maybe a serape and sombrero. Your Spanish is more fluent than some Mexicans. It's September and you're dark from summer."

He nodded again, wanting to tell her what he was thinking. He didn't because it was so preposterous.

Mama looked at him, measuring him in that way of hers that told him she had something to say. He waited, amused, because he had something to tell her. She hesitated and obviously thought better of it.

They sat together, silent, under an awning in the lumberyard until Pa returned, carrying a burlap sack of vegetables. With a sigh, he sat down beside them and handed five dollars to his wife, looking at both of them.

"What's this? A delegation? Did I do something wrong?" The smile left his face. "Brother Finch found you, I guess."

Ammon nodded.

"He came to the *mercado*, and I told him you had come out with the others. Are you crossing the border to bring back Addie?"

Ammon nodded again.

"Thought you might."

Keeping her voice low, Mama explained what had happened. She looked around, then opened her apron pocket a little for Pa to see the money. Pa whistled.

"Guess my five dollars didn't impress you too much today!" he joked.

"He's going to give you another five hundred if I die down there," Ammon said.

"I have it in writing," Ma chimed in.

"I think he expected me to be all noble and say I'd find Addie for nothing, but I'm tired of being noble, and we have plans."

Ma looked at him, startled. He touched her arm.

"Yeah, this is my business voice; I usually keep it in Pearson. My sisters have plans; you know they do. Elise has her heart set on going to the academy in Provo, and Joannie wants to study nursing. Susan wants to teach home economics someday, and June . . ." Ammon frowned. "Junebug would just like another set of play dishes like the one she left behind. We're strapped, Pa, and we need Brother Finch's money, plain and simple."

They sat in silence, then Pa cleared his throat. "Get Addie out fast and hurry back to us, son."

Ammon shook his head. "No. I intend to take my time getting Addie out, provided I can find her. Just an extra day or two."

Pa just stared at him. Ammon glanced at his mother, who was smiling a private little smile, even though it made her lips tremble.

"Were you going to suggest that, Ma?" he asked.

She nodded. "I thought you might think I was crazy. Mothers don't *send* their children into danger. They pray them out of it, except that's not what happened when I prayed."

"You're not crazy. I had the same thought in the depot." He turned to face his father. "If I just whisk Addie out of Mexico, I doubt I'll see her again. Brother Finch will bundle her away, and I don't want that."

"She made her intentions pretty plain, son," Pa reminded him, as if he needed reminding.

"She did. I haven't seen her in two years and certainly haven't lived with her in two years. Pa, I'm sealed to her for eternity, so maybe Addie and I should figure this out. Eternity is a long time to hold a grudge."

Pa opened his mouth to argue, then closed it.

Here goes, Ammon thought. "I'm also going to try to get the cattle out."

"Going to disguise them as a herd of antelope?" Pa asked and shook his head.

"I . . . I don't have a plan yet. Maybe Addie has one."

"Maybe you have rocks for brains."

"Maybe I do."

Pa gave him a blessing before he left El Paso. Ammon knelt in the dust of the lumber stall with all his family around, and Aunt Loisa sniffed into her brother's handkerchief. Junebug complained that Mama was holding her too tight, and Pa told him to listen to the Holy Spirit, something he was already planning to do.

Mama walked Ammon to the edge of the lumberyard. He waited for her to offer all kinds of advice, but she only handed him her Book of Mormon. "You're named after Ammon for a reason," she said, her voice small and pinched. "So far, I've never figured out the reason. It's your turn to try." She kissed his cheek. "She's a proud woman, Ammon. I think Addie still hurts as bad as you do. She probably regrets every word she said, but it's hard to forget what we say . . . and hear."

He had to know. "Am I a fool to try this?"

She shook her head and moved him toward the street. "You'd be a fool not to try." She kissed his cheek again. "I'm going to turn around now and not look back. *Vayas con Dios, mi hijo.*"

There was no one on the westbound train that he knew, and Ammon was glad of it. When he arrived in Hachita, Brother Adams, whose ranch now hosted many of the Colonies' horses, tried to talk him out of returning to Mexico. He gave up when Ammon said nothing. A tall man, he clamped his hands down on Ammon's shoulders, forced him to the ground, and slapped his meaty hands on Ammon's head for another blessing. Ammon knew better than to say his own father had just done that, because Brother Adams wasn't a man who ever lost an argument.

When he finished, he gave Ammon a slap on the side of his head. "That's from my wife for being stupid," he muttered.

He started to laugh then, and Ammon laughed too, as soon as his ear quit ringing. Hands on each other's shoulders, they went into the ranch house, where Sister Adams glared at him, her lips tight, and fed him within an inch of his life. When she gave him a handful of tortillas and a pot of beans after he finished, her eyes dared him to thank her.

He did anyway, because he knew her heart. He also knew how hard she was working right now to help keep his friends from the Colonies fed in their encampment near New Mexico's border. He kissed her cheek.

"That's from my mother," he told her, then kissed her other cheek. "And my Aunt Loisa."

In what little shade remained on the porch, he told her about Addie. "I have to go back and fetch her out, if I can."

"You can," Sister Adams told him. She gave his arm

a little shake. "Sometimes women go a little crazy when they lose a baby."

So do men, he thought. *So do men*.

He didn't say it out loud, but she seemed to sense his private pain and kissed his cheek. "She was probably worn out with hearing 'It's God's will,' and 'You'll have other children,'" Sister Adams said. "Some people are idiots."

She clapped him on the back then, a wallop that reminded him how equally yoked Brother and Sister Adams were. "Go get your team and that smart horse that knows how to open all our gates!"

Ammon laughed out loud. "I should have warned you about Blanco."

She walked him to the horse corral, keeping up a commentary about the families camped on the border, itching to return home. As they neared the corral, she stopped and lowered her voice, as though the horses would overhear and pass it on to their owners in El Paso.

"Do you think even half of those folks will ever see their homes again?"

Ammon shook his head. "It's going to take people with nerves of steel to go back and face armies of desperate men."

". . . and women," Sister Adams added. "We went to the border and used binoculars to watch a skirmish near Topia yesterday. It looked like two different guerilla armies, fighting each other. You ever seen *soldaderas*?"

He nodded, remembering the hard-faced women, some of them barely older than his younger sisters, riding alongside their men. He hoped Sister Adams hadn't seen what they could do with machetes and shovels to a fallen enemy.

When they reached the corral, he swung up and sat on the fence. He looked and then whistled for Blanco, who stood nose to nose with one of his teaming horses by the distant fence. With a smile, Ammon watched his gelding's ears twitch forward. Blanco tossed his head, pranced a bit for good effect, then started toward his master with that mincing step of the Arabian he was. He took his time.

"You old show-off," Ammon said. "Let's see how smart you really are."

When Blanco was twenty feet away, Ammon clapped his hands three times. Standing beside him, Sister Adams gasped as Blanco began to limp, the kind of limp that meant the next stop was the slaughterhouse.

"What happened to him?" she asked Ammon, bewildered.

In answer, Ammon clapped his hands three times again, and Blanco pranced forward, fit as ever.

"Yeah, he's smart enough to open your gates, my stable latch in Pearson, and most of the back doors in García," Ammon said as Blanco stopped in front of him. "Good boy. You remembered." Grasping Blanco's mane, he swung onto his back. "If I do run into Red Flaggers or *federales* on the prowl for horseflesh, three claps, and even they won't want a broken-down lump of future dog food."

In a short time, Ammon had his team rounded up and hitched to his freight wagon. He tied Blanco on the tailgate once more, blew a kiss to Sister Adams, and started for Dog Springs. He didn't look back, because the temptation was strong to remain. He could hire out his team and himself to the army and someone else could find Addie. The moment passed, because he knew, with a dread that filled his whole soul, that someone else would be guerillas. "Please not that, Father," he murmured in Spanish.

In another hour, he saw the mountains of Mexico to the south, which put the heart back in his chest. Soon the late summer sun would turn them pink and then purple. If he traveled steadily tonight, he would be in the sheltering pines of the mountains tomorrow, holed up somewhere and safe until night's cover protected him. Two days of that would see him home to García.

He went right to the quartermaster depot when he arrived at Dog Springs, an army outpost so small he doubted it was on anyone's map. He frowned to see the tent village there, where more of his friends and neighbors camped and waited. Drying clothes fluttered on lines strung between tents. He smiled to see garments strung discreetly between lines of sheets and towels, the better to hide them from prying eyes.

"Yessiree, we are peculiar people," he said out loud to his team.

He went right to the sergeant who had helped them two days ago and offered to lease his rig to the army. "I know you're hauling more because of us," he said.

The sergeant nodded and took him directly to the lieutenant in charge of quartermaster stores. In less than an hour, he had signed a six-week haulage lease, and directed any money to be sent to David Hancock, care of Walter Long's Lumberyard, El Paso.

"I hear folks are living in the wood stalls there," the lieutenant said after he blew on the paper so the ink could dry.

"It's true, sir." Ammon smiled. "Do you know, my mother made salmon tamales out of government rations?"

The lieutenant shook his head. "How long will they wait there?"

"Until it's safe to go back, or until they give up and move somewhere else."

The lieutenant looked him in the eye. "Are you going back to Mexico? I could probably detain you, if that's your plan."

"You can't, sir. I was born in Mexico and it's my country."

"There was a fight in Topia yesterday. The whole region could still be crawling with rebels fighting against each other."

"Or they could have melted back into the desert by now," Ammon countered.

"Your funeral," the lieutenant said with a shrug and turned back to his paperwork.

Ammon left the army outpost and rode Blanco back to the tent city, knowing he'd find friends and something to eat and probably more advice than he wanted. He ate with the Rouse family, near neighbors back home, content to remain silent and let the conversation swirl around him. It pained him to hear it, but the Rouses were moving to Bluewater to start over. The Rouse brothers had pooled their slender resources to lease a farm because they couldn't see a future in Mexico.

He walked through the camps, listening to other conversations, blending into the shadows. When it was dark enough, he went to the *tienda* on the border, the little grocery store he had noticed when they rode in from Mexico. Some coins bought a few tortillas and beans to supplement Sister Adams's parting gift, and there was a *paisano* eager to trade his sombrero for Ammon's Stetson and toss in a serape too.

"My own sainted mother wove this for me," the man said, as he handed over a serape that had seen better days and smelled like it had last been used to line a dog box.

"Then I will wear it in good health," Ammon replied, just as polite. A child of Mexico, he understood the manners of doing business.

The desert chill had settled in for the night and he pulled the serape over the scrap of quilt his mother had insisted he take along, grateful for the warmth now after the day's furnace.

After kneeling in prayer on the New Mexico side of the line, asking Heavenly Father to protect fools, Ammon Hancock crossed the border at midnight. The moon was bright and the desert landscape bare of any animals or people. In the silence that grew bigger with each mile he traveled, he learned that it was one thing to travel out of the country with two hundred and fifty well-armed men, and quite another to travel back alone into a country in revolt.

He relaxed gradually as Blanco set a sedate pace not designed to attract any attention. Smart horse, indeed.

Not a light shone anywhere as he approached Topia, the first town across the border. He felt himself relax a little more, grateful the guerillas had left. Once through the town, he planned to turn toward the mountains and not take another road until he reached García. He remembered the well in Topia's plaza, where he could fill the canteen he had not filled in Dog Springs because he knew the water was better in the village. He turned onto the plaza and pulled back suddenly on the reins, his heart in his throat.

Stretched before him, as far he could see by moonlight, lay a sleeping army.

FOUR

AMMON COULDN'T TURN back. His involuntary act of jerking Blanco up sharp had wakened the guerilla lying on the ground right in front of him.

Idiot, idiot, idiot, Ammon thought, as the man sat up, rubbing his eyes. His heart pounding in his chest, Ammon casually pulled his leg from the stirrup and rested it across his saddle in that careless way he had seen Mexican riders do when they wanted to stop and chat.

"*Hola, hermano,*" he said, hoping he sounded like a man with all the time in the world. "*¿Qué pasa?*"

To his incredible relief, the man muttered something and lay down again, pulling his sombrero back over his face.

Thank you, Lord, for blessing a stupid man, Ammon thought, as he backed up Blanco, careful not to step on any of the other sleeping men.

Too late. Another man sat up and casually put his Mauser rifle across his lap. "And who are you?" he asked in Spanish, much more alert than the first man.

Ammon closed his eyes, hoping there wasn't a password. "Endalecio Salinas," he said, perjuring himself with the name of his father's foreman. Never tell anyone too much at a time, his father had advised two years ago, when the revolution started and men were shot for merely babbling. "The more lies you tell all at once, the harder it is to sound convincing," Pa had said. Ammon waited, hoping his rescue of Addie hadn't ended before it began. He yawned, trying to looking both tired and bored.

"Where are you headed, my brother?" the guerilla asked, his tone kinder now. He rubbed his eyes.

"Message for Captain Pepe Lopez," Ammon said promptly, pulling a name out of his head. Brother Adams in Hachita called all Mexicans Pepe Lopez. Hopefully this guerilla had never crossed the border and worked for Brother Adams.

The guerilla's eyes narrowed and his hand caressed the Mauser. "I don't know him."

"No one does around here," Ammon said and gestured vaguely. "From the south somewhere."

He knew his Spanish was impeccable. He returned the gaze leveled at him, wishing he looked more Hispanic and hoping for clouds to cover the sudden sin of being Anglo.

After another long moment, the guerilla nodded. "Hurry on, then."

"*Claro*," Ammon said and held Blanco to a slow, steady walk down the street crowded with sleepers, even though he wanted to dig his spurs into his horse and make tracks. And from the way Blanco trembled, he figured he would be in good company.

The men slept where they had dismounted, their horses nearby. Some of the *soldados* had wrapped their reins around their wrists, ready to mount at the slightest necessity. The horses looked well-ridden, but that was nothing surprising. The Hancocks and their mountain colony neighbors had lost many horses to guerillas and *federales* alike who had roared up on shaky mounts practically walking on their knees, leaped off their jaded horses, "borrowed" the Mormon horses, and raced away, leaving behind lathered and quivering animals that Ammon usually ended up shooting.

"That's the way they are," his father had said. "They'll ride a horse to death, bite it on the ear to get it up, then ride it another twenty miles. Just life during a revolution, son."

The street was endless, like looking down the wrong end of a telescope. Soldiers slept everywhere, some on the board sidewalks, others even curled around the town's well, where Ammon had hoped to fill his canteen. Good thing he wasn't thirsty anymore.

Blanco picked his way carefully among the sleepers, his hide quivering every time a man rolled over or coughed. The horse seemed to sense that this was no ordinary situation. Ammon kept his hand on Blanco's neck and whispered to him in Spanish.

Ammon looked around. The soldiers had obviously just come from a raid. Their saddlebags bulged, and some of the horses even had sausages and hams tied together and draped over their necks. *Colony food,* Ammon thought; food his friends and neighbors had worked for. He thought about his folks in the lumberyard with their army-issue hardtack and canned salmon.

Ammon let out his breath slowly as he came to the

end of the street. He kept Blanco's pace deliberate until he noticed a row of bodies lying under a pepper tree. They could have been sleeping, but they were laid out so straight. He rode closer out of curiosity.

Three dead men lay there—four, if he counted the young boy lying with them. When he got closer, he realized what had attracted his attention. They lay close together under a white tablecloth. The cloth was blood-stained, muddy, and torn, but even in the light of a waning moon, he recognized the blue border of cross-stitched flowers.

His heart began to thump in his chest as he dismounted and walked closer. Ammon squatted on his haunches by the bodies and fingered the tablecloth. It was the same one that had covered Grandma Sada's dining room table when Addie threw her wedding ring at him.

So the rebels had been to García; maybe some of them were still there. He thought about his wife and closed his eyes. "Addie, please be the resourceful woman I married," he whispered as he mounted Blanco and continued his deliberate pace until he was out of town. When he reached the small river that fed the town's *acequias* in wet weather, Ammon gave Blanco his head. The gelding leaped the river, which was just beginning to flow again with fall rains, and lit out for the mountains.

Ammon knew Blanco couldn't continue that pace for long. He had already ridden him quite a distance from Hachita, and they were still one hundred miles from home. He let him run, though, alert for a good place to hide for the day. He wanted to ride Blanco farther, but daylight was coming, and he wouldn't be deep in the mountains on those unused Indian trails until tomorrow evening. Just the purest chance had gotten him through Topia alive, and he knew he couldn't count on that kind of luck again.

As dawn made its usual way to Mexico, Ammon felt his uneasiness grow as his instinct to hide increased. He halted Blanco and dismounted, gathered the reins and walked, even though he wanted to ride as hard as the guerillas. His horse nudged him.

"Sorry, Blanco. One of us has to see a bit of reason, and it's more likely going to be me," he said. "I don't have any grain for you, so we'd better take it easy." He grinned as Blanco nudged him again. "Want to share some salmon?" Over his protest, Ma had slipped several cans in his saddlebags.

He found what he was looking for a mile down the trail: a small spring set back in the pepper trees a short distance from the almost-dry river that flowed nearby. The river itself still contained enough water to satisfy anything but small armies, while the spring was set farther off the main route. He could stake out Blanco behind the screen of pepper trees and sleep until nightfall.

As he walked toward the spring, he felt exhaustion settle around his shoulders like concrete. What with traveling out of Mexico, taking the night train to El Paso, trying to sleep in a noisy lumberyard, then taking the train back to Hachita, he hadn't had a peaceful rest in more than a week.

It was longer than that, if he wanted to be honest.

He doubted he had enjoyed a good rest since he kissed Addie good-bye before teaming to the logging camp and breaking his leg two years ago. He stood in complete misery as he remembered the honest pleasure of a good night's rest with his wife beside him. She had a funny way of blowing bubbles in her sleep, and her hair always smelled of lavender. She never minded a cuddle either, unless it was really hot. That last night, they had talked about the baby that was two months underway, making plans already.

"Adaline." He couldn't say anything else because the pain was too great.

This is getting you nowhere, hombre, he thought, as he gave the reins a little tug and went deeper into the pepper trees, still shrouded in early-morning darkness.

He couldn't see far in front of him; thank goodness his horse was smarter. Blanco jerked his head up and whickered. Ammon heard an answering whinny and looked down just before he stepped on a soldier.

"*Ay de mi*," he muttered and stepped back, waiting for the man to sit up and shoot him.

He waited. When nothing happened, he squatted on the ground and stared at the figure until the barest light penetrated the grove of pepper trees. He knew the man was alive because he heard him breathing. When his own heart quit pounding, Ammon listened to the breathing that stopped and started, slower and slower, and knew he was listening to a dying man.

He had to be a guerilla. Maybe if he hadn't been thinking of Addie and feeling remarkably tender just then, Ammon could have backed out of the shelter and found another spot. He knew the area had springs the farther he angled toward the mountains.

He waited in silence as the sun rose higher, curious now more than frightened. He sat back and dropped the reins, knowing Blanco wouldn't move. The guerilla's horse was still just an outline on the other side of the spring. Ammon thought the animal might circle the spring to sniff out Blanco, but he did not move. His big head drooped, and Ammon knew it was one of those horses ridden almost to death. He swallowed and felt a sudden rush of sympathy for the dying man and his desperation—a wounded animal's desperation—to find a place to hole up and perish.

The feeling grew, and Ammon did something he hadn't intended: he bowed his head and prayed for the unknown man's release. He had never prayed for a guerilla before, but there was something about this lonely setting that compelled him. He knew he wouldn't much care to die alone.

Maybe it was one thing more. While he had waited for the sky to darken last night at the little store on the border, Ammon had taken out the Book of Mormon Ma had loaned him and turned to the book of Alma. True, the store had been noisy, and the bench in front met no requirements to allow serious contemplation of the scriptures, but he had skimmed that chapter about Ammon the Nephite and former reprobate, traveling alone into danger after he had parted from his brothers.

Too bad he couldn't ask his namesake how he felt about traveling in the land of the Lamanites, but as he sat there by the dying man, Ammon felt a surge of love for the dangerous land he traveled in now. Mexico was his home, and he wanted more than anything to stay in the land of his birth. *You ever feel like that, Ammon?* he asked in his heart. *I'd sure like some advice about now.*

Fear left him as he watched the man and thought about Ammon, who had gone with nothing but faith to preach to the great enemies of the Nephites. "What would you do?" he asked in a whisper and realized he had asked in Spanish. He also knew exactly what Ammon would do. He realized with a start that maybe the book of Alma wasn't scripture; maybe it was a lesson manual for him. Maybe it always was.

He knelt beside the man, hesitating for just a moment. He placed his hand lightly on the man's forehead, trying to think of all those things his mother used to do when he was sick. He knew it was the most puny of gestures, but it wasn't his imagination when the soldier sighed.

He heard someone weeping then and looked up, startled, alert. Dawn had sneaked up steadily, and he saw a woman sitting on a fallen log. She had a Mauser rifle in her lap and *bandoleras* crisscrossed on her chest, and he knew she was a *soldadera*. He had heard tales about the ferocious women of the revolution who rode beside their men into battle. He knew there were mothers in Colonia García who frightened their misbehaving children into obedience by threatening them with the *soldaderas*.

Silent, Ammon watched her, his eyes on the Mauser and then on her face. During one of the skirmishes fought near García last year, he had taken his father's binoculars—lost shortly after to guerillas—and watched the action from the second floor of their home. Amazed, and then appalled, he watched a *soldadera* shoot a *federal*, then scalp him.

He didn't see a knife, and this *soldadera* was more of a girl, probably not much older than his little sister. Joannie would have started her second year at Juárez Stake Academy this fall if they hadn't been forced to flee Mexico. Now she was thinking about working as a maid in an El Paso hotel. Times change.

As the light grew, he watched her face and saw nothing there except misery of the acutest kind. *I do believe she's afraid of you, Am*, he thought as he took his hand away from the dying man's forehead. The light was better, so he looked down. The dying man was only a boy too. He looked back at the girl.

"Your brother?" he asked.

She nodded.

"I won't hurt you." He gestured. "Please come closer. You know, we're not that far from Topia. If we move him closer to the road and you ride there, you might find a doctor among the soldiers."

She shook her head, her eyes wide and terrified now, and he knew without her saying anything that she and her brother had been on the losing side. They were hiding too, same as he was.

Ammon looked back toward the road. In the better light, he saw the bloody trail they had left as she dragged her brother into the sheltering grove. "We have to fix that," he told her, wondering if she would ever speak to him.

He stood up, and the Mauser came up automatically

out of the girl's lap. "Careful, careful," he murmured. "I'm going to cover our tracks." He pointed to the bloody trail. "Someone's going to see that."

He watched a war of emotions play across her face as she obviously toyed with the idea of just shooting him and getting it over with. He squatted down again and thought of that earlier Ammon. "How can I help you?" he asked, thinking of Old Ammon the Nephite.

"Cover the tracks," she said and lowered the rifle to her lap again.

She had a little girl's voice, soft and high-pitched, so he glanced at her again, wondering just how old she was. *You wouldn't scare too many García Colony children into good behavior*, he thought as he turned his back to her, hunting for a branch.

So far, so good. He hadn't heard the click of the hammer being pulled back on the Mauser. He broke off a hanging limb of the nearest pepper tree, walked back to the road, and brushed behind him as he walked backward to the spring. It probably wouldn't hold up to close scrutiny, but the guerillas wouldn't be looking for a boy.

He returned to the wounded boy, pleased to see that the young girl had moved closer. He doubted she was a day older than fourteen, now that he could see her better. He also noticed that her once-white skirt was stained and bloody.

"Are you wounded too?" he asked gently.

She shook her head. "It is my brother's blood," she told him as tears left dusty tracks on her face. "Señor, will he die?"

"I fear so, Adelita." He called her the generic name of the *soldaderas* from a military song. He could do better, since it looked like they were going to share this spring today. "What *is* your name?"

"Serena Camacho." She gestured to her brother. "This is Felipe." Her chin trembled. "He said revolution would be an adventure."

He smiled at her, at a loss what to say, except that he did know what it felt like to be a big brother. "Serena, *my* sisters never believe me when I tell them something like that."

The wisp of a smile crossed her face and she edged closer. She took her first good look at him. "You are not one of us."

"I am. I was born in Mexico." He wondered about the virtue of telling her his religion but figured the real Ammon wouldn't hang back. "I'm a Mormon from Colonia García."

"We came through there a few days ago," she said, much closer now. She sat beside her brother.

"Did you . . . did you see anyone there like me?" He had to know.

She shook her head, then looked him in the eye and glanced away, embarrassed.

"Some of the soldiers took hams and sausage." She sighed. "We didn't get any of that."

I don't suppose you did, he thought, feeling strangely compassionate, considering that bandits like her and her dying brother had been robbing them blind for two years now. Youthful soldiers like Serena and Felipe Camacho were probably pretty far down any military roster.

Felipe groaned, and Serena sucked in her breath. "I don't know what to do, señor," she said. "Do you?"

He didn't, but he couldn't tell her that, not when she was giving him that patient look, expecting him to have some ideas since he was older and possibly wiser. He didn't want to disturb the young soldier, but Ammon ran his hand along Felipe's head, feeling for a wound. Nothing.

He looked at Serena. Without a word, she pulled back the serape across his middle, and he had to look away until his stomach settled. Felipe Camacho was not going to leave the grove of pepper trees. He touched her hand and she surprised him by grasping his fingers.

"I'm afraid," she whispered. "Can you help him?"

You've seen his stomach. No, I can't, he thought, but he knew she didn't want to hear that. *All right, Ammon. I know what you would do.* He reached into his shirt pocket and took out a small bottle. *I'm either the biggest fool on the planet or all this girl has.*

"This is consecrated oil," he told her, holding out the bottle. "Go ahead and smell it. Just olive oil."

She did as he said, as obedient as one of his little sisters, who always expected him to do the right thing. She looked at him, expectant.

"I can't heal your brother, but you know that already, don't you, *chiquita*?" He couldn't help himself; the little endearment slipped out.

She nodded, her eyes filled with misery. "But what *can* you do?"

"I can put a drop of this on his head and pray that

nuestra padre celestial will take him quickly. He has suffered enough."

For a long moment, she stared at her brother, watching the rise and fall of his chest as he struggled to breathe. "Do it then, señor," she said, her voice scarcely louder than the breeze that ruffled the low-hanging leaves of the pepper tree overhead. "I believe you."

He thought suddenly of Adaline, wishing with all his heart that he could have been by her side for a blessing when she needed him. He did as the girl said, administering the oil and then asking an all wise, knowing, and quite compassionate Father in Heaven to welcome this soldier into paradise without any delay. Eyes closed, he thought of all the times he had wished all the armies and guerillas of Mexico to long and painful deaths and silently added to his prayer, asking the Lord to forgive him for being stupid and human.

When he finished, he put the bottle back in his pocket, sat back on his heels, and watched Felipe Camacho take one breath, let it out, and breathe no more. *Thanks, Lord*, he prayed silently.

Wonder of wonders, the Camachos had an entrenching tool, probably stolen from a *federal* in one nameless skirmish or other. While Serena sobbed, Ammon dug a hole deep enough to discourage wolves and mountain lions. The ground by the spring was soft, and all things considered, there were worse places to wait for the morning of the resurrection.

With her help, he put the boy into the ground, arranging the dirt just so, covering him with the black earth of Mexico. When the only thing left to cover was his face, Ammon sent Serena to her own horse, telling her to bring him closer for a drink from the spring. It was the most superficial of errands. She must have known what he was going to do, so she knelt first and made the sign of the cross on her brother's forehead before she stood up gracefully and—with such dignity—did as he asked, turning away.

He touched Felipe too, then shoveled dirt over his face. He smoothed down the dirt, patting it here and there the way he remembered his mother tugging up the quilts around him when he was much younger.

He watched Serena try to tug her horse closer. *I should ask the Lord to take you too, old fellow*, he told himself, and did just that. As he stared, amazed, the horse sank to his knees, then rolled onto his side, dead.

Well, my goodness, Heavenly Father, he thought. *That's probably enough for now.*

Serena stood a moment, her hands on her hips, as she contemplated the horse. In another moment, she was sitting close beside Ammon, close enough for their shoulders to touch. Again he was reminded of his sisters.

"Señor, will you get me home?" she asked finally. "I don't want any more adventure."

"Where do you live?"

He winced as she told him Santa Clarita, a village ten miles west and far from the relative safety of the mountains.

It isn't supposed to be like this, he told himself. *I'm supposed to rescue my wife.*

"*Claro.* Of course I will."

FIVE

*I*F ONE BIT of inspiration destined to humble him was good, then two were even better: Serena loved canned salmon.

At first he thought her enthusiasm was due to starvation. By mutual, if unspoken, consent, they had withdrawn deeper into the grove of pepper trees, taking Blanco with them. When she set down her heavy rifle, Ammon picked it up, opened the chamber, and smiled to himself. Empty. "You should probably load this," he told Serena, handing it back and indicating the *bandoleras* crisscrossed on her chest.

While she loaded the Mauser, Ammon inventoried his saddlebags—tortillas and four cans of salmon that Ma had insisted he take along. He had, because he was a dutiful son, and figured that if he ran out of ammunition, he could chuck the cans at the guerillas. He took out the little can opener Aunt Loisa had given him in the lumberyard and worked it around the top.

When he finished without lacerating his fingers, he looked up to see Serena watching his every motion. His heart softened a little more to see her hunger. "It's canned salmon," he told her, all the while perfectly aware that neither word registered in her mind. "I'll show you."

He took out a tortilla and set it on a rock, then scooped the canned salmon into the center with his fingers. "Use the tortilla like a plate," he said, holding it out to her. "You can eat the salmon with your fingers."

Without hesitation, she took the tortilla from him, careful to hold it level. She paused only a moment when she brought the first bite of salmon to her lips, then downed it. Her eyes widened. "Fish," she said.

Ammon nodded. "Salmon comes from the Pacific Northwest, where it rains all the time and nobody shoots at anyone else," he explained, giving her three bits of information that had no place in her world, or his, either, come to think of it. "Maybe we should all move there. How about it, Serena?"

She wasn't listening to his gentle teasing, focusing her heart and soul on the salmon that everyone in El Paso's lumberyard had grown weary of. Her expression told him he had given her something priceless. He watched her, suddenly aware of the education he was getting, free of charge and courtesy of the enemy, if he could call Serena an enemy.

Serena didn't waste a scrap. She carefully spread the last bit of salmon around the tortilla with her dirty fingers. She folded each side in on itself until she had a tidy package, not losing a single bite. She held it out to Ammon politely, but he shook his head. Even if he hadn't eaten anything since he had polished off his beans at the border, he knew he had eaten more recently than she.

When she finished, she looked at him with a frown.

"How does it get into the can?" she asked.

He considered the question and realized that he probably didn't know any more about the process than she did. "Perhaps the cans just lie on the ocean floor and the salmon curl up in them," he teased.

At first, he regretted his foolishness when she nodded, serious. He changed his mind. His lame explanation probably made more sense than trying to describe a big factory where thousands of fish were cleaned and packed.

It hardly mattered. Here they were, twenty miles inside Mexico and he was so tired he was having a hard time keeping his eyes open. It was time to level with Serena Camacho, late of one guerilla army or the other, who wanted to go AWOL from the revolution and needed an escort home.

First things first. He took the can and started to bury it, but she stopped him. When she gestured, he handed the odorous can to her. She went to the spring and washed it out using sand. When it was clean, she dipped the can in the spring and drank from it.

"Very good. You have a cup now," he told her, impressed with her resourcefulness. He handed her the lid, sharp where the can opener had carved little demon ridges. "Careful now."

She washed it the same way, then took a scrap of leather from the saddlebag he had taken off the dead horse. She wrapped it around half of the lid, giving herself a safe way to hold it, then wrapped it in the remaining bit of leather. "I could probably kill someone with this," she said.

You probably could, he reminded himself, unnerved. Maybe she was more of a *soldadera* than he thought.

She interpreted his expression correctly and smiled. "I would not hurt you, señor, because you helped me."

"I'm relieved," he said in English, then switched back to Spanish when she frowned. "It's this way, señorita: I think neither of us dare to travel by daylight. You are trying to leave the army and go home, and I am a Mormon trying to get back to Colonia García and find my wife."

"You lost your wife?" she asked, interested.

"I did."

"How careless."

I suppose it was, he thought. *More than you know.* "It is a long story and I am too tired to tell it. I'm going to sleep here today and then tonight I will take you to Santa Clarita."

"That is a long way from Colonia García," she reminded him. "Señor, I did not see a woman or a man in Colonia García. Are you so certain she is there?"

"No, I'm not, but I have to see for myself."

She thought about that and nodded. Her face took on an expression of shame. "We did not leave anything there for you to eat. I am sorry for that, now that I have met you."

"Well, never mind. I can always eat *nopal*," he told her, gesturing toward the spiny-leafed cactus behind them. "I'll take some with me tomorrow." He yawned. "I'm going to sleep now, and I advise you to sleep too."

"Should one of us watch?"

Trust a soldier to be smarter than he was. "Would you watch first, Serena? I've been awake a long time."

She nodded and pulled the loaded Mauser into her lap, sitting quietly on the fallen log, as he had first seen her when the sun rose. He asked God to protect them both and closed his eyes.

She woke him hours later, when dusk approached. He sat up, immediately alert. He knew how quickly he could go from snoring to wide awake used to startle Addie, who preferred to wake up in stages. Serena didn't seem surprised. She was used to soldiers and men always on the edge of activity.

Night had fallen, and she had let him sleep all day. "Serena, you were supposed to wake me, so you could get some rest," he chided her.

"Your need was greater," she replied simply. "Besides, I can sleep in the saddle."

He took out two tortillas and opened another can of salmon, dividing the tin between them this time. She ate with the same economy of effort. When she finished, she went to the prickly pear cactus and carefully cut off several leaves. She handed him two and kept two for herself, trimming the edges expertly, the same as he did, and cutting off the spiny eyes. She cut hers in strips and he cut his in chunks and they finished dinner.

Ammon filled his canteen from the spring, mindful that the dead horse was starting to bloat and give off mysterious gassy sounds. He picked up Serena's saddle-bags, poor limp affairs too light to be holding anything.

"How did you get enough to eat?" he asked her, thinking of Topia, and the guerillas' saddlebags stuffed with food.

"You have to be fast and if not fast, then know someone who is," she said with a shrug. "Felipe and I . . ." Her voice trailed away and she looked to the mound of dirt.

"Then it's time to go home. Blanco can carry us both."

Ammon gave her a moment's privacy as she knelt beside her brother's grave, patting the earth as he had done earlier. After wishing he had grain for Blanco, he saddled his horse and mounted, holding out his arms for Serena, who nimbly put her foot in his stirrup and swung up in front of him. Her *bandoleras* of bullets were uncomfortable, so she took them off and slung them on the saddle horn, the Mauser across her lap. She tried not to lean against him, until he teased her for being silly, as he would tease one of his sisters. With a sigh, she settled back.

He thought she slept, as they rode west toward Santa Clarita. She smelled of wood smoke and sweat, same as he did, and he missed the fragrance of lavender in Addie's hair. Serena had been kind to let him sleep all day. She was a child at war and so far from the image of a *soldadera* that he wondered how he could have been such a fool.

"The soldiers came through our village two years ago," she said out of the blue, when he thought she slept. "They promised us land and cattle if we would take up arms for Francisco Madero."

My land and my cattle, he thought, but had the sense not to say it. "Did your father get any land and cattle?" he asked instead, curious more than irritated.

She shook her head. "I suppose we were never first in line there, either." She half turned in the saddle. "Señor, you are a wise man. Why does the fighting go on and on? Why do allies turn against each other?"

"I'm not that wise, Serena," he said. "Go to sleep."

He held Blanco to a walk as they crossed the big valley. The moon was large and bright and felt like a parabolic mirror, pinpointing them as they passed through what he prayed was empty space. He saw no armies, but he also knew how the land that looked so level contained furrows and ridges capable of concealing men and horses.

As Serena slumbered in his arms, he considered Old Ammon the Nephite, separating from his brothers and heading into his own wilderness, living rough and on the alert for Lamanites. *I hope you don't mind if I talk to you now and then, Ammon*, he thought. *Were you as frightened as I was? Did you have to take a detour on your journey, or was the whole thing the journey? Addie, I hope you're alive. I'll find you when I can. Addie, my own Adelita.*

Dawn was breaking and he was stiff from the saddle when he saw the winking lights of Santa Clarita, a few lights here and there; it was a small village, as villages go. He sniffed the air and smelled smoke from cooking fires. He often hauled grain to Santa Clarita for

Rancho Chavez outside of the village. The *hacendado* raised racing horses, and his *mayordomo* had taken the trouble to show Ammon the stables and arena where they broke the beautiful horses to the saddle. Two years now after the revolution began, he wondered if that land owner was still alive and what had become of his horses.

Serena would know. When she stirred and stretched, he pointed to Santa Clarita and felt her huge sigh.

"Did you think you would never see it again?" he asked.

She nodded. "Before every battle."

"I have never been in a battle."

She twisted to stare at him in disbelief, a true daughter of the revolution. "*How* old are you?"

"Twenty-six, Serena, and not everyone goes to war," he said in his own defense.

She just shook her head.

Blanco must have known there might be a stable and hay, if not grain. He picked up the pace of his own volition. Ammon obliged him, eager to be under cover somewhere, now that dawn was breaking.

"Serena, I know this revolution is about land." He gestured to the series of buildings just south of Santa Clarita, still black humps in the distance. "Did your family get any of the land from Hacienda Chavez? I can't imagine the *hacendado* is still in residence there."

"His bones might be," she replied. "General José Inés Salazar cut him up a piece at a time until he died."

I'm glad you owe me a favor, Ammon thought, disturbed. "And the general divided the land amongst the

68

paisanos of Santa Clarita?" he asked, ready for an answer with a happy ending.

She shook her head. He could tell she was choosing her words carefully. He could almost sense her weighing each syllable before it left her mouth, as if measuring the revolution in his eyes, or maybe her own for the first time.

"The general decided he needed it more than we did," she said, her voice soft, as if to speak louder would bring down the wrath of a revolution that had turned on the people it was supposed to benefit.

"I'm sorry for that," he replied. He shut his mouth, thinking of all the harassment and duplicity he and his neighbors had endured at Salazar's hands. So much for a revolution of the people, something easy enough to proclaim in crowded plazas full of potential soldiers, and less easy in hay fields and stables full of blooded stock. "He needed it more than your family did?"

She shrugged, that refuge of all Hispanics when words wouldn't do.

"Oh, Serena, stay home now and prosper," he said softly.

They were in Santa Clarita by the time the sun rose, riding through quiet streets—too quiet. For a moment, Ammon wondered why it was so silent. His first instinct was to set down Serena and gallop from the village immediately. Then he realized that there were no dogs barking. He listened, a frown on his face. No roosters announced the dawn, either. What he thought were cooking fires was the nearly burned remnant of a building, collapsing in on itself. This wasn't the Santa Clarita he remembered, with its small but noisy marketplace and dogs everywhere. This was a dying village.

"Where . . . where is your home?" he asked the *soldadera*, his mouth suddenly dry. Amazing how fear could leech out saliva.

Wordless now—she felt so wooden in his arms all of a sudden—she pointed down a side street, where pepper trees hung low.

Please let there be a house and people in it, he prayed silently.

"Here, señor," she said, indicating an adobe house with a grindstone in the front yard. "My father is a knife sharpener. Mama cooks for the *hacendado*, or at least, she used to."

Business obviously hadn't been good lately. Too bad General Salazar didn't understand that when his army killed the landowners, they killed the people who provided livings for the villagers. He spoke to Blanco, who obligingly stopped. Serena stepped down as nimbly as she had mounted and Ammon followed, stiff from a night in the saddle. The little *soldadera* stood silently in front of her home, then squared her shoulders and went to the door.

"Mama? Mama?" she called, her voice soft, as though she had enough second thoughts about Santa Clarita to match his own. She went inside. He waited.

She came out a few minutes later and gestured for him to come closer. Looking around, Ammon led his horse through the gate and tied him at the side of the house, out of view of the deserted street. He followed her inside, observing the tears in Serena's eyes, even as she tried to look away so he could not see them.

When his eyes accustomed themselves to the late-night gloom that lingered, despite the sunrise, he saw three men sitting at a table. They were as thin as Serena, with blank expressions that told him all he needed to know about the success of the revolution in Santa Clarita.

"I didn't mean to disrupt your breakfast," he said. "I can wait outside."

His quiet words seemed to rouse them from their stupor. The oldest man, perhaps Serena's father, rose and leaned heavily on his chair. His voice shook, but he welcomed Ammon with all the hospitality Ammon remembered from visits to Mexican homes.

Serena stood beside him, telling them of his help in burying Felipe and getting her home safely. The men nodded, their eyes wary.

"My father, my uncle, and my other brother," Serena whispered. She bowed her head, and whispered, "They tell me Mama died last winter when everyone starved."

And no one's doing much better now, Ammon thought, appalled. "How can I help you?" he asked Serena.

"Papa said there is a bowl of nettles in the kitchen. That is for the evening meal, but if you are hungry . . ." Her voice trailed off.

"You would give it to me, wouldn't you?" he asked, touched. "Serena, I'm not hungry, except for these *nopales*."

He sat down at the silent table and picked up the knife, running it deftly around the spiny leaves of the prickly pear, then cutting out the sharp eyes. He remembered that Serena had cut her *nopal* into slices last night, so he did the same thing, all the while telling the silent men how he had come upon Felipe and Serena. The men all looked the same age, a testimony to what starvation could do. When he finished, there was a pile of cactus strips.

"I'll be back," Ammon said, getting up.

Blanco was cropping what little grass remained by the side of the house. Ammon took out his few tortillas and the remaining tins of canned salmon, wishing he had not laughed at Ma when she offered him more for his journey.

He handed the tortillas to Serena, noticing the sudden interest of her relatives. "I wish there were more," he said simply. He set the cans of salmon on the table, along with the sharp little can opener. *Please, Lord, turn it into loaves and fishes*, he thought, as he nodded to her and left the house.

Serena followed him into the yard. "Papa said the village is nearly deserted now," she told him. She looked away, embarrassed. "He said his heart breaks that he can offer you no hospitality. He assures you that no one in the Camacho house will ever say that you were here. He told me to kneel and kiss your hand."

Ammon shook his head. "I just wanted to get you home, Serena. Would you ask your father where I might hide myself and my horse until nightfall?"

She went back inside. When she came back, she handed him a knife. "This is for bringing me home and for burying Felipe. Papa wants you to have it."

"I can't take that," he protested.

The *soldadera* gave him a look so fierce that he felt his insides rearrange themselves. "Haven't you lived in Mexico long enough to know not to turn down a gift? It's ever so sharp because he is a fine grinder of knives." She said it with all the dignity of her people, a most polite race.

"Very well. Tell him thank you." He took the knife from its sheath and admired the razor-thin edge. "He *is* a fine grinder of knives."

"He also said for you to go to Hacienda Chavez. No one lives there now and you will be safe this day in the stables. I will watch over you from the field and warn you of trouble."

He knew better than to argue, but every instinct rebelled at leaving this little soldier the same age as his younger sister in a place no better than where he had found her. He had to do more.

He pocketed the knife and felt the few dollars left of the twenty-five his mother had coaxed out of his father-in-law as part of the deal to find Addie. He hoped with all his heart that it would look like an enormous sum to the Camachos, who sat in their house waiting to die.

He held out the money and Serena backed away, frowning. He took her hand and put four dollars in her grimy palm, closing her fingers over the money. "Don't give me trouble," he warned. "In the United States, there is a custom that if someone gives you a knife, you have to pay a few pennies for it, or it's bad luck. I don't have any pennies, so I'll give you what I do have."

Serena looked down at the dollars in her hand, then up at him. "Go with God, señor," she whispered. "Hurry now, before the sun is any higher." She touched his arm. "I hope you find your wife, señor. If you do, don't lose her again."

He nodded. "I won't." He took her hand and kissed her cheek. "And you remember how the salmon got in those cans, *chiquita*."

His reward was the ghost of a smile, and it nearly broke his heart.

Six

AMMON KNEW BETTER than to hesitate. With a smile he forced on his face, and a wave, he mounted Blanco and rode back the way he had come, through silent streets. He didn't look around because he knew people behind curtains watched him. All he could do was stare straight ahead and pray that no one was curious about who had brought Serena Camacho home.

The sun was high overhead now, and he knew it was not safe to travel, even to the deserted *hacienda*. He also knew he had no choice.

To lessen his own danger, he rode Blanco west until he was out of Santa Clarita, then dismounted at the top of a small rise that commanded the view. He crouched there in the tall grass, watching the village. After an hour, when no riders followed him or started for the rebel army he thought was somewhere to the north, he mounted Blanco and rode back toward Santa Clarita, then south to the *hacienda*. *I wonder what a bullet between the eyes feels like*, he thought. *Probably I'll never know what happened.*

Nothing. Relieved, he rode through the sagging gates of Hacienda Chavez, once so majestic and now just ruins swinging on creaking hinges. Probably by winter, the people of Santa Clarita would knock down the gates and use the wood in their fireplaces. With a jolt, he realized that would happen to Colonia García if none of the Mormons returned.

Once through the gates, he stared a long moment at the *hacienda*. Someone had set it on fire—who knew which army? He sniffed; the burn smell lingered, suggesting this latest insult to a lovely estate was of recent origin. If General Salazar had claimed it for himself, as Serena insisted, some guerilla group or other had taken what his father would call "poor man's revenge."

He rode closer, looking at the hanging baskets once filled with some exotic red flower Addie could probably identify, dangling limp now that most of the cords anchoring the baskets to the porch ceiling had been cut.

He had admired those flowers earlier this summer when he freighted grain to Señor Chavez for his beautiful horses. There had been ladies sitting on the porch, sipping tea like the English and paying him no mind, except for Graciela Andrade, daughter of the *mayordomo* on the San Diego Ranch near Colonia Juárez. Eyes lively, she had nodded to him. As he remembered, she had started to rise from her wicker chair when the blonde woman next to her—Señora Andrade—put her hand on her arm and whispered something, probably that he was a dusty Mormon gringo.

"Where are you now, Gracie?" Ammon asked the empty, half-burned porch.

Like most of the young men at Juárez Stake Academy, he had fallen in love with Graciela Andrade, whose father had taken the unconventional step of enrolling his daughter in the school of the *mormones*. Tongue-tied and shy, Ammon couldn't believe his good fortune when his English teacher made Graciela sit next to him so he could help her. He couldn't think of another time in his life when grammar ever mattered so much.

After one term, Papa Andrade decided he had been too unconventional after all. Graciela had cried on her last day at the academy when she came to collect her books. He sent her to Chihuahua City for the rest of her education. Ammon had written a number of letters to her, then discarded them.

He sat there a moment longer, until Blanco reminded him with a shake of his head that there had to be a better plan for the day. Ammon tipped his sombrero to the long-gone Graciela. Revolutions being what they were, he hoped the rumor was true that she had married a doctor from Chihuahua City and moved to Spain. It was just as likely she was dead in a ditch somewhere, revolutions being what they were.

No one fierce for revenge had burned the stables, to Ammon's relief. The doors swung wide, and he rode Blanco inside, but not before taking his rifle from its scabbard and setting it across his lap. He sniffed the air, smelling cats and something more cloying and dense. He knew the odor, which made the hairs on his neck do a little dance. Ammon patted his horse and continued a slow walk past the empty stalls.

One stall midway through the stable wasn't empty. Ammon looked and glanced away quickly, trying to take shallow breaths. He thought at first they were stable boys. He peered closer, shocked to see bodies in long skirts, flung at random against the back wall of the stall. "Please, no," he whispered. He couldn't tell how many there were because of the advanced state of decomposition, and he didn't feel curious enough for a closer look.

"Why the women?" he asked, before raising his bandanna to cover his nose. Pray God they had not suffered long.

Shaken to his boots, he continued to the far end of the stables, his heart sinking lower and lower as he suspected what had become of the beautiful, dainty-stepping horses. Whatever faction that had raged through Hacienda Chavez had likely commandeered all the blooded stock and rode it to death.

He knew there was an *acequia* on the far side of the stables. He dismounted on shaking legs, leaned against Blanco for a moment, then led his horse to the irrigation ditch, choked now with weeds. As Blanco drank, Ammon looked between the other outbuildings to the *hacienda* in the distance, wondering who else lay dead there. He hoped it wasn't Graciela.

He touched his saddlebag where his mother's Book of Mormon was stashed next to several leaves from the prickly pear that Serena had insisted he take along. He just touched the book for comfort, wondering if the original Ammon had seen sights like this in the land of the Lamanites. It was the paltriest kind of reassurance, but it kept his heart beating.

The last thing he wanted to do was go back inside the stable with Blanco, but he did, moving more slowly this time. He got as close as he could stand to the stall with the rotting corpses, knowing that anyone snooping around would back away before they saw him.

It could have been worse; maybe his new friend and ally Old Ammon the Nephite was watching out for him from some celestial perch. Blanco perked up, gave a low whinny, and headed for the darkest corner of the loose box. He went right to a barrel and stuck his head in. Ammon peered inside.

"Well, well," he said. "Blanco, you won."

Somehow, hungry horses and pillaging armies had overlooked a quart or two of grain deep in the barrel. Blanco strained to reach it, so Ammon tipped the barrel on its side, after moving away rancid straw with his feet.

When he finished, Blanco left the loose box and went to the next stall, and the next, until he found another stash of grain. When he finished, he came back to Ammon.

"Smart, smart horse," Ammon said, tying the reins around a post. "Smarter than your rider."

The stench from the corpses was overpowering, but he knew he could bear it. He sat next to the now-empty barrel in the back of the stall, said a prayer, thought about Old Ammon the Nephite, and closed his eyes.

"Señor? Señor?"

Ammon opened his eyes, alert at once. The stall was deep in shadow now, so he knew he had slept the day away.

Serena stood silhouetted against the open stable doors. She had hesitated on the other side of the dead bodies jumbled together. *A corpse or two a day keeps the guerillas away*, he thought. He stood up and called her name before she shot him with her brother's Mauser.

"I'll come to you, Serena," he said. "You don't want to come closer."

He untied Blanco and walked toward her, turning his face away from the death in Loose Box 14.

There were deep circles under the *soldadera's* eyes, and he knew she had kept her word, watching out for him in the field, staying awake to keep him safe. Ammon wasn't sure he was that valuable to anyone, considering the danger.

"*Gracias,* señorita," he told her.

He thought she might smile at that, considering that probably nobody ever called her anything so polite. Instead, she took his arm and gave him a little shake, her eyes deadly serious, reminding him all over again that she had ridden with desperate armies for two years while he ran a business, made money, and whined over his misfortunes with Adaline.

"Señor, the army of the north is on the move again." She shook him again for emphasis. "You have to leave, and fast."

He hurried with her out of the stable. "Who told you?"

"The butcher's boy, when I took your money to his father for some food," she said. "He heard it from José, who sells eggs when there are any, who heard it from the man who lights the lamps at night."

"Impeccable sources, eh?" he joked.

He should have known better. Serena gave his arm

the butt end of the Mauser, which would have knocked him down if Blanco hadn't been there to break his fall.

"*Tonto!* I am trying to save your life!" she declared, enunciating as though she spoke to an idiot. "You have to ride, even though it is not entirely dark yet."

He was only a fool on occasion. Ammon mounted Blanco, as serious as his unlikely protector now. "Should I just go back across the open plain or detour south to throw anyone off my trail?"

"Go across the plain to the mountains. Don't delay by taking a roundabout way." She handed up the Mauser.

"I have my own rifle, Serena," he reminded her.

"Take this too," she insisted. "The soldiers always roam through Santa Clarita, trying to squeeze food out of starving people. If they should find this Mauser and they realize I was in the Topia fight, our lives won't be worth kindling in a hot fire."

He took the rifle and reached for her *bandolera* when she took it from around her neck. "Come with me."

She hesitated and he knew she wanted to put her foot in his stirrup again and ride with him. She stood there, indecisive, then shook her head. "You have brought me home safely, and that is enough," she said simply.

It was Ammon's turn to hesitate. "If forced, will one of your neighbors tell how you came home this morning?"

Serena shrugged. "All they saw was a man in a serape and sombrero, maybe a soldier, maybe not. If they say something, well, that is war."

"But, Serena, your life . . ."

She shrugged and turned to go back to Santa

Clarita. He leaned down and touched her head, which made her smile.

"*Vayas con Dios*, Serena," he told her. "I mean that," he muttered in English, under his breath.

Still he hesitated. "*Chiquita*, do you know what happened to the Chavez family here?"

"My uncle tells me it was nothing good. All dead. Probably still in the *hacienda*. All dead."

Not all in the hacienda, he thought. "And you still don't have any land!" he burst out, unable to help himself. He closed his eyes a moment against the memory of the lovely ladies sipping tea on the veranda in June.

He opened his eyes when Serena slapped Blanco. "Go away, señor! You cannot find your wife if you never make it to the Sierras!"

He gathered his reins and held Blanco back from the kind of gallop that would signal to any army that here was a man desperate to get somewhere, anywhere, out of his enemies' reach. Better any advanced guard think he was just a *paisano* intent upon his business in the mountains, but in no particular hurry.

He couldn't bring himself to look at the *hacienda* again as he passed by, but he did glance back at Serena, a smaller and smaller figure as Blanco ate up the distance in a gentlemanly fashion. For one stupid moment, he wished he could wave his hand and transport the little *soldadera* to a safer place where salmon spawned and ended up in cans somehow.

He saw the army's scouts as merciful darkness

found him nearing the foothills of the mountains. They thundered along at the usual breakneck speed designed to chew up horses and leave them worthless. His heart nearly stopped when two of the riders veered and wheeled in his direction. Ammon unslung the Mauser from his shoulder in a reflex action, wondering at the same time what Blanco would do if he fired the gun. He had never trained his smart horse to stand still for rifle fire. Never needed to.

Almost afraid, he looked back at the scouts. He could have fallen to his knees in gratitude to see them arguing with two other vanguard riders, possibly wondering why they wanted to follow a lone rider into the mountains, where everyone knew there were Indians.

"I like it so much better when you fight with each other," Ammon told them softly. He turned his back on the four quarreling guerillas and continued his steady climb into the foothills. When he looked back a few minutes later, the *soldados* had rejoined the others.

"Thank you, Ammon, you Old Nephite," he said. "Now keep an eye on Serena, will you?"

He rode steadily upward as twilight descended on the valley that stretched out far below him now. He stopped for a long moment, letting his breath out slowly, reminding himself to breathe as he watched the guerilla army that had defeated Serena's faction at Topia on the border. It snaked along, strung out for miles. He hoped the soldiers would bypass Santa Clarita. Surely by now they knew how little remained in the village, picked over by one faction or the other, not to mention the *federales*.

To his dismay, the long column turned west toward

the village, where even now the egg man and the butcher's son and Serena's father and uncle were probably trying to hide whatever pitiful supplies remained to them. He wondered how Serena would fare, and he wondered why it even mattered so much to him.

The answer was simple, and something his father had told him once, after *federales* "requisitioned" two of his best horses.

"Just you wait, son," his father had said as Ammon fumed watching his best horses ride away. "They'll go home to wives and children who love them."

At the time, Ammon had stared at his father as though all his brains had dribbled out. He understood now, as he thought of the young girl and her dead brother, following an army that promised land and couldn't deliver it. He had buried Felipe, ridden with Serena dozing in front of him, trimmed prickly pears in her father's house, and made no objection when she watched over him while he hid in the stable and slept. He knew them now as people, and he worried about them.

He continued his steady climb into the mountains, stopping finally when it was too dark to see, and he feared he had lost the trail. Feeling older than old, he gave Blanco his head and knew his smart horse would find water.

When Blanco did, Ammon dismounted and flattened himself by his horse as they both drank deep from one of the little springs in the high mountains. The water was cold and sweet, and a far cry from the silty, warm water of the Rio Bravo that separated his country from the United States. When he finished, he lay on his back and stared at the stars high overhead. He didn't move until Blanco nudged him.

"No grain for you and no food for me," Ammon said. He debated a long moment, then took off the saddle and turned his horse loose to graze. Ammon drank some more water until it filled his stomach. He could look for prickly pears in the morning and be in García by nightfall.

The saddle made as good a pillow as he was going to find this side of García, provided guerillas hadn't ripped open the pillows and let the feathers blow to the winds. He lay there, remembering with a pang how well Addie fit by his side in their bed in García. As water sloshed in his empty stomach, he settled back and closed his eyes, wishing for her warmth as the cold settled into his bones on the mountain, so far from the hot plains.

Addie was still in his thoughts at first light, burrowing into his side as she liked to do because he had a bad habit of stealing all the bed covers. She nuzzled, nudged, and prodded until he opened his eyes and found himself staring up at a circle of Indians staring back at him, one of them prodding him with his foot.

"Good morning, gentlemen," Ammon said in Spanish, alert and stupid at the same time. "Would any of you like this Mauser?"

SEVEN

A S IT TURNED out, the Indians did want Serena's Mauser, and Ammon's rifle too. So much, in fact, that to keep his own weapon with its high-powered scope, Ammon had to promise them five cattle from the box canyon where he and his father had hidden them before they left Colonia García.

The trade was a fair one, considering the stories he had heard of miners and loggers disappearing in the Sierra Madre. He was acquainted with the Indian who had been prodding him in the ribs, so he did not appeal to strangers. Joselito usually came around García in the fall to do odd jobs, and Ammon's father always hired him. Ammon saw how thin they were, almost as worn down as the villagers of Santa Clarita.

He gave up the Mauser cheerfully, happy to have it in Indian hands where it probably wouldn't come to the attention of any of the factions. The rifle was a hot potato, and he was glad to have it off his hands. The Tarahumara had been retreating farther and farther into the remote canyons of the Sierras since the revolution began.

If only there was something to eat. He yawned,

rubbed his eyes, and looked around, but all he saw was *nopal*. Joselito saw his glance and sliced off a few leaves with a wicked-looking knife, handing them to him.

In a few minutes, they were all trimming *nopal*. "I am getting tired of this," Ammon said in English.

Maybe Joselito knew some English. The Tarahumara glanced briefly at Ammon and looked away just as quickly, polite not to stare. Without a word, Joselito opened the leather pouch around his skinny waist and pulled out two or three beetles, already squashed and ready for dinner.

Ammon gulped and carefully took the beetles from the tip of that knife. He gestured to his chunk of *nopal*, and Joselito nodded.

The Indian chuckled when Ammon stared at the beetles for a long moment. He wondered if Old Ammon the Nephite had eaten bugs when he traveled into Lamanite land and figured the answer was yes. He decided that the matter probably got lost in Joseph Smith's Book of Mormon translation because it wasn't all that important. He spread the beetles on his prickly pear chunk. He told himself to chew it and think about Addie's crunchy toffee that she made at Christmas. To his relief, it stayed in his stomach.

The Indians watching Ammon nodded their approval. Joselito ate a few more beetles without benefit of prickly pear, then stood up. "We will follow you to your cattle," he said in good, workaday Spanish.

"Then you will know where my herd is," Ammon pointed out.

Joselito shrugged. "We can take your rifle, if you

wish." He said it so politely, his hand on that wicked knife, ample proof to Ammon that if he wasn't exactly a prisoner of the Tarahumara, he was as close as he ever wanted to be.

"It appears I am turning into a philanthropist," Ammon replied, which made Joselito smile. The Indian had no idea what a philanthropist was, obviously. Either that, or he did and he liked a good joke.

Ammon mounted Blanco and led the way, the Indians trotting along beside him. He knew the Tarahumara were renowned for their long distance running, but he also saw how worn down they were. If he kneed Blanco into a gallop, he could put miles between himself and the Indians who wanted—no, needed— the five promised cattle. He thought about it just long enough to remind himself that Addie's father would have done precisely that and rejected such a blatant betrayal of his word.

He rode all day, hungry, sleepy in the warm sunlight, impressed with the steady pace the Indians set, even in their weakened state. When he slowed Blanco into a sedate walk, Joselito looked at Ammon and smiled his gratitude.

Ammon decided to camp that night in the box canyon where he hoped his cattle still resided. Maybe he could appeal to the better natures of his Indian escort to leave the rest of his herd alone, but he doubted it. Barring that, he intended to read a few more chapters in Alma by the light of the campfire, just to get an idea of what Old Ammon the Nephite would do. Mama seemed to think reading about Ammon might give him some idea, and she was generally right. At least the Indians wouldn't want his Book of Mormon. They didn't read.

They reached the box canyon while shadows rappelled down the walls, turning them the dull gold of wheat ready to harvest. The days were beginning to shorten, and he knew the night would be cool, so high in the mountains. He breathed deep of piñon pine and it settled his heart.

The Indians nodded their approval when he came to a barely visible fence and tugged on it, pulling back a brush cover to reveal a narrow opening to the canyon, one of many in the area. With a smile on his face, Ammon took off his sombrero and grandly ushered them inside. He closed it behind them and walked Blanco to the head of his curious escort column, amused now more than dismayed by the upcoming loss of his cattle.

What was that Pa had said before he left El Paso? It had irritated Ammon then because he was worried about Addie and wondering how the Hancocks were going to survive, and here was Pa, getting all philosophical. Pa did have a tendency to woolgather. Thomas Finch was not entirely wrong in that regard.

Am, if you want to find yourself, sometimes you have to lose yourself. It says so in Matthew, Pa had told him. Ammon shook his head, reminding himself that Addie was the one he was trying to find. So far, he had helped a little *soldadera* bury her brother. The little *soldadera* had watched over him in a field while he slept, then warned him that the army was on the move. Now he was going to help some starving Indians. He was still alive, and maybe that was enough for now.

The canyon was narrow, and he took his time. No rush. Maybe his Mexican neighbors were right about *mañana*. He couldn't think of anything that would keep the Indians from taking all his livestock, so why hurry his family's ruin?

To his relief, the Hancocks' cattle were right where he and Pa had left them, grazing steadily throughout the small canyon. With its stream, ample pasture, and the sheltering mountains, he knew they could stay there, multiply, and grow fat until either the revolution ended or he figured out how to get them across the border. Ammon sat there a long time, admiring the cattle, calculating right down to the penny what they would fetch in Stateside markets.

Ammon reminded himself that if he had possessed a lick of sense, he would have holed up last night in a safe place and not just flopped down on that river bank. He kicked himself mentally a few more times, then shrugged and gave it all away.

"Here they are," he told Joselito. "Cut out the five you want and leave the rest."

It was utter fiction; he knew it and they knew it. Still, he could try. "Joselito, my family could use these cattle too. If you need more in a while, take them, but don't take them all, if you please."

The Indian nodded. Ammon glanced at his fellows squatting there, exhaustion writ large. He knew they were used to hard times, but he asked himself how many hard times it would take to break even these resilient people. Ammon's stomach rumbled loud enough to make Blanco prick up his ears.

"Joselito, pick out a good one right now, will you? I'm hungry and I suppose you are too." *I can't do it myself,* Ammon thought. *I just can't butcher my family's future.*

The Indian spoke to one of the squatting men, who got up in that enviable, fluid motion of his tribe and walked toward the herd, nocking an arrow to his bowstring as he walked. One well-placed arrow to the lungs and the cow dropped in her tracks. It happened so fast that none of the other cattle did more than glance around and continue grazing.

They ate the best pieces immediately, some of the Indians so hungry that they didn't bother with a cooking fire. Ammon let his chunk sear and then turn a moderate shade of done, when the juices dripped and hissed in the fire. He always carried a tin plate and a little salt in his saddlebag, so he prepared his own feast while the blood dripped off Joselito's chin. Any misgivings about dinner vanished with his first bite, pure heaven after several days of *nopal* cactus and canned salmon.

He ate all he could and so did his dinner guests. Eyelids drooping, Ammon lay back in that simultaneous agony and ecstasy of overconsumption and watched the Indians cut up the rest of the beef with their own wicked knives. He wondered what they were going to carry it in, until they took off their loin cloths and bound up the raw meat. *Resourceful,* he thought, smiling a little to imagine what Addie would think of all those bare rumps.

When they finished, Joselito returned to Ammon, squatting down and holding up his bloody hand in a gesture that could have meant anything from "Thanks, chump," to "Look out for rustlers and card cheats."

Joselito put his fingertips near Ammon's hand, and Ammon understood. He had seen the Tarahumara Indians touch fingertips in greeting and farewell, but never with a white man. He held up his hand too, impressed by the delicate gesture and its implication.

"Watch your backs, boys," he called after them as they cut out five of his fattest beeves and chivvied them on foot toward the entrance to the box canyon. Joselito gave him an answering wave, and they disappeared as quietly from his life as they had entered it.

He toyed with the idea of moving his cattle, but he knew it was pointless, now that the Tarahumara knew the general location of his herd. He looked at his fingertips, bloodied by Joselito's gesture, and smiled, pleased with himself.

He added more piñon to the campfire until he had a blaze big enough to warm him and light enough to read by. Lonely now that his dinner guests had left, he read aloud the chapter in Alma where Ammon and his brothers head for the land of the Lamanites. Belly full, he made himself comfortable, and read until the fire burned down.

As near as he could figure, Old Ammon just went about doing good, even if he was in the land of his enemies. He went to King Lamoni and asked how he could be of service. Am frowned at the well-thumbed pages, wondering how that figured in his current situation. He flipped to Second Nephi, hunting until he found what he wanted. He settled back against his saddle.

He smiled over "He hath confounded mine

enemies," well aware that the only person confounded by the Tarahumara Indians had been Ammon Hancock. He flipped another page and found what he wanted even more: "Wilt thou deliver me out of the hands of mine enemies?"

It was a good question, but with a start, he found himself thinking more of Adaline than himself. He was well-fed and doing fine out here by a little fire, and he possessed a rifle. He had no idea where his wife was or in what circumstance she found herself at this moment. He didn't think it was anything good, so he prayed for her. "For goodness sake, keep her safe, Father," he murmured.

Not so comfortable now, he kept reading, then found what he had probably been looking for since she had thrown his ring at him. He read it twice, then closed the book, satisfied and ready to sleep.

"'Wilt thou make my path straight before me?'" he asked out loud, as Nephi had probably done.

Ammon woke up to his cattle grazing all around him. He watched them, content for a moment, then felt a pang and the certainty that the next time he came through this canyon, if ever, they would be gone. It hurt less than he thought it would, confirming a long-held suspicion that he was a better freight hauler than stockman.

He had wakened before daylight. Breakfast was more chunks of beef cooked over a fire. "I'm cooking one of your *compadres*," he announced to the milling herd. The only response was a level look, then back to cud-chewing, reminding him that he ranked a little higher on the food chain, but not by much, considering the wisdom of his recent decisions. Addie would likely agree.

He was in the saddle before daybreak and out of the box canyon after carefully securing the camouflaged gate. He rode Blanco steadily into the dawn, not taking any time to admire the beauty of the sunrise. Addie called it pagan of him, but he had long been in the habit of raising his arms to the rising sun, as he had seen the Tarahumara do. Maybe she was right.

He came to Colonia García on a morning much like the one when he and the others had ridden away more than a week ago now. The few streets looked just as deserted, and he felt himself relax. His first stop was his house, where he stabled Blanco in the kitchen again. Nothing had disturbed the grain he had left for his horse, which gratified Blanco to no end and relieved Ammon.

He gave the house another close look as he left it, walking backward. Burning the front room had been the right idea, and heaven knows he didn't ever plan to live there again without Addie. Set well back in the trees, the house looked like a ruin. *Much like my life*, he thought. He wondered if Old Ammon the Nephite, former reprobate, had left behind anyone he loved when he went on his fourteen-year mission to the Lamanites.

As much as it seemed the same as last week, something had changed in García. Staying in the early morning shadows, Ammon walked toward the town center. Movement in the cornfield caught his eye and he stopped. Colony cattle grazed among the corn now, so he knew some faction or other had passed through, probably taking what they wanted, then turning the cows into the corn so they would be even fatter when they came back to rustle some more.

A door banged behind him and he raised his rifle, stepping back farther in the shadow. It was the front door of the Odegaard's house, which he knew had been closed and locked when they left town. The slight breeze had slammed open the screen door, which already hung on one hinge only.

Silent, still, he waited, just watching the house. When nothing happened, he looked both ways and crossed the street. When he got closer, he saw that the inside door was slightly ajar. He pushed it open slowly, then stepped inside.

The sight before him made Ammon suck in his breath and just hold it, until he reminded himself to breathe. Someone had ripped open the little lace-covered pillows that Sister Odegaard placed on her settee and wing chairs, scattering stuffing until the room looked like García after a snowstorm. The backs of the settee and chairs had been ripped open too, and innards spilled out like gaping wounds.

Worst were the pictures of the Odegaard's parents. Someone had thrown jars of bottled fruit at the frames. Cherries and peaches, moldy now, adhered to the shattered glass and the wallpaper around the pictures.

Ammon walked as far as the door to the kitchen, his boots sticky with fruit juice and pillow stuffing until he looked like one of Mama's exotic Cochin chickens with the feathery legs. The kitchen was a ruin, partly burned where wood from the firebox had been spread around. The pie safe had been thrown onto its face. Shattered crockery lay everywhere.

Lips tight together, Ammon stared at the mess. He knew the Odegaards had already left for Provo. He was grateful they would probably never see the desecration of what had been one of the loveliest houses in García. He couldn't have counted how many times he had sat on the side porch there and turned the crank to the ice cream freezer.

Leaning against the doorframe, he heard a grunt and squeal coming from the pantry. He raised his rifle, angry enough to shoot, then lowered it when two hogs tried to squeeze through the narrow door. They were stuck, which gave him time to avoid them. He turned on his heel and left the house, suddenly not curious to look into another house as he continued down the street.

He couldn't help himself. He went only as far as the open doorway to the bishop's house, sick at heart to see the piano, the family's pride and joy, caved in by an axe still imbedded in the top. The piano keys had been yanked out like a deranged dentist had been at work, which made him run his tongue over his own teeth.

He backed out of the house, nearly ill and disturbed at what he might see at Grandma Sada's house. *Addie, what have they done to you?* he asked himself in horror.

He knew the town was deserted now, so he hurried through the little business district and down the second side street, where other doors hung open. The Flynns' residence had burned to the ground, with just the chimney remaining, at least until a strong wind came along and toppled it. He doubted the chimney would survive the winter.

Ammon stood for a long moment in front of Grandma Sada's house. The door was closed, which only disturbed him more, for some reason. He opened it, ready for the worst, and was not disappointed.

The same wreckage greeted him that he had seen in the other houses. What hadn't been looted and carried away had been ruined so no one could ever use it again. He glanced into the dining room. He already knew the tablecloth was gone because he had last seen it covering corpses on the outskirts of Topia. The table had collapsed under the weight of the massive sideboard that had been pulled over on top of it. He looked away. Grandma Sada had always been such a tidy housekeeper.

This wasn't finding Addie, he knew. The main floor was a ruin. He started for the stairs, not wanting to climb them, but determined to search the entire house. He stood a long time at the foot of the stairs, saying one of those wordless prayers that he hoped made sense to Heavenly Father, steeling himself for what he might find.

"*¿Hay alguien aquí?*" he called, not realizing until he had said it that he had spoken in Spanish. "Anyone here?" he repeated in English this time but softer.

Nothing. His rifle at his side, he started up the stairs. Since he and Addie had lived with Grandma Sada until their own house was finished, he knew which treads creaked and avoided them. Silent, he checked the room he and Addie had shared, which was as tidy as it had been every day they lived there. Addie never left a bed unmade unless she was in it.

He closed the door and walked down the hall, unwilling to open what he knew was the door to Grandma Sada's room. The other doors were open, and he looked in them, surprised that no guerillas had come upstairs to destroy the rooms' contents.

Indecisive, Ammon stood outside Grandma Sada's closed door. Finally, he tapped on it with his knuckles, just a little tap. "Grandma? Addie?" he asked. *"Abuelita? Abuelita?"* he called louder. Grandma Sada liked it when he called her "little grandmother" in Spanish.

No answer. He tipped back his sombrero and leaned his forehead against the door frame, unsure what to do. The room was empty, and he had no earthly idea where to search for Addie.

This was getting him nowhere, and the sun was up now. Time to hide. He turned the handle and walked into the room.

Or tried to. He stopped, transfixed at the sight of a shotgun pointing right at him. The barrel shook, because Addie held it. He had never stared into such terrified eyes.

His relief at seeing his wife made him sigh, and then yelp and slide down the doorframe when she shot him.

EIGHT

ADDIE! YOU SHOOT better than you throw," he managed to gasp out before he flopped over sideways on the rag rug.

When the darkness and spinning stopped, his head rested in Addie's lap. He noticed her shirtwaist was stained with perspiration and her sleeve was ripped. This was not the tidy Addie that he remembered.

But there was this matter of his bleeding arm. He had never been overfond of blood, especially his own, when it was supposed to stay inside and chug merrily along. Addie had managed to stop the flow from that fleshy part of his shoulder by pressing a handkerchief against it. The wound was already starting to ache. He grimaced with the pain, maybe a little more than he needed to, but his wife *had* shot him, and that hurt too.

Then he looked into her eyes, those big blue ones he had once labored to describe in a dreadful poem he wrote her during a long week freighting, when he really wanted to be home with her. Addie's eyes were still wide with terror and the worst kind of loneliness. He knew she had her gripes, but for that moment, at least, the last thing she wanted in the world was for her estranged husband to bleed to death and leave her alone again.

It was time to put her out of her misery and not play on her sympathy. His arm wasn't *that* bad. Maybe she would have looked at any man that way who spoke English and wasn't out to hurt her, but right now, he was the man.

"Addie, it's not that bad. You just blew some skin off my arm."

She was in tears now, holding him closer to her marvelous bosom, and he figured explanations could wait. His father-in-law had complained once that Hancocks spent way too much time enjoying the moment and not enough time planning ahead. Probably he was right. Addie was still a woman to admire at this particular moment.

"Hey, hey, don't cry over this," he chided gently. "Help me sit up and we'll see how bad it is."

Her sob ended on a shudder, but she did as he asked, helping him into a sitting position on the floor at the end of Grandma Sada's bed. He leaned his head against the footboard and smiled at his wife.

"At least we didn't wake up Grandma," he said.

Addie sobbed again, then put her hand against her mouth in a futile attempt to stop. She shook her head. "Grandma died last night."

"Oh, Addie." He closed his eyes. "And you've been waiting here for . . . for what?"

"My father said he'd send some help but no one came," she said, staring at his bloody arm. When she looked in his eyes again, it was a long-distance stare, something he never cared to see in a woman's eyes. "I suppose I've just been waiting for the guerillas to return and find me."

Again the look of terror came into her eyes, and Ammon knew she was on her last nerve.

If she were a child, he could soothe away her fears, but she was a woman, one with different fears. "They're not here yet, but the army of the north is on the move. We need to act quickly. You have any scissors?"

She got to her feet, rummaging in Grandma Sada's bureau until she found a pair of shears. As Ammon watched, she carefully cut up his sleeve and through his garments until the wound was exposed. He glanced at it and looked away, frowning. He looked at Addie then, and she gave him the barest smile.

"You never have been much of a brave man about blood," she reminded him. She gave herself a little shake, as if gauging how close the bullet had come to something vital. At least, he hoped that was so. "All . . . all I heard was something in Spanish, then someone coming up the stairs."

"I should have known better, but I've been speaking nothing but Spanish for days now. I forgot."

She nodded, then took away the handkerchief. It was her turn to frown.

The bullet had tracked through the top few layers of skin and kept going. "If I bind it really tight, I think the bleeding will stop," she told him. "You're going to have a dimple there. Hold this handkerchief."

He did as she said, watching as she cut a length off Grandma Sada's sheet and bound his arm, leaving the handkerchief in place. A knot over the wound made him wince, but he knew she was right.

When she finished, she leaned against the footboard too. She closed her eyes and he could almost feel her exhaustion. He was starting to feel stupid and groggy, even though he knew it wasn't much blood, not in the greater scheme of things—certainly not as much as Serena Camacho's brother had spilled. All he wanted to do was lie down and sleep, and he knew that was a bad idea. Still, he was almost touching shoulders with his wife right now, and he liked the feeling.

But here too was Grandma Sada, not getting a moment younger.

"Addie, you've been watching Grandma all this time?"

She nodded. She moved a little closer until their shoulders really were touching. Or maybe he had started to lean a bit.

"Papa had been so sure she was dying this time and told me he'd be back." She sighed. "Why did everyone in García vanish?"

Funny how such a small wound was making him dizzy. He leaned his head against her shoulder, not because he wanted to—well, maybe he did—but because he didn't seem to have a choice.

"You haven't heard anything?"

He felt her shake her head because his eyes were closed now.

"President Romney sent out the women and children to safety on August 1, and the men followed last week. We didn't think anyone was here."

She sighed. "She was so sick and I didn't know what to do."

She said it in a small voice, then drew her legs up and rested her forehead on her knees. "I'm hungry, I'm tired, it's hot, and I still don't know what to do. Please, Ammon, stay awake."

He forced himself to pay attention to her, even as he knew he was drifting into shock. "I'm feeling awfully cold, Addie. Can you get me a blanket?"

She just stared at him and he realized he was speaking in Spanish. Too bad Thomas Finch had never wanted his family to learn Spanish. "Our leaders have told us to keep separate," his father-in-law had primly reminded him once.

"A blanket," he repeated in English. "Something."

He lay down on the floor, unable to keep his eyes open, while Addie sobbed out loud and took the blanket off the foot of Grandma Sada's bed.

He would have slept then, except that his ear to the floorboard alerted his groggy brain to vibrations that could only be an entire troop of horses thundering toward García. He opened his eyes and looked at Addie.

"Quiet!"

It must have been English, because she was silent, her hand to her mouth, her eyes full of misuse.

"Listen!" he hissed at her.

She did as he said, and he watched the color drain from her face. Without a word, she crawled from the footboard to the open window, where lace curtains fluttered in the breeze. Rising up, she looked out, then sank back, her look of misuse changed into terror again.

"It's a whole army!" she gasped and crawled back to him. She shook his good arm. "Ammon, an army!"

The news was bad enough to fight against the shock that threatened to send him to sleep. "I wasn't fast enough," he said. "Help me sit up."

Her expression frantic now, she helped him into a sitting position again, then held her hands against both sides of his face until she had his attention. "Don't you dare go to sleep!" she whispered. He had never heard such desperation in anyone's voice before, and certainly not from well-bred Adaline Hancock.

"We have to hide right now," he said, weary beyond belief. He looked at his arm. Maybe he had lost more blood than he thought. Luckily, most of the blood was on his shirt and pants and not the floor.

Addie fumbled in her apron pocket. She held out a piece of paper, much creased and folded. Her hand shook. "It's a safe conduct pass," she told him, speaking in his ear so he could not misunderstand her. "From General Salazar. I'll take it downstairs and wait, then show it to their leader."

His arm felt like lead, but he latched onto her wrist. "It could be the wrong army out there. Addie, it's not safe for you to go *anywhere*. We have to hide right here."

She looked around wildly, then pointed to a half-size door that he remembered led into a narrow attic that ran the length of the second floor. "It's full of boxes and trunks," she said, tugging on his good arm now.

She stopped and he watched the tears well in her eyes again. "They'll find us in there because they've ransacked everyone's houses, even this one."

"But not up here, not this floor."

"No. The doctor—I'll explain later—the doctor told everyone to stay off this floor." She couldn't help her tears then. "You're sure this is a different army?"

"Sure enough not to want you standing in an open doorway downstairs," he said. "It's the attic for us. Help me up."

She whimpered and put her hands over her ears when the *soldados* passing down the main street fired their weapons. She burrowed as close to him as she could in the mindless terror of a small, cornered animal.

"They sure are fond of wasting ammunition," Ammon said in what he hoped was his most casual voice, trying to calm her. He didn't think Addie was the hysterical type, or at least, he hadn't thought that until two years ago. "Addie, Addie, it's a lot of noise. They're good at that. Help me into the attic."

"What's going to keep them from finding us?" she asked as she helped him to his feet.

"Grandma Sada," he told her, pointing to the still form on the bed.

Addie had pulled the sheet up to cover Sada's face. He stood there a moment, weaving from side to side, thinking how much he loved the old lady. He wanted to glance sideways at the woman beside him, holding him up with her arm around his waist, but his eyes didn't want to cooperate. He turned his head to see her.

"You're not going to like this," he said and held out his good arm. "Take off my shirt and rub the blood all over her sheet."

Addie stared at him as though he had lost his senses,

and he pressed his hands against her face this time. "They won't come up here right away. By the time they do, the blood will have dried. Trust me, Addie. We have to frighten them away from wanting to do *anything* in this room, or they'll find us."

He watched her face, then let out a long breath as understanding came into her eyes. She nodded. "I can do this," she whispered, more to herself than him as she helped him out of his shirt.

Moving quickly, Addie smeared his blood all over the white sheet, squeezing it until the blood dripped. Her hands shook as she pulled back the sheet and gently stretched out Grandma Sada's arm until it hung off the bed. Her eyes fierce with concentration now, Addie squeezed the blood onto her arm and fingers until it dripped on the floor.

"Take the ring off her finger," he said.

She didn't hesitate or question him, removing Grandma's ring and putting it on her own finger.

"Open the attic door and toss in my shirt." He chuckled. "It's the only one I have."

Addie seemed to catch the spirit of what he was trying to do, to keep her calm. "Ammon, you never were too kind to your wardrobe."

"You meant my shirts and pants, and that suit that never fit?"

"That one."

He could tell she was steeling herself for the ordeal to come, on top of this one. "It'll get better, Addie," he said gently. "But right now, we have to hide."

She wiped her fingers on her apron, then used a

clean corner of the apron to open the door. She helped him inside the attic, exclaiming when he moaned as she forced him to double over to get through the short door. He dropped to his knees and one arm, and shook his head to clear it.

"Hurry up," he said. "Don't . . . don't . . ."

He didn't know what he wanted to say. He watched as she looked around the room, then flipped over the rag rug to hide the blood. The horses sounded so loud in his ears, and for one horrible moment, he thought the *soldados* were climbing the stairs on horseback. *I am out of my mind*, he thought.

"Addie, please!"

"In a minute."

She moved out of his sight line then, and he heard her light footsteps in the hall. She came back in a moment with a canvas bag, which she stuffed under Grandma Sada's body. He heard her sob.

"What . . . ?"

"Tell you later." She glanced at him, and the last thing he remembered was her look of real purpose. This was the Addie he remembered. He closed his eyes, feeling reassurance all out of proportion to their situation as she crept into the attic and shut the little door. He decided he was woozier than he thought: For the first time in two years, he felt safe.

Ammon had no concept of time. When he woke, or regained consciousness—he didn't know which—Addie's hand was suspended just over his mouth. The attic was too dark to see her hand, but he could smell the faintest bitter almond of Jergen's Lotion, mingled with dried blood—his.

"I'm awake," he whispered.

"They're downstairs now," she whispered back, her lips close to his ear. "I was afraid you might cry out."

She was shaking; he could feel it. "This is what's called an adventure, Addie," he whispered and chuckled when she flicked his cheek with her middle finger.

That went better than he thought it might. He knew she wasn't going anywhere. He had no idea what Old Ammon the Nephite would do at a time like this, but he had a good idea what *he* would do.

"Could you stand a little cuddle?" he asked. "I'm just about scared to death."

"That's two of us," she said and lay down next to him, her head on his chest.

The attic was far too hot for a cuddle, but he didn't care. He raised his arm, wincing with the pain, because he felt something furry near in his face. "What in the world . . ."

Addie chuckled this time. "One of Grandma Sada's fox fur stoles, the ones with little beady eyes on each end. I dragged you under a clothes rack."

She jumped when something downstairs crashed, and he tightened his grip on her. "Just breathe in and out, Addie," he murmured. "Where's my rifle? And your shotgun?"

"Beside me."

"Hand mine over."

She did as he said and couldn't help her sharp cry

when they heard footsteps on the stairs. Ammon put his hand on her head and turned her face into his chest. "Not a word now."

They were silent as several guerillas tromped upstairs and down the hall, their spurs jingling. Addie winced when they heard them yank family pictures from the walls and throw them to the floor, the glass tinkling. Her tears wet his chest.

He heard them walking from room to room and the tinkle of glass as more pictures were thrown to the floor. Ammon knew when they were in the room they used to sleep in and the room Addie must have been using. She tensed in his arms when she heard the sound of cloth ripping as they destroyed her clothes.

He tensed too when someone banged with a rifle butt on Grandma Sada's door, the only door on the floor that had been closed, if he remembered right. "Jeez Louise," he murmured, "just turn the doorknob."

With an effort, he put both arms around Addie now, because she was shaking so badly. "'Sweetest little feller, everybody knows,'" he sang softly in her ear. "'Don't know what to call you but you're mighty like a rose . . . '"

It was the stupidest song, but one that Mama used to sing to Junebug and all he could think of. *Please, God*, was all he could manage, but he knew Heavenly Father was wise enough to understand their current need.

Then the guerillas slammed open the door and stood in Grandma's room. Terrified, Addie tried to burrow inside his chest like a frightened animal. He smoothed her sweaty hair, twisting his fingers through her curls.

Funny how her hair curled when the weather got so hot.

I know these men, he wanted to tell her. *Just hang on a moment longer, wife. I know what they will do.*

There. They came into the room no farther than he had before Addie shot him. He heard them whisper to each other, then back out and quietly close the door. They couldn't get down the stairs fast enough. *Thank you, Grandma Sada*, he thought, relieved beyond words. *I'm sorry what we had to do to you, but we had to do something.*

Addie raised up slightly, listening intently now, still shaking. Gently he put his hand against her head and she lay down again with no protest. "We're not going to move," he whispered. "For all we know there is someone still standing in the room, waiting for this door to open."

He knew there wasn't, but he also knew if they were going to survive to the border, they had to be cautious to the point of absurdity. Addie had no argument with him. She rested her head on his chest again like an obedient child, which soothed him right to his soul.

Silent, sweating, they listened to more banging about downstairs and then another bang as the screen door swung wide and closed behind the soldiers. In a few moments, they heard horses trotting down the street, and then quiet. Ammon waited until wrens began to scold each other in the cherry trees again before he let Addie even sit up.

To his relief, she didn't question his great caution. She stood up and stretched and went to the little door. She just stood there, her hand on the knob, then sat down beside him again.

"I'm afraid," she said. "I'm thirsty and I'm dirty, but you're the one I shot. You need some water."

He was still too tired to say anything, which made Addie touch his good arm and give it a tiny shake, as if determined to make sure she was not alone. He had to say something in the face of her terror.

"I *am* thirsty, Addie. Is there anything to drink?"

"There is, but I have to go across the street to get it." She moved closer to him, then shook herself as though discarding fear.

He had seen her do that before when she was much younger, the time she had jumped into an irrigation ditch in Juárez after her little sister, who had upended herself and went under the water. Of course, the water was shallow and her older sister had only laughed at them both, but Ammon remembered watching determination banish fear when Addie had to act. He hadn't laughed, and he didn't laugh now. He doubted supremely that her older sister would even be alive today if she had been left in charge of Grandma Sada and not Addie.

"That's my girl," he said. "Help me through that door, will you? Then bring out my rifle."

She took his arm and guided him through the small door, mimicking his own sharp intake of breath with one of her own, as though she felt his pain.

The room spun around a few times, but Addie held him steady until the furniture quit sliding across the slanted floor.

"That's better," he said finally.

She looked at him as though she didn't believe him. "Really, Addie. Maybe all I needed was a good rest in a hot attic with fox furs just overhead looking at me with beady eyes."

She smiled as he hoped she would, and it was a genuine smile.

"You're too much."

She went back for his rifle and brought out both weapons. Then she stood beside him, both of them looking down at Grandma Sada.

The blood all over the sheets had dried to a dark brown now, and Grandma's features, usually so firm, were starting to slide. Ammon sniffed. "It doesn't take long in a hot climate," he whispered, as though he didn't want the usually impeccable old lady to give him one of her stares.

"It's not Grandma yet," Addie told him. "It's what I put under her before I went into the attic."

While he watched, mystified, she took a deep breath as though steeling herself, then pulled a canvas bag out from under the dead woman. "I knew it would be safe there."

"Bravo, Addie," he said, proud of her ingenuity.

The canvas bag looked familiar to him. "Uh, where did you get that?"

She held it at arm's length away from them both, her face turned away. "It stinks, but it has some dollars and pesos in it. The doctor who looked at Grandma gave it to me to take to his wife in exchange for the army leaving us alone. General Salazar wasn't happy at all, but the doctor insisted." Addie looked at him, uncertain. "I know you want to get us out of here as fast as possible, but I gave my word, Ammon. I have to take this stinky money to his wife."

Ammon laughed out loud; he couldn't help himself. Addie glared at him, reminding him immediately of the dear old lady on the bed in front of them.

"Addie, turn over that bag. Do you see a double H?"

She did and held it closer to him. He laughed harder, wishing laughter didn't make his arm hurt. He wanted to sit down on Grandma's bed, but that seemed inappropriate. He leaned against the bureau instead and took the bag from Addie.

"Addie, the HH stands for Hancock Haulage. The good doctor stole it from my privy in Pearson and gave it to you to give to his wife, who lives *where*?"

Addie stared at him, her eyes wide. "You won't like this. In San Pedro, some distance south of here. *Your* money?"

"Some of it. I adopted that design and name, after I . . . we . . . after I moved to Pearson," He thought of days hauling lumber, sleeping under the wagon, slapping mosquitoes, mooning over Addie, dodging guerillas, avoiding Indians. A week ago he would have been incensed that a rebel doctor had swiped money he worked so hard to earn. Today, it made him laugh. "Trust a doctor to actually use my privy," he told her. "I knew the guerillas would never go in there. That's what happens when you give a man an education, I suppose."

Addie stared at him, mystified, then shook her head slowly. "You need to tell me what's going on."

"After you get me something to drink."

He must have looked convincingly pathetic because she nodded. She put her arm around his waist and led him toward the window overlooking the empty street.

He nearly told her he thought he could stand by himself, but he stopped in time, content to relish her nearness.

"You see the Thayns' back porch? That's where I'm going." She gulped and took a step closer to him. "I'm still afraid to leave the house."

"I'm going to sit right in the window with my rifle. I've got you covered, Addie."

She gave him such a look then. It took away the sting—if it was a sting—of losing some of his outhouse money. He looked out the window, almost content for someone who had been shot by his wife and now had to go with her even farther into dangerous territory.

"You're going to find water on a back porch?" He kept his tone light and teasing because he knew she was steeling herself to leave the house now.

He knew Addie. She raised her chin, squared her shoulders, and went to the door. "You're not the only smart Hancock."

She left the room and he nodded. *So you're still a Hancock*, he thought, pleased and touched at the same time.

NINE

AMMON HEARD ADDIE sob out loud when she saw the damage in the upstairs hall, but she didn't hesitate. She was quiet on the stairs and out the front door with no hanging back. She looked up at him once—for reassurance?—and he waved to her, his rifle on the window ledge.

He watched the street for any movement. The only sound was the distant rumble of thunder. Curious, he watched his wife reach under the steps on the Thayns' side porch and take out a pry bar. Deftly, she pulled up two of the boards and reached down, taking out two quarts of something dark. He couldn't tell what it was, but his saliva started to flow. It had to be better than his diet of *nopal* and nothing.

From the far end of town, rifle shots rang out. Addie looked up, startled, then pulled out another quart that looked like apricots. Working quickly, she replaced the boards and tamped them down with the pry bar, then hid it under the porch steps again. She picked up the three quarts and stood there a moment as more shots sounded. Looking both ways, she darted back across the street and was upstairs in moments.

She set the jars on Grandma Sada's bureau. "The Thayns hid all their bottled fruit under the porch before they left. I watched them from where you're sitting. They were so secretive." She grinned at him. "I'm worse than a *soldadera*!" She grew serious quickly, anxious now. "I don't think the Thayns will be back. Ammon, do you think *anyone* will return here?"

His eyes were on the jars. He wiped his mouth. "Hard to say."

He had to do better than that, according to the expression on his wife's face. "I know the Thayns won't mind that you took their bottled fruit. In fact, I hope there's more." He started for the bureau. "I really need some of that now, whatever it is."

Ever the cook and nurturer, Addie sat him down on Grandma Sada's trunk by the attic door and lifted up the metal hasps on the jar. She looked around. "I need a spoon."

He reached for the jar. "I don't." He took a cautious sip: blackberries in sugary juice. "Oh my word, Addie," he said and downed the juice, reaching in when he finished to scoop out the berries.

"You have no manners at all, Ammon Hancock," she scolded, but gently, her eyes on the jar too.

"Hold out your hand," he ordered and she did. He teased out the rest of the berries and put them in her hand.

She ate them fast and opened the other jar, drinking half the juice before handing it to him. Her mouth had a ring of purple around it. Impulsively, he leaned over and kissed her, then went back to stuffing the rest of the blackberries into his mouth.

She laughed, which relieved his heart in a monumental way, and reached for the other bottle containing apricots so symmetrically arranged that he almost didn't want her to open it.

She held it up, turning the bottle this way and that to catch the light. "I try to be this perfect, but I never am. It bothered my father."

"Doesn't bother me."

She turned the jar around. There was a dreamy smile on her face, and for a moment it was as though she forgot where they were. "Mama took me to a county fair in Logan once. This is what all the jars looked like."

He didn't ever want her to look any other way, even though he knew she would remember in a moment that Grandma Sada lay dead and guerillas occupied García.

"Let's give it a blue ribbon and open it," he said, hating to intrude on her pleasure, but still so hungry.

She flipped the hasps on this jar and handed it to him. He drank half the juice, slower now, and disrupted the symmetry of the apricots in a major way. When he handed it back, she only ate a little.

"I'll save the rest for you," she told him, even as she gave the bottle a lingering look. She set the Mason jar on the floor and gave a little jump when the guerillas started shooting again. He was still sitting on the trunk, so she joined him there, probably afraid to be alone.

"What do we do?" she asked quietly.

"We wait."

The afternoon may have been long, but at least it wasn't hot. The growl of thunder to the west in the Sierra Madres finally amounted to something, a drenching rainstorm that Ammon knew heralded the arrival of autumn in the higher elevation.

"Maybe they'll leave town," Addie said, inching closer. Ammon felt more comfortable leaning against Grandma Sada's footboard, and she had joined him there.

Ammon shook his head. "What they'll do is hole up here in these empty houses until the storm lifts. We'd better go back into the attic."

He knew she didn't want to. She even opened her mouth to tell him so, he was sure, but just then they heard the sound of horses on the street. Addie grabbed the empty jars and what was left of the apricots and crouched through the small door. She got the guns next, then looked around to make sure nothing else was out of place.

"Hurry up!"

He put his finger to his lips, and she went a shade paler. She sat down on the floor beside him, as though her legs wouldn't hold her. It was worth a try, so he put his good arm around her, and she burrowed in close.

"Listen a minute," he whispered.

She was beyond listening, so he just put his hand on her head and pulled her closer.

"They're right below us in the street and one of them is telling the others about a dead woman." He let out a sigh when the horses and their riders moved on down the street. "Grandma Sada was always good to us. She still is."

Addie nodded but did not leave whatever puny protection she thought his chest offered. Women were funny that way, he decided.

"Maybe they'll tack up a sign on the door," Addie said finally, her voice so wistful. "You know: to warn others away."

"They mostly don't read." He chuckled. "Or generally use privies. Trust a doctor to find my money. That chaps my thighs!"

He was only trying to distract her, and it worked. He felt her low laughter right against his heart.

"Did you just leave it in plain sight? I know you're smarter than that."

"I'm way smarter than that," he agreed. "I left the money in a little wooden box where I kept—um—some pages from an old Sears and Roebuck Catalog. You know, sort of like I was hiding my stash. Some dollars, some pesos—not much, really."

He knew she was smart, and let her think about it for a moment. "So it was just a decoy! You wanted whoever stole your money to think that was all, and leave." She nudged his chest. "And that maybe you weren't too smart."

"I couldn't have fooled you. Guess where the actual strongbox is?"

"I don't even have to, because you're a rounder. Is it a two-hole privy?"

"Of course. I'm sociable," he teased, and she jabbed him. "I added a little shelf to the inside of one hole, just out of sight. It fits my strongbox. I, uh, don't use that hole."

She shook her head. He couldn't see her face to tell if she was impressed, but he felt her chuckle and decided she was.

They stayed close together at the foot of the bed and he dozed as the rain poured. He woke up when Addie shook him, not surprised that his head was resting in her lap now. He heard the guerillas downstairs before she said anything.

They crawled quietly into the attic and closed the door as the men started upstairs. Addie started to shake again, and he held his hand close to her mouth, just in case. Huddled in each other's arms, they sat by the little door.

The midday invasion was repeated as shadows lengthened across the room and the air smelled of rain and something else now: Grandma Sada mellowing.

Practically holding his breath, Ammon heard someone light the lamp on the bureau. He let out his breath—or maybe Addie was doing the same thing; they were so close it was hard to tell—when the men in the room shrieked like girls. They must have tried to go through the door at the same time, because he heard wood splinter. They ran down the stairs, missing a few treads, because they sounded jumbled together in a heap. The next sound was horses galloping away. The next smell was wood burning.

Before he could act, Addie leaped up, cracked her head on the little door, and ran into the room. As he watched from the doorway, she took the rug and beat out the flames from the lamp, which the men must have upset in their terror to leave the room.

"We don't need a fire right now," Addie said decisively as she dusted off her hands and rejoined him in the attic.

"You're a cool-headed woman."

She shook her head. The attic door was still open and he winced at the fright on her face. "I just don't want to die, or . . . or be interfered with. Women always have more at stake."

He nodded, thinking of Serena then, and the laughing ladies on the porch of Hacienda Chavez that he had admired earlier that summer. He had heard something in her voice of her determination to see his money got safely to the doctor's wife, and now he understood it.

"Did the doctor protect you?"

She nodded. When she spoke, her voice was small as though she was reliving the experience. "I have some awful bruises on my arms, but Doctor Menendez got to me in time."

"Oh, honey." He hadn't called her that in two years. "We'll get that money to the doctor's wife somehow," he assured her.

"I only wish it were more," she replied simply.

So do I, he thought, surprising himself again how little his hard-earned pesos were starting to mean to him. Come to think of it, Old Ammon the Nephite had probably lit out for his mission among the Lamanites with basically nothing except his brothers. *If he can, I can.*

She was silent then, but busy, giving herself something to do, which he understood. As he watched in the fast-fading light, she rearranged their attic space until she had created a nest of clothing that looked almost comfortable.

I simply have to feel better in the morning, Ammon told himself. *I'm in charge here.* He smiled in the dark. *At least I think I am.*

"Lie down and go to sleep," Addie said when she finished.

He hesitated. "Nature is calling."

He saw the fear again. "You can't go outside."

"Didn't intend to. Grandma Sada wouldn't like it, but I'm just going to pick a room and let it go at that."

She opened her mouth to protest, then just nodded. He smiled at her. "And you can pick a room too."

"There'll be worse in here after we leave, won't there?"

"Probably."

They went in opposite directions down the hall. He started to laugh.

"Stop laughing right now or I'm going to thrash you into next Tuesday, at some point," his sweet wife muttered.

The nest of clothing was so comfortable that he went to sleep immediately when he returned to the attic. He was dimly aware when Addie joined him, gratified that she wasn't going to thrash him anytime soon because she cuddled close with a sigh of her own.

He woke up in the middle of the night, probably because the rain had stopped and the house and street were silent, just the way he wanted it.

"Are you all right?" She sounded frightened, maybe worried that he would run a high fever, turn delirious, develop red streaks up his arm, die of gangrene poisoning before dawn, and leave her alone with two dead bodies.

"I feel better, actually," he assured her, and it was true. "Where's that quart of apricots?"

She handed it to him, and he drank some of the juice and fruit, wanting to leave more for her. The apricots went down cool and sweet.

"I didn't mean to wake you up," he told her as he lay down again stretching out his good arm for her to pillow her head, if he was so lucky.

She didn't accept the invitation, if that's what it was. "I couldn't sleep. One of us should stay awake."

He couldn't see her in the dark, but he knew her well and figured there was more. He waited, pretty sure what she wanted to know and not certain how to respond.

"Why are you here?"

Her voice was so quiet, almost as though she didn't want to hear his answer.

"Your father had been asking around the lumberyard—we were all staying there—trying to locate you. When the García men came out, he found me. I figured you'd gone to Juárez earlier on that last train out. None of us knew you were here with Grandma."

"He told me to watch over her," she said, her voice even smaller. Another long pause. "Did he offer to pay you?"

"He did."

"And you told him you wouldn't take any money?" She sounded so hopeful.

Lie or tell the truth, he thought and knew he had

no choice, because he wasn't a liar. "I almost did, then I changed my mind."

He knew she was too kind to thrash him into next Tuesday because she needed him right now as much as any woman had ever needed a man. He couldn't help himself, but in his mind, he saw all over again her fierce anger, so far from her usual serenity, when he had tried to explain himself, standing there with crutches. Maybe some things were impossible to forget. She was listening now, so he chose his words with infinite care.

"My folks came out of García with one trunk among the eight of them. My father and I managed to hide most of our cattle in a box canyon, but I ran into trouble on my way here, and I doubt the cattle are there now. We Hancocks have busted out. We're dead broke. Dad's working in a Mexican *mercado*, culling bad fruit, and my mother, aunt, sisters, and cousins are living in a stall in the lumberyard."

He heard her sigh, but she said nothing. At least she didn't leap up and leave the attic, he thought grimly, then his humor surfaced. As if she could. He had a captive audience, the thing he had wanted most for two years. Thank you, Mexican Revolution.

"I told your father I would rescue you for one thousand dollars."

She gasped. "I never thought he would . . ." She stopped.

"Pay that much for you? Addie, you're worth much more."

"What will you do with all that money?" she asked

after another long pause, and he heard the icicles hanging from her words.

"It's not mine. The deal was he would give five hundred dollars right away to my father to help him start over."

The ice started to thaw. "And the rest?"

"If I die and don't get you out, it goes to my father too," he told her. "If I succeed, the five hundred is yours. Those were my conditions."

"Noth . . . nothing for you?"

He thought he heard more uncertainty, but she had to hear what he was telling her. "I don't need it. The US Army has contracted my team and wagon to haul freight for our friends and relatives camped along the border who are trying to decide what to do. If I return, I'll keep hauling freight somewhere, hopefully back in Pearson, because Mexico is my home. That's it, Addie. Go to sleep now."

"What am I supposed to do with the money?" she asked, so uncertain that his heart ached.

"I suggest you file for divorce and start over some place where *you* want to live," he said, not mincing his words. "I told you the truth when I said no one told me about your . . . your . . ." He stopped, feeling his own pain. "No, *our* miscarriage. We both said some harsh things."

"Is it too hard to un-hear them?"

She said it so softly. He nodded, then knew she couldn't see him in the dark. "*Quizás*," he said, suddenly unsure. Maybe it was, maybe it wasn't. He had started this rescue of his wife thinking he could teach her something. Now he wasn't so sure who had to learn the most.

Silence. At least she wasn't in tears, which meant she was thinking about what he said, using her head instead of her heart. She lay down, burrowing into the pile of old clothes she had arranged for them both, not close to him, but not across the attic, either. He was content with that. If they could stay alive, time was on his side.

He thought of Old Ammon the Nephite, who went into a foreign land where everyone wanted to kill him. Before he left, his father, King Mosiah, had been promised by the Lord that no harm would come to his beloved son. Ammon didn't know if Heavenly Father had cut the same deal with his own father, but he didn't know He hadn't, either.

Ammon looked toward Addie, lying so still now, even though he didn't think she was asleep. *I will not force her hand*, he thought, chilled to realize how close she had come to what he suspected was a woman's worst fear. How in the world could her father have left her alone in García, in charge of an elderly woman who had been threatening to die for four or five years at least? He considered the matter. In fairness to Thomas Finch, his father-in-law had no idea when he left García that the whole matter of Mormons in Mexico would change so quickly, when word came to pull out of the country.

I wouldn't have done that to my daughter, he thought. *Just call me Señor Self-Righteous.* This was not a comforting thought to coax him to sleep. The rain on the roof did that. If Addie wanted to stay awake and guard them, that was her business. He closed his eyes, more perplexed than usual.

TEN

E WOKE IN the morning to the sound of horses trotting down the main street of García a block over. He sat up alert and on edge, but too slow for Addie, who was already sitting by the open window, watching just out of sight, the rifle in her lap.

The rebel army—which faction he had no idea— was on the move again, heading south. He would have preferred to see them ride west toward Sonora, especially since Addie had to deliver his stolen money to a doctor's wife south of them. Maybe if they hung back long enough, the guerillas would have swarmed through that area like locusts and moved on to victimize another village.

Ammon watched Addie from the attic doorway. He sniffed the air, smelling smoke. Stifling a groan, he crouched his way out of the attic, grateful all over again that Addie was such a poor shot.

"Smoke," he said, and Addie nodded, pointing with the rifle toward the south.

"It's probably Brother Barrett's place," she told him. "I think it was his cattle they shot yesterday."

She spoke calmly, almost as though he were just

an acquaintance, and not the man she had knelt across the altar from in the St. George Temple four years ago. Maybe he shouldn't have been so plainspoken last night.

He considered the matter and decided he had been right. His journey south, bad as it was, had convinced him that he did not want to leave this nation of his birth. If Addie decided to stay with him, she had to weigh all the possible delights with the danger. He would see that she had five hundred dollars, which would at least give her breathing room to think it through on the safe side of the border. And if she decided to stay with him, there was time to worry about that later, once she was safe. If not—he gave himself a mental shrug—he wouldn't be the first man who had made a mistake.

"We're going to bury Grandma Sada as soon as the army rides away," she said in a tone of voice he had never heard from her before. She had always been so gentle and pliable. This time, she spoke with firmness that told him if he did not agree, she would do it by herself.

"I'm not sure I can dig too well, Addie," he told her, stating the obvious truth but also curious to hear her reaction.

She didn't raise her voice. "I'll do what you cannot." She stepped back from the window and toward him, where she could not be seen from the street, if some *soldero* had dared to look at the house with a dead woman inside. "The ground out back is soft from all that rain. I'm going down the hall to our . . . my . . . room, to see if the guerillas left me a needle and thread. I intend to sew this coverlet around Grandma."

"That's a good idea," he said, not because he wanted to placate her but because she was right.

She hesitated a moment before the closed door, as if she expected to see a rebel standing just outside it when she turned the doorknob. She looked back at him. "Will I always be afraid?"

"What you will always be is cautious," he said. "That's even better."

The glance she gave him then was full of gratitude. She seemed to stand a little taller when she opened the door. He heard her rummaging around in their former bedroom, and then a "woo hoo!" which made him happy to know that not even war was going to take all the fun out of his wife.

She came back to Grandma's room, needle and thread on one hand and a necklace in the other.

"The ravaging hordes missed your necklace?" he joked, looking at the gold chain and locket he had given her on their first anniversary, when life was good.

"I hid it in the box where I keep my monthly supplies," she said, her face reddening. "I suppose not even guerillas like to plough through stuff like that. Wish I had put more of my jewelry in there. Everything else is gone."

"Addie, you're resourceful."

She undid the clasp of the necklace and walked to him, turning around so he could work the stiff clasp, his job with this particular piece of jewelry. He did so with pleasure, enjoying the fragrance of her, even if she wasn't any cleaner than he was.

She stood for a long moment looking down at

Grandma Sada, who definitely needed to be buried. Ammon saw the tears on Addie's cheeks and started to gather up the sheet for her. He stopped, remembering.

"Does she have temple clothes?"

Addie nodded and knelt by the bottom drawer of the bureau. She took out the packet containing the temple clothes and handed it to him without a word.

"We can't put her in them because she's a bit far gone for that, but we'll do our best." He looked at her. "Are you square with that?"

She nodded, the muscle in her jaw working as she tried so hard not to cry. He shook out the temple clothing and spread it across Grandma Sada, grateful that he knew Heavenly Father straightened out everything in the eternities. He had believed that all his life, but he understood it on a deeper level now as he prepared a fine old woman for the best grave they could manage in such desperate times.

Ammon returned his attention to the task before him, gathering the sheet and pleating it back and forth until Grandma Sada was hidden from view. As he worked, Addie threaded the needle. She sat on the bed when he finished and with a delicate stitch, sewed the pleats together. Ammon watched her, ready to take over if she faltered. Instead, her face grew more calm with every stitch, until Addie had regained the serenity that had attracted him to her in the first place.

Without a word, Addie followed his lead and gathered the bottom sheet in her hands. When he nodded, she lifted her end and they carried Grandma, a light bundle, down the stairs, and out the back door. They lowered her gently to the porch.

"Do we have a shovel?"

"The Thayns do. I'll get it."

"Can you get a few more bottles of fruit too?"

While she was gone, Ammon looked around the backyard, wishing with all his heart that they could do more for such a fine lady. The ground was softest under the clothesline. The cord hung limp from all the rain, and he remembered the times he had helped Addie hang clothes. Once the sheets were up, she was easy enough to entice inside the sheltering dampness for a kiss. Probably not today, though; maybe never again. The thought troubled his heart. Maybe he wasn't as immune to her as he had tried to make himself believe.

Addie returned with a shovel and two jars of black-berries. She flipped the clasps and handed him one, which he drained, tipping out the blackberries until the jar was empty. He handed it back to her.

"Dry it out well, and get a piece of paper," he said. "Write who is buried here, and include birth date, death date, and place of birth. Maybe next of kin. Whatever you think is important."

She did as he said, returning to the house for paper and pencil. He began to dig, wincing against the pain, but grateful for the night's rain that had softened the ground. When he had to stop, Addie took over without a word. She dug until she ripped out the other sleeve of her blouse. She had pushed up her sleeves until he could see the bruises on her arms, which were turning an unsavory green now. Ammon closed his eyes and thanked God for the doctor who had saved her virtue and probably her life too. The least he could do was see that the physician's wife got the money her husband stole from him.

It took them two hours to dig Grandma Sada a grave that was deep enough to discourage wild animals. Ammon had no idea what guerillas might do to such a mound in the back yard. His arm pained him so much that he started to shake. Addie frowned and bit her lip to see him so weak, but he couldn't help himself. She held out her hand to help him out of the hole, but he shook his head, fearing that if she pulled him out, he would never be able to get back in to finish the task.

"Can you pull Grandma Sada from the porch?"

She nodded finally and did as he asked, gasping when she had to bump Grandma Sada down one step. He knew better than to assure her that Grandma had no idea what was happening. He remembered the old lady as a woman with a real sense of humor, who relished a good practical joke. He hoped she was chuckling now, watching them from the spirit world.

Addie tugged her grandmother to the edge of the grave. Ammon reached up and gentled Grandma into his arms while Addie watched him, her eyes anxious. He knew it was the perfect opportunity to deal himself a sympathy card and groan a little, but he resisted. Addie was under enough strain.

He settled Grandma Sada in her resting place, thinking of Felipe Camacho and his grave under the pepper trees. Addie handed him the glass jar with Grandma's name, death date, and place of birth—Daviess County, Missouri, 1837, plus her nearest of kin. Ammon looked through the glass. Addie had written, "I am the resurrection and the life," from the book of John.

"I wanted something so elegant for Grandma Sada, but here we are," Addie said as she sat beside the grave. "Is it enough?"

"It wasn't until you added that verse from John," he told her, reaching up to touch her leg.

Her eyes filled with tears. "When she was nine years old, she stood holding one corner of a tarp over her mother who was giving birth in the mud beside that trail from Nauvoo. After her mother died, Grandma carried her little brother all the way to Winter Quarters." She bowed her head, and he increased the pressure on her leg. "Why did she have to leave this world in the middle of a revolution?"

"You were with her, and we all know how she felt about you, Addie."

She stood up, all business again, even though tears ran down her face now. She held out her hand for him. "Come on out. It'll take us a while to bury her, and you still have to dedicate her grave."

She helped him out, then went to her knees, head bowed, while he dedicated Grandma Sada's makeshift grave, the home for her body until the resurrection, when the dead would rise again. "Make this a hallowed place, Lord," he prayed. "Addie and I have done the best we could for a fine lady." He stopped, unable to say any more. Addie leaned against him until he could whisper a close to his prayer and hope that he had said the right things. Amazing how many new experiences had come his way since he rode into Mexico.

She brought him the shovel, but he knew he didn't want her to watch while he shoveled the first few layers of dirt over her darling grandmother. Addie looked so uncertain standing there, so young, reminding him of another girl at another grave he had dug only days ago.

"How about you go inside and try to find some better clothes," he suggested as he leaned on the shovel, trying to look so casual, when he could barely stand upright.

"Everything's ruined."

"Not the clothes in the attic," he reminded her. "See if you can find a full skirt. Something that'll work on horseback. I have an idea."

She nodded and went inside, maybe thinking he really did have an idea. After a few moments gathering his strength, Ammon shoveled the good dark earth of Colonia García over a kindly woman who knew what trouble was and who had pioneered her whole life. She had always treated him well, even when Addie wasn't speaking to him.

He was taking a break when Addie sat beside him on the porch step, clothing in her arms. "You'll laugh, but I found a wonderful skirt that I remember wearing a long time ago for a Cinco de Mayo celebration." She shook out the gathered folds.

"I won't laugh at all. That's perfect, Addie," he told her. "Do you have a shawl?"

She held it up, triumphant. "Now all I need is a *bandolera* to look like a *soldadera*!"

"I have an extra one where I stashed Blanco."

"You're serious," she said, her eyes wide now.

"Never more so. Addie, we have to blend in, if we're going to even get close to that doctor's wife in . . . in . . ."

"San Pedro." She looked at the skirt. "There was a shirtwaist in the attic that might work too."

"Change clothes and I'll finish here."

He wasn't done when she came down again, wearing the full skirt and white blouse he had seen on many a señorita. She had found a red sash for her waist, and sandals.

"You'll do," he said, admiring her, which he found as easy to do as it had ever been. She was a lovely woman, maybe not the beauty that her sister Evangeline was, but something better. He had decided early in their marriage that Addie was the sort of woman who would grow more lovely as she aged. He figured Evangeline was about to peak any day now. Not Addie.

Without a word, she took the shovel from him and continued where he had stopped. "You go upstairs now and see what you can find," she said.

"I can fin—"

"Go."

He went, taking his time, mainly because digging the grave had exhausted him, reminding him that he had probably lost more blood than he had thought at first. Food would help, something more substantial than blackberries and apricots. He thought about the canned salmon that everyone in the El Paso lumberyard was tired of and then about Serena Camacho. "I hope you're still alive, Serena *la soldadera*," he said as he went into the attic.

He found two white shirts that must have belonged to Grandpa, dead a long time and buried in a much grander plot in Colonia Juárez. If he was still alive when

135

this whole adventure ended, Ammon knew he would get a coffin for Grandma Sada and take her down there to lie beside her husband.

He pulled on one of the shirts, and in a moment of whimsy—maybe he wanted Addie to laugh again—draped the two fox fur stoles around his neck. Their black glass eyes still gave him the willies same as they had when he was three.

He walked down the hall, brushing aside broken glass with his boots, shaking his head over so much destruction for no good purpose. He stood for a long moment in the doorway of the room he had shared with Addie before their own house was built. There had been mornings after he had come home from a week or two of freighting to just lie there with his wife, talking, laughing, and then putting the quiet time to better personal use. Grandma Sada had never even rolled her eyes at them when they finally came downstairs. She was a woman in a million, much like her granddaughter, whom he had let slip through his fingers like a fool.

Ammon went downstairs and into the dining room. Maybe it was like a tongue seeking out an abscessed tooth to stand there in that doorway and remember Addie's ferocious anger that he was only beginning to understand.

He looked at the sideboard pulled onto the dining table, glasses and dishes broken and scattered, the table caved in. The corner cabinet hadn't been pulled over, even though the bowed glass front that hadn't even cracked coming across the plains was now a ruin.

Ammon found a scrap of a rug in the parlor and returned to the dining room to spread it over the glass fragments. He knelt on the rug and gingerly felt under the china cabinet. He smiled as his fingers closed around his wedding ring that Addie had thrown at him two years ago. Stubborn woman! She had just left it there, too proud to retrieve it. They needed it now. No telling what they could barter for with that ring.

A look into the kitchen turned up a battered canteen with no stopper and a moldy loaf of bread that even the mice had ignored; he ignored it too. From a forgotten wooden box, he coaxed a handful of brown sugar, hardened into shards, which he put in his pocket. He wrapped some loose salt in one of Grandpa Storr's handkerchiefs, also retrieved from the attic. And that was it. Anything else that might have been eaten had been carted away or rendered inedible by someone's call of nature.

"I would say we are not beloved among the various rebel factions," he announced to Addie when he sat down beside her again on the porch.

Addie looked at him and laughed to see the fox furs around his neck—precisely the reaction he wanted. He started to remove them, but she put her hand on his arm.

"They're the latest fashion! Leave them on."

He did, happy to humor her, especially when she looked back at her work. She had finished burying Grandma Sada. He could feel her sadness in the way she seemed to deflate and then lean against him as though her strength was gone.

"No, they do not love us," she said, looking at

the bruises on her arms. "Father wouldn't let us learn Spanish or mingle."

Ammon never thought he would feel inclined to defend his father-in-law, but he reminded her that early Church leaders had advised just such a course. "I know they wanted us to remain neutral." His voice trailed off and he shrugged. "My father thought otherwise, so we learned Spanish."

They were both silent until Ammon handed her the wedding ring. Her face grew rosy, but she took it from him. She started to slide it on her finger, but he stopped her.

"Put it on that chain around your neck."

She gave him a hurt look. She opened her mouth as if to speak, then closed it, her lips in a firm line.

"It's not what you think, Addie," he told her, choosing his words carefully, because sitting there beside his wife, he wanted more than anything to see his ring on her finger again. "It's safer for you on the chain. When I was freighting near Hacienda Muñoz in Sonora, I saw a rebel chop off a woman's finger to get to her rings."

She gasped and turned slightly so he could undo the clasp. Her hand shook as she handed back the ring to slide on the chain.

They sat together in silence until Addie cleared her throat. "What do we do now? You said you have an idea."

"Just a small one," he said, wondering why on earth he had ever told her he had an idea. "We're going to get Blanco and ride into the mountains. We'll sleep today and ride at night. It's safer that way. We're going to hope we look like peasants or a *soldero* and his *soldadera*. We'll take that money to the doctor's wife in San Pedro, then turn around and head for the border."

"What are we going to eat?"

"We'll take as much fruit and juice as we can manage, and this country is full of prickly pears. It would be better not to fire the guns."

She nodded and stood up. She hesitated a moment, then held out her hand to help him up. He almost shook his head to tell her he didn't need any help but changed his mind. He took her hand and she boosted him to his feet.

"Let's get Blanco," she said. "García is starting to make me nervous."

He pried up the Thayns' floorboards this time, while she reached inside for four more quarts of blackberries. He ate and drank two quarts of peaches, then insisted that she do the same. Addie shook her head after the first quart.

Before he tamped down the boards again, Addie wrote a note of apology and stuck it inside one of the empty peach bottles. "I hope they aren't too angry," she said after she put the jar back under the porch.

He had married such a tender soul. Ammon didn't have the heart to tell her that it was highly unlikely the Thayns would ever return to García. He looked up and down the quiet street, memorizing it for the last time because he doubted he would return, either.

They took the back alleys to the north side of García, where their house was set back from the road in a grove of pepper trees. On the way, he told her how he had burned the front of their house so anyone riding by wouldn't bother to stop.

Still, he saw the tears on her cheeks when they came to their home. "I used to go back here now and then, after you . . . you left," she said, her voice soft. "I'd sit on the porch and rock."

"Did you ever go inside?"

She shook her head. "You weren't there." She stopped and set down the two quarts of blackberries in her arms. It took her a long moment to raise her eyes to his, but she did it. "I owe you such an apology, but it's probably not possible to un-hear hard words. I know I can't un-say them."

Maybe we can both try, he thought. Before he could put his thoughts into words, Addie had picked up the bottles and started walking. He hurried to walk beside her, wanting to take her hand, but he was holding the other two quarts of fruit.

She stopped at the front of the house, shaking her head. When she set down the bottles again, he set his down and took her hand. Without a word, he kissed her fingers, then held her hand to his chest.

"I used to love it when you sat on the porch, just humming and knitting," he said. "You almost always fell asleep."

She nodded and gave him such a shy glance that it was almost like the look she used to give him at Juárez Stake Academy, when he decided he was in love. And here they were, standing in front of their ruined house, the one that hadn't fared any better than their marriage.

"Did you break the windows?" she asked, dismayed.

"I did, and ripped your lace curtains too. It had to look ruined, Addie, or I wouldn't have done it."

She nodded, her expression thoughtful. "Where is Blanco?"

"I left him in the kitchen with a lot of water and grain."

He still had hold of her hand, so he gave it a gentle tug. She followed him around the house to the kitchen, where there was no Blanco.

Ammon took a deep breath and another. He looked around, calling his horse's name. Nothing.

He wanted to cry, but not with Addie on the tender side of tears herself. She had not released his hand; in fact, she was rubbing his chest in that way she used to when she knew he was upset about something.

"Addie, I—"

"Señor, *un momentito.*"

ELEVEN

AMMON YANKED ADDIE behind him. He looked around and saw nothing, then wondered why he was such a fool to leave both rifles in the front yard. He couldn't even keep himself safe, let alone a wife. Too bad Addie married an idiot.

"Over here, señor. Fear not."

He forced himself to calm down. Addie spotted the man before he did. He heard her sharp intake of breath as she pointed to the pepper tree beside his smokehouse. An Indian stood there, Mauser in hand, probably the gun he had turned over to the Tarahumara Indians who had so politely stolen his cattle. And he knew the Indian.

"Joselito?" At least his voice didn't squeak like a teenager's.

Addie whimpered, and Ammon patted behind him to reassure her. She pressed so close to him that he almost expected to see her pop out of his chest.

"You are careless. Maybe you need my help."

"Perhaps I do, my friend. Addie, I know him."

Joselito came no closer, squatting beside the smokehouse. The way he took a sudden interest in his rifle, looking down, made Ammon suspect the Indian had his own experience with frightened wives. It was a nicety he hadn't expected.

Addie was breathing so fast he feared she might faint. Ammon turned around and held her so close he could feel her heart beat. He gestured for Joselito to come closer.

"I lost my horse," he said, speaking over Addie's head.

"No," the Indian said. He came closer, but not too close, obviously aware of Addie's terror. "The guerillas came near this house, so I moved him."

Preoccupied with Addie, it took Ammon a moment for Joselito's words to register in his brain. "Hush, Addie," he said finally, tired of worrying about her reaction. He pried her from his body and put his arm around her, walking close to Joselito, dragging her with him.

"You've been trailing me? Why?"

"You helped me. My people have food now." He looked at Addie, whose face was still turned in Ammon's chest, as though she didn't want to see an Indian on top of everything else that had happened. "Señor, there was a guerilla watching your woman when she crossed the street and pried up the boards."

"Joselito . . ."

The Indian put out his hand in a placating gesture. "He watches no more."

"Thank you," Ammon said simply. "I did not expect this of you."

Joselito gave Ammon the kind of look a person would give a not-so-bright child. "What else could I do? When you rode beside us that day, I know you could have galloped, and we could not have kept up with you because we were so hungry."

May you never suspect that the thought crossed my mind, Ammon told himself.

"My women and children are alive because you were kind." A ghost of a smile crossed his face. "Señor, I did not expect that kindness from a white man, but I had to try."

Ammon swallowed and looked away. He felt Addie's hand on his chest, ever the nurturer, even in such a tight spot.

Joselito watched them both, his smile lingering. "Ah, well. You would not have come through all this danger to find a woman you didn't like much."

Ammon chuckled, looking at Addie for her response, then remembered they were speaking Spanish. "I suppose I would not." He knew he could afford to be generous since the matter of the Hancock's cattle was entirely out of his hands. "You may take all my cattle you need."

It was Joselito's turn to laugh. "We will, with or without your permission, señor."

They regarded each other in perfect charity. By now Addie was calmly watching them both. Ammon kissed her temple. "We're all right," he told her, then said it again in English, because he kept forgetting.

Joselito gestured and they followed him, after Ammon snatched up their weapons from the front yard. Walking before them, and so quiet, Joselito led them north into the woods close to the river, where Blanco calmly cropped grass.

Ammon undid the reins from the lower branch of the tree. "Thank you again, my friend," he said.

"Now you will ride swiftly back to the land of the black soldiers," Joselito said.

Ammon shook his head. "I cannot. My woman must repay a debt in San Pedro. Then we will ride north."

The Indian frowned. "You can't expect me to protect you, if you will ride into danger."

"No, I cannot," Ammon said. "You have done enough. In fact, how can I repay *you*?"

Joselito was silent a long moment, reminding Ammon suddenly of Old Ammon the Nephite's encounter with King Lamoni in the Book of Alma, and Lamoni's long pause. *He wants something I have*, he thought. He looked at Addie. No, not Addie. She would drive him crazy within a week or two. The thought made him smile and think, *She would probably shoot him, but she'd miss*.

"What's so funny?" Addie whispered.

You are, he thought and had the good sense not to tell her. "Tell you later." Maybe much later, if he ever worked up the nerve.

The silence continued. Ammon looked at Blanco, so calmly filling up, as if he were abducted by a Tarahumara Indian every day of the week and had no complaints. Come to think of it, this had to be better than being cooped up in a kitchen. No, not Blanco.

Ammon followed Joselito's gaze. He looked down at the fox furs around his neck, and knew. He thought a moment, knowing he needed to charge the occasion with considerable ceremony. "No laughing, Addie," he whispered to his wife and started to sing the grandest church hymn he could think of, which happened to be "The Morning Breaks, the Shadows Flee." He sang it loud and slow as he carefully took Grandma Sada's fox stole with the beady glass eyes off his neck. He watched Joselito's face and knew he was right.

When he finished the first verse, Ammon lowered the stole around Joselito's shoulders. "For you, my friend. This is powerful medicine."

His eyes lively with the thrill of it, Joselito touched the fur piece delicately. "What animal is this that has all-seeing eyes on both ends and joins as one in the middle?"

"The rarest I know," Ammon said. "I will give you its mate, too."

He started to lift the remaining stole off his neck, but Joselito stopped him. "No, my friend. If you are going south like a fool instead of north like a smart man, you need that one for your own protection."

"Very well, if you insist," Ammon said, after a show of reluctance. "Thank you for saving my horse."

Joselito nodded. He smoothed down the fox fur, crooning his own little song to it. He took another long look at Ammon. "How did you hurt yourself?" he asked, indicating the bandage.

"My woman shot me."

Joselito barely blinked. "She's not a very good shot, is she? Keep that totem around your neck or be nicer to her."

He waved his hand and blended into the woods once more. Addie stared at Ammon. "That's going to bring him good luck?" she asked, amazed.

"Maybe anything'll bring you good luck, if you think it will."

"Why did he . . . why did he save Blanco?"

He tugged on Blanco's reins and started back to García. Taking a chance—after all, he did have a powerful totem—he held out his good arm to Addie and she let him drape it over her shoulders, almost like she used to, except she didn't put her arm around his waist. Better than nothing.

As they ambled along, he told her about the Indians sort of capturing him on the river bank and making him give up some of his cattle. "They were in bad shape and I probably could have outrun them on Blanco, but I gave my word." He nudged her. "Kind of like you gave your word to that doctor."

"I had to give my word to him."

"I know you did." He took another chance and hugged her shoulders. "I'm glad you did." He stopped. "We'll just stay here today, a little deeper in the woods. Joselito would be glad to know I'm getting smarter."

"We'll travel at night? Do you know the way in the dark?" she asked, anxious.

"Addie, I've been freighting these roads for a long time. I know my way." He turned toward the river, looking around until he found the trail, little-used since he had left García for Pearson. After Addie threw his ring at him and while his leg healed, he had come here often to fish and think. His thoughts generally led him nowhere, but Ma had appreciated the trout.

"I spent some time here while my leg healed," he told her. "No one can see us from the road." He gestured toward the path that led to the river. "Ma used to wonder where I was."

She blushed and turned away. He watched as she squared her shoulders, let out a shuddering breath, and turned around. "I don't expect you to forgive me, but I want you to know I'm sorry for what I said. And if I'm being too much trouble by making you go south, I can try it alone." It came out in a rush all at once, as though she had been working up the nerve to say that much for a long time.

"You wouldn't get very far by yourself," he said, touched. What he wanted to do was grab her and hold her, and he wasn't sure what stopped him. Maybe it was the shame on her face, the look of someone without any hope. *Would you even believe me if I told you I still love you?* he asked himself. *If you don't believe me, it doesn't matter how I feel.*

She let him take her hand, even though she wouldn't look at him. He walked her to the river and sat her on the fallen log where he used to sit. He sat down beside her. "Addie, I'm here to get you out of Mexico," he began. He stopped and couldn't help his smile. "So far I haven't done a bang-up job."

"It would help if I didn't shoot you." She said it gruffly, tentatively, and he knew that tone in her voice. It was one of his favorites, because he knew how playful she could be.

He laughed, just a low laugh, the kind between two people with a few things in common. "Yeah, that would help. You've taken pretty good care of me since then."

"Have I?" she said it eagerly, sounding so hungry

for his approval that his mood took another shift as she nearly broke his heart.

"You have. You are, Addie," he told her gently. "If we're going to ride tonight, we need to go to sleep now. Wish I'd been smart enough to bring along a blanket. Ground's a bit hard."

He reached for his rifle, tucking it beside him as he lay down by the log. He hoped Addie might lie down on his other side, but all she did was slide from the log and prop herself against it.

When he woke, Addie was gone. He sat up, startled and groggy to find himself covered with her shawl. Blanco still cropped grass close to the river. Birds chirped, and he heard a fish splash. It could have been any peaceful afternoon in early fall before the revolution.

"I'm going to tan your hide if you started walking south," he said out loud, looking around. He sighed with relief to see the odorous money bag lying beside her shotgun. He knew she wouldn't have left without the money for the doctor's wife. He doubted Addie even knew where San Pedro was. If there was a more ill-equipped adventurer than Addie, he didn't know who it could be, unless it was him.

He walked up the path to the road, looking both ways. Nothing. He told himself not to panic; she was a grown woman and not a stupid one. As he stood there wondering what to do, he saw her coming toward him, blankets around her shoulders in the heat and dragging something behind her.

Relieved beyond measure, he walked toward her slowly. As he came closer, he saw how dirty she was, this fastidious wife of his who bathed every night and who used to make him shine her shoes every Saturday night. Her hair must have bothered her because the pompadour was gone, replaced by pigtails which made her look so young.

"I missed you," was all he said. He could have scolded her for giving him such a fright when he woke up alone, but he was beginning to suspect that she had been berating herself for two years and didn't need any help from him.

She gave him a grateful look, reminding him again how eager she seemed to get things right.

"I found these two blankets in the attic. You know how cold it gets at night, and fall's coming." With a little effort, she tugged the burlap bag that she had been dragging toward him. "I dug potatoes."

He looked in her eyes and saw something deep and sweet. A few years ago, she might have just said, "I love you." She was a woman of no confidence now and not brave enough to take a chance and say that, but she had dug potatoes, something he knew she had never done before. Thomas Finch's daughters never went into the field; it was almost a colony joke.

"Addie, you're a wonder," was all he said.

She gave him a shy grin. "At first I thought maybe I could just pull them up by tugging the leaves, but my goodness, they're really in the ground and all wound up in each other."

"That's the way potatoes grow," he said, amused.

"Did you go back to the Thayns for the shovel?"

She nodded and started tugging the burlap bag toward the river. He took it from her and she gave him a grateful look. "I knew they were potatoes. I got the shovel and dug around."

She looked tired but he had no intention of scolding her. What she had done was so kind. He walked her back to the fallen log, then handed her his canteen. She took a long pull on the canteen then gave a contented sigh, followed by a frown. "They were Brother Odegaard's potatoes. I wanted to leave him a note to apologize, but I didn't have a paper or a pencil."

"He won't mind. You know you're a favorite of his," he reminded her. "I wish I had a nickel for every time he asked me why such a pretty girl married me."

Her smile was genuine, which eased his heart. He took her dirty hand and turned it over, tracing the blisters in her palm. She looked away, as if struggling with herself.

"You need more to eat than blackberries," she said in a small voice. "I can wash these potatoes in the river and you can make a little fire . . ."

Her voice trailed off when he kissed her cheek. She inclined her head toward his. "And the fun part? I guess I didn't know this about potatoes: You never know how many you're going to get with each shovelful. It was almost a treasure hunt."

"That's a pretty small pleasure, Addie," he observed.

"I know. Evangeline used to tell me I didn't think large enough. She probably wouldn't have had much fun digging potatoes."

"That *is* the fun thing about potatoes," he agreed, happy even though his shoulder ached and his stomach was about to gnaw through his belt buckle.

While she washed the potatoes, Ammon built a little fire, one of those smokeless kinds he had become adept at creating while freighting through lonely spots after the revolution started. She brought him a handful of potatoes and he gave her his knife to pierce the skins. She sat quietly, watching the fire burn down and turn into ashes.

"I'll stick them in the ashes and we'll just be patient," he told her. "I have some salt too."

They sat together in silence on the log, but it wasn't the uncomfortable silence he had almost dreaded. It was just Addie-silence, because she was a quiet woman. *I have missed this*, he thought.

While the potatoes baked in the ashes, Ammon cut more prickly pear and showed Addie how to trim them. "Are these for Blanco?" she asked.

"They're for us. They taste better than you think."

She objected to staying alone while he rode bareback to their burned shell of a house to retrieve his saddlebags. After he mounted, he held out his hand for her and she scrambled up in front of him, unaccustomed to horses and draped across his lap like a sack of meal. She righted herself and chuckled. He remembered how graceful Serena had been and wisely kept his mouth shut.

He kept well back in the trees, circling behind the smokehouse.

"The guerillas are gone," she said. "Why . . . ?"

"The villagers aren't. We can't really trust anyone, and the sooner we're gone, the better."

She shivered despite the heat of late afternoon. "I should have been more cautious, shouldn't I?" she asked as they neared the house.

"Maybe, but if we see any villagers and they know you're with me, we'll be all right. Dad always made a point of getting to know his neighbors, including the Mexicans."

"My father never did," she told him. "I can't even speak Spanish."

"Maybe you'll learn some."

She nodded and was silent the rest of the way to García. She stood quietly by while he saddled Blanco, then she walked into their shell of a house, picking her way carefully because Blanco had been stabled there for two days. He saw her going from the parlor to their bedroom and into the spare room, where she stood a long moment. He watched her, his heart tender, because he knew she was thinking it would have been a good nursery. He watched her shoulders raise and lower, her head bow, and then she gave that little shake to her shoulders that heartened him. He knew she was a hard woman to discourage and wondered again at her frightening tirade when she flayed him alive in Grandma Sada's dining room.

As he watched her regain her composure, it struck him with considerable force just how much she had wanted their baby. The whole terrible experience must have unsettled her mind. He knew now, as sure as he knew Heavenly Father was real and Joseph Smith was a prophet, that the emergency had rendered her helpless. He wondered if she had the courage to try again, then asked himself if *he* had the courage.

Dusk came as they returned to the riverbank. He had showed her how to put her foot in his stirrup and mount more gracefully so she had nothing to be shy about.

"I'm not sure how comfortable we'll be, riding like this, but I don't have another horse," he started.

". . . and I'm not much of a rider," she finished.

She got off as gracefully as Serena when they returned to their hiding place. Ammon used the shovel to pull the potatoes from the ashes. Addie's face fell when she saw the blackened lumps.

"Never fear," he told her. "We'll use a knife to scrape off the outside, like this. See? It's fine inside, and I have some salt."

She let him put a potato on her tin plate and she did as he said to the potato, revealing an inside soft and white. "I only need one," she assured him, when he shoveled out another potato.

He ignored her and put it on her plate too. "Here's the thing about adventures, Addie: You never know when your next meal is coming. Eat both of them."

"After we have a blessing," she said.

When he blessed their pitiful meal, the familiarity of that ordinary event touched a tender spot in his heart. He thought of their other meals together, and then all his solitary meals in the past two years. So often he hadn't bothered with a blessing, not because he forgot, but mostly because it pained him not to hear her soft, echoing "amen." He listened for it this time, and another pound of discouragement slid off his shoulders.

Dusk had dimmed the harsh light and heat by the time they ate the potatoes and put out the fire. While he led Blanco to the water, Addie carefully poured the juice from the blackberries into their two canteens and added river water to fill them. She scooped the berries into one jar and tucked it in the burlap sack with the potatoes, cushioning it. She drank half the peach juice and ate some peaches, then gave him the rest.

"I wish we could save this jar too," she said, wiping her mouth with the back of her hand, something she never would have done a few days ago.

"Too big a chance it would break. This is where we take a page from Joselito's book," he explained. "When food is plentiful, we will eat all we can. When it is scarce, we will starve."

She nodded and gave that low laugh he had missed so much. "My sister in Logan is probably having a new dress made right now to wear to general conference in October." She looked down at her dirty white skirt. "And probably complaining because it won't be quite right."

He nodded, remembering Evangeline's pointed distaste the day he drove up to the Finch's ranch in all his freighting finery—bib overalls, rough brogans, and a sombrero—with Addie so proper beside him on the wagon seat. He reminded Addie of that day, and his wife laughed.

"Oh, and when you quoted Psalm 37 . . . I can't remember . . ."

"'A little that a righteous man hath is better than

the riches of many wicked,'" he quoted promptly. "Made her angry enough to give me the hairy eyeball."

They laughed together, but he grew serious quickly. "Addie, you and I both need to look dirty and shabby and like every other revolutionary *soldado* and *soldadera*, just in case. Mostly we'll try to stay out of sight. It's fifty miles to San Pedro. Got the money pouch?"

She wrinkled her nose. "Can't you smell it?"

He nodded and mounted Blanco, holding out his hand to her. "We have a debt to discharge. Let's ride, *chiquita*."

TWELVE

THEY WERE FOUR days getting to San Pedro, four days of riding so close together, walking to relieve Blanco, and staying against the tree line between the river and the main road. The first day was hot and dusty, the second day cold and rainy, and on the third day, the complex woman he had married saved his life.

When she dozed during the first night as they rode so slowly, Ammon felt just tired and groggy enough to imagine ways he could appear to some advantage with this wife of his. He was sort of rescuing her, but it wasn't turning out to be a heroic venture at all. He had noticed quickly in his rescue of his wife—if that's what it was—that she seemed so ashamed that she could not look at him for long. Her terrible anger, his eventual withdrawal, and the long days of watching everything crumble around her as Grandma Sada grew weaker and weaker had turned her into a woman of no confidence.

In better circumstances, maybe he could have started visiting her in García, just sitting on the porch to chat a minute and reacquaint her with the man she had married. Ammon doubted there would have been much resistance from Addie's father-in-law, who had been so eager to uproot his family and seek greener pastures in a safer place than Mexico.

But war had interfered. As each day passed, Ammon was discovering how little war and revolution cared about reconciliation. Where life used to be measured by a slow pace in Mexico and little acts of kindness, revolution had blown all that away with the hot winds of destruction, want, and misery.

So he fretted and schemed to no avail as they followed slowly in the wake of a guerilla army. That first evening, they learned, to his dismay, they were following General José Inés Salazar's army, the man most responsible for driving their family and friends from Mexico.

They learned that when they surprised two deserters staring, dejected, at a small fire on the bank of the river, not far from García. They were only boys, brothers probably, who leaped up and clung to each other after Ammon let Addie down in the tree line for safety and rode toward their little fire, cocking his rifle as he came. The metallic sound had been enough to cause them to raise their hands high over their heads. They had no weapons.

They must have thought he was an officer from Salazar's army, sent to round up deserters, because they went to their knees, pleading for their lives, begging the Virgin of Guadalupe to intervene between them and General Salazar. Their fervid petition told Ammon everything he needed to know about how the mercurial Salazar dealt with youngsters tired of war.

He kept his rifle on them as he dismounted, then told them not to worry. All he wanted was information, which they eagerly supplied in their relief to be alive. Ammon motioned Addie forward as the story of their fight on the border at Topia tumbled out, and their increasing hunger as they traveled through villages already stripped bare of provisions.

"We are going home to Morelos," the older of the brothers said, breathless with his tale. His frightened eyes followed Addie as she came into the light of the campfire, her shotgun held in front of her like she meant business, even though Ammon alone knew what a wretched shot she was.

The sight of his wife calmed them further; they must have reasoned that any man traveling with a woman meant them no mischief. *You just don't look like a soldadera*, he thought as he watched Addie too. Still, there was something about the set of her mouth and the way she held the shotgun that made him happy enough not to be her target this time.

"Please, señores, do you have any food?" the younger deserter asked, his hands together.

Ammon turned to Addie. "What about it—do we have any food?" he asked her in English.

She didn't answer right away but returned her calm gaze to the young boys still cowering in front of them. Ammon watched her eyes soften, and her shoulders rise and fall in the sigh of all women when confronted with want among children.

"Am, tell them we will share our potatoes," she said.

No one else would have understood the sweetness of that moment. Maybe Addie hadn't even intended it, but she had used her little nickname for him, back when days were better. He swallowed, knowing he couldn't turn into a blubbering idiot in front of young boys, yes, but soldiers.

He nodded and told her to keep her weapon trained on them, the shotgun he didn't even think was loaded. He fished four potatoes from the burlap bag and handed them to the older youth. He was obviously unfamiliar with potatoes, but his mouth watered anyway.

Ammon told them to sit by the fire and squatted there with them, explaining how to poke the skins with a knife, if they had one, and put the potatoes in the ashes for a while—*un poco tiempo más o menos*—he knew they didn't have a timepiece. He took a little salt from Grandpa Sada's handkerchief and set it on a smooth rock beside the fire, telling them to scoop out the potatoes and sprinkle on the salt.

The boys watched him, their faces serious, and nodded with each instruction. When they did nothing, Ammon smiled for the first time and took out the knife Serena Camacho had given him when he left Santa Clarita.

"Do you have a knife? A weapon?" he asked.

They shook their heads. The older, braver one said, "We won at Topia, but somehow we lost too. How is that possible?"

He could picture it: the boys fighting, and then throwing down their weapons and running when the tide turned, not knowing it would turn back again, as others from the American side of the border had described the fight to him. Ammon was surprised Salazar had not killed them for cowardice.

"Were you flogged for losing your weapons?" he asked gently.

They nodded, so sober. The younger boy turned around and raised his shirt, which made Addie gasp and look away.

"Now you are going home?"

"If we can find it," the older one said. "Before this year, we had never been farther than our village." His face fell. "We might be lost."

"Your village?"

He knew the village they named. By the light of the little fire, while the potatoes roasted, he used the knife to draw the Bavispe River and the pass between the mountains to cross the plains and find their home. When he finished, he handed Serena's knife to them and told them not to lose it.

Ammon gestured to Addie and helped her into the saddle. The boys were staring at the knife, as if amazed at the smile of good fortune, which they probably hadn't seen in a long while. He returned to the campfire.

"I have given you a knife and food. What else should I know about Salazar?" he asked.

"The army is hungry and short of weapons," the younger boy offered. He ducked his head. "We were not the only ones to drop our rifles and run."

The older boy seemed to have a better grasp of tactics. "The army is going to join up with more soldiers at Namiquipa."

"Then will they head south?" Ammon asked, hopeful.

The boy shrugged, then grinned, telling Ammon

that not all the fun was gone from his young heart. "Señor, General Salazar did not take me into his confidence."

Ammon laughed and touched the boy's head. "*Vayan con Dios*," he told them.

He took the reins from Addie and walked Blanco deeper into the trees.

"Stop a moment," Addie said, when they could still see the two boys.

He did as she said. They both looked back to see the boys scrabble in the ashes of the fire, pulling out the potatoes that were still mostly raw. Again he heard her sigh. He reached up and gave her foot a tug, because he couldn't speak, either.

He mounted and they rode in silence under a full moon. Gradually, Addie began to lean back against him and he just as gradually tightened his arms around her. She was quiet, but that was Addie. Leaving out the little detail of Grandma Sada's tablecloth covering four dead bodies at Topia, he told her about his encounter with Serena and Felipe Camacho.

"And you prayed that Heavenly Father would take him?" she asked, amazed at what he said.

"He couldn't live, and I couldn't help him," he pointed out. "And there was Serena, so frightened."

"A *soldadera* afraid," she mused. "It's hard to believe. Why did you stop to help?"

"You'll laugh."

"I doubt it. Really, why stop? The boy couldn't harm you, and . . . and Serena wasn't going anywhere. These people are our enemies."

"I've been reading that part in Alma where Ammon . . ." He gave a self-conscious chuckle. "I've been calling him Old Ammon the Nephite—where Ammon goes to preach to the Lamanites. As near as I can tell, he just went around asking what he could do to help."

Maybe it did sound strange. Good thing Addie couldn't see his face. "I thought I could help."

"Sounds like you did, Old Ammon. I doubt anyone helps much in a war."

He shrugged. "I'm starting to think that all anyone wants is just to be left alone to grow a little garden."

He heard the humor in her voice. "My father would say that's what's wrong with the Hancocks: no ambition." Her humor changed to embarrassment as the woman of no confidence resurfaced. "I should never have said that."

He took a chance and kissed the top of her head. She was as grimy as he was now, but he didn't care. And her words didn't sting. "He'd be right. Our ambitions don't go much beyond land and cattle." It was his turn to feel embarrassed. "You know, Addie, I like my freighting business, but it kept me away from church now and then, didn't it?"

She nodded. "It's hard to get started when you don't have much capital to begin with," she said, excusing him so gracefully that he couldn't help smiling. "I thought my father might offer to help you financially, but he never did."

"He never saw me as a sure thing."

"That's where we differed," she told him, her voice soft.

She didn't say anything else. In a few minutes, her head lapsed to one side and he knew she slept. The night was warm, but he knew his warmth came from inside. Maybe somewhere under all the hurt and shame, she might still think he was a sure thing.

He was so tired in the morning that his eyeballs felt as though they had been removed, dipped in sand, and shoved back in. Addie had slept most of the night, so she was wide awake. Once Blanco was unsaddled and hobbled by the small stream, Ammon yawned, sat down under a tree and closed his eyes.

When he opened his eyes, the sun was high overhead. He lay on his side, his hands tucked under his cheek like a child. He heard a splash from the stream so he turned over quietly in time to see his wife washing herself. She was as lovely as he remembered, even though it was obvious that the last few weeks of deprivation had taken a toll on her. He could clearly see the vertebrae in her spinal column. When she raised her arm to wash under it, he could have counted her ribs.

Considering the current tentative nature of their relationship, if there even was a relationship, he turned over again and devoted his attention to the tree he slept under. She splashed a little more and then was silent. When he heard the rustle of her clothing, he yawned and then coughed. After a few more minutes, he yawned again and rolled onto his back. When he looked in her direction this time, she was dressed and combing her damp hair with her fingers.

When she finished, she came closer, holding out several prickly pear leaves. She had trimmed them, but he would have known that just from looking at her fingers, which were pricked and bleeding.

"I'm not too good at this yet," she apologized.

He examined one of the leaves elaborately, which made her smile. "You're being silly," she said. "What do I do now?"

"I cut mine in chunks, but Serena Camacho cut hers into strips. Your choice. Are the potatoes gone?"

"We're saving them," she said as she cut the *nopal* into strips. "If you want to wash in the river, it's shallow there by the bank." She sniffed. "In fact, I recommend it."

She looked at him with just the hint of a twinkle in her eyes, which made him want to wriggle like a puppy.

"Yes, ma'am," he said promptly. "I'll do it for you, but would you take off the bandage? Maybe I should let some air get to my arm."

She helped him out of his shirt and untied his garments and helped guide his arm out of the sleeve, wincing as he winced. Her face was serious as she unwrapped the dirty bandage. They both looked at the wound, which had started to granulate, to Ammon's relief. Her eyes filled with tears.

"I could have killed you."

"Not with that shot," he replied, keeping a light tone. "Let me give you some advice, in case you decide to fire that shotgun again: keep your eyes open and hold your breath, then just squeeze the trigger."

"How did you know I had my eyes closed?" she accused.

"I was watching your face."

He went to the river's edge and unbuttoned his pants. "Well, to quote the punch line to a bad joke my father told me once, 'Close your eyes, ladies, I'm coming through.'"

He stripped and waded in, glancing back at the bank to see Addie looking the other way. He chuckled and sat down where the river was sandy, using some of the grit to scrub away more grime than even he was used to. Freighting was dirty business, but war even more so, he decided. He hummed to himself, remembering a few memorable moments in a tin tub with Addie scrubbing his back. He wondered if she ever thought of those times he knew he would never forget, since they were all he had now.

When he finished and looked around, Addie was still facing away, but she must have tossed her shawl toward him to use as a towel. It was still damp from her efforts in the stream. When he was dressed, he joined her in the shade. She had a pile of prickly pear leaves. Like the good Relief Society sister he knew she was, she had arranged them, spoke-like and organized, on the tin plate.

She asked a blessing on their pitiful breakfast and handed him the plate. "Evangeline tells me that her husband is getting flabby," she told him, maybe aiming for some breakfast table conversation.

It amazed him how quickly some women could adjust to life's bare bones. He hadn't really known that about Addie. What she said also made him laugh inwardly.

Maybe not so inwardly. "What's so funny?" she asked.

"You are," he teased. "You know I'm not flabby. Confess: did you peek when I dried off?"

Her face turned rosy. "I was merely wondering if you might need some help getting into your clothes again," she told him with some dignity. "You will *never* be flabby."

Well, a compliment. Funny how it made the tasteless *nopal* go down better. "He was flabby before Evangeline married him. I don't think bankers work too hard outdoors."

He could barely keep his eyes open after they finished breakfast, but Addie was still alert, and he wasn't about to shut her down by going to sleep. After he assured himself that Blanco was well-hidden, he found a comfortable-looking spot that a deer and fawn must have vacated, and moved them in.

He settled himself against a sun-warmed boulder, Addie close by, but not too close. He told her about sleeping in the deserted stables on Hacienda Chavez, claimed by General Salazar now and destroyed by one faction or another. He couldn't bring himself to tell her about the discarded ladies, not when she had suffered her own brush with the cruelty of war on women.

"What happened to the owners?"

"Serena told me some of them were probably dead in the burned-out *hacienda*."

Addie digested that. "I remember Hacienda Chavez from your company books. You knew them, didn't you?"

He nodded and told her about his last visit, and the lovely women on the porch. "One of them was Graciela Andrade. Remember her?"

"Of course I do! You and all the other boys in our class were in love with her. Evangeline used to complain all the time that none of them even looked at her when Graciela was around."

"Did that bother you?" he asked, his eyes starting to close.

"Why would it?" she asked in turn. "I was never in her league, or Evangeline's, for that matter."

You were always better, he wanted to assure her, but sleep took over.

He woke up to rain, the kind of cold rain in early autumn that he always welcomed because they lived in a parched land. It didn't feel so welcome now as it dripped off his nose and chilled him to the bone. Addie had kindly covered him with one of their blankets and wrapped herself in the other, but her teeth chattered.

There was too much rain to build a fire. The only thing to do was ride, even though it wasn't full dark. They had passed occasional ruined buildings as they cautiously followed General Salazar's line of march. Maybe there was one set back from the road that had a roof left, and they could find shelter there. He could hope.

He was starting to worry about Addie, who shivered continuously now when he saw what he knew must be a chicken coop. Some of the locals dug below the ground to build coops cool enough to shelter chickens during Chihuahua's scorching summers. The level above ground generally housed more hardy animals or was used as storage space.

The structure was set well back in the trees. Blanco shied and stepped around as they approached, so he dismounted and left Addie by the coop. He led Blanco beyond the building and down to the trees by the river, where the gelding seemed to settle down.

By the time he returned with his saddlebags and weapons, Addie had already crouched her way into the coop, pulling the potato sack with her. The chickens were long gone, but the odor made him wrinkle his nose.

"Be it ever so humble," Addie said doubtfully.

He could barely see his hand in front of his face, much less his wife, but at least the coop was dry. He looked around when his eyes accustomed themselves to the dark. At least they weren't sharing the space with anything except moldy straw and an egg better left uneaten.

"We'll stay here the rest of the night, and probably tomorrow." He sat down and leaned against the wall. Addie was just the barest outline now, but he held out his arms, hoping she would accept the invitation.

After a moment's hesitation, she did and sat on his lap. He put his arms around her as she continued to shiver. The rain was noisy on the roof above and dripping through in places. Without any comment, Addie took off her sodden skirt and spread it out on the floor. She sat on his lap again and wrapped her blanket around them both.

"That skirt will never dry," she said through chattering teeth.

Ammon put his finger to her lips, listening. Above the sound of the rain, he heard something stirring on the floor above them. It was just a little rustle, like an animal circling around to find a better spot, probably the equivalent of a human turning over a pillow to find a cooler place.

"What's wrong?" Addie whispered.

"Nothing. Some animal. I hope it's not javelinas, because they stink."

"So do we," she pointed out, then put her hand over his mouth in turn when he started to laugh.

Ammon held Addie in his arms, relieved when she finally stopped shivering. Her head grew heavy against his shoulder as he listened and then slept too.

He woke before she did. The rain had stopped and silence was everywhere now. He listened. Nothing. He let out a quiet sigh of relief. Javelinas could be nasty if cornered. No wonder Blanco had been so jumpy.

It suited him to just lie there, hold Addie in his arms, and remember better times. He could see her distinctly because it was daylight and the rain had stopped. Her lips were chapped from the eternal dryness of their high desert climate. He used to get beeswax from Brother Odegaard just for her. She added a little vanilla and was so sweet to kiss.

He wanted to kiss her again. Maybe if she was deep in sleep she wouldn't know. When he moved a little closer, his stomach started to growl. Her eyes opened and she watched his face. She always came awake so peacefully, another part of her serenity he hadn't discovered until they were married and shared the same bed.

She was ordinarily such a busy person, active all day, that this new facet of her personality was a tonic to him. It had remained so, he discovered, holding her in a foul-smelling coop in Nowhere, Chihuahua.

He couldn't tell by her expression whether she wanted him to continue what was probably pretty obvious to her. He sat back, choosing to err on the side of discretion. He really wanted to watch and see if she was disappointed, but his courage failed him.

His stomach rumbled again and Addie sat up. She colored slightly, looking down to see her one petticoat up around her knees. "I hope my skirt is dry," she said in her rusty voice of early morning.

Ammon reached for it as she stood up. "Dry enough," he told her, his voice as rusty as hers. He might have been more thirsty than hungry. It was easier to remedy the thirst when he went to the river to check Blanco and kick himself a few times for being an idiot. His hunger was starting to require more than food; he wanted Addie more than he wanted a real meal.

She pulled on her skirt, smoothing down its stained folds much as he remembered her smoothing down her best Sunday dress. He almost expected her to do the little twirl in front of her floor-length mirror in their bedroom that she always did. Too bad the mirror had been carted off to someone's *casa*, and the house was a burned-out shell with horse manure in the kitchen.

She pressed her middle and winced. "I don't know about prickly pear," she said. She picked up her shotgun. "See? I'm going to remember this from now on."

"Wait for me, Addie."

"Nope." She shook her head. "I have to . . . uh . . . evacuate."

He grinned at that. His wife was so proper. "That's not what I call it."

She gave him a pointed look and shook the weapon at him. "I *know*," she said. "Am, at some point, I think I'll just be happy when you say . . . say . . . cow dung instead of, well, you know what you say!" She crouched her way from the coop.

He watched her go, almost holding his breath. What she had said implied there might even be a future. Maybe he'd have to try out dung instead of you know. He heard a sudden, familiar sound and looked up, quiet now and listening. He hadn't heard anything earlier, but there it was again, not javelinas but something bigger, something that purred but was far from domesticated.

"Addie," he called. "*Cuidado. Vuelva a mí.*" He slapped his head. *In English, you fool,* he thought. "Be careful! Come back!"

THIRTEEN

HE COULDN'T HAVE put a sequence to what happened next because it happened so fast. The noise was almost directly overhead, so he jerked open the trapdoor above him to stare into cat eyes, smell a cougar's breath, hear a snarl, and feel a swipe that just caught the tip of his nose as he reared back.

He yelled and put his hand to his bleeding nose. The puma, as startled as he was but much quicker, settled into a quivering crouch only seconds from launch when the door on that upper level slammed open.

"No, Addie!" he screamed as the cougar sprang, her shotgun went off, and the animal collapsed on top of him, half in and half out of the trapdoor. He felt the heat of the cougar's blood as it dripped onto his face. The cougar gave another half-hearted swipe that hooked into his neck. The claws flexed in and out, then the animal dangled there, dead.

Ammon shook his head to clear it, wiping cougar blood from his eyes, fearful it was his at first. He felt no pain except for the sting on his neck and nose, which hurt less than the last time someone had aimed that shotgun his way. His ears rang with the close range percussion, and he yawned to relieve the unpleasant pressure.

Addie. He leaped away from the dangling cougar and scrambled out of the coop, calling her name. She sat slumped in the doorway, the shotgun in her lap, her head down. Fearful, he touched her shoulder and she toppled over in a dead faint, probably as startled as the cougar had been.

He cradled her in his arms, holding her until she regained consciousness. Her eyes fluttered open and she gasped. He had forgotten about the cougar's blood all over his head. Her eyes started to roll back in her head again, so he patted her cheek, crooning to her, " Sweetest little feller,'" because it was the only song he could think of, what with his pulse still racing and his ears ringing now.

"Addie, I'm fine. That's not my blood," he told her. "You saved my life."

"Don't shout so loud," she protested, then burst into tears, clinging to him.

He held her close. When her tears tapered off into a sniffle, he pulled up her skirt and commanded her to blow into it. She blew her nose, then just shivered in his arms.

"I did what you said," she told him finally, her voice still breathless. "I kept my eyes open and held my breath."

"Worked, didn't it? Addie, let's get out of here."

She made no protest as she stood up, staggered, and let him hold her close until she could stand on her own. She looked in the upper room again, her eyes huge, her mouth open, to see the cougar she had killed, probably while it was pouncing.

"I did *that*?"

He heard the amazement in her voice, mingled with something that sounded like pride, which made Ammon want to shout hooray. "No one else did it. You saved my life."

She leaned against him, her arm around his waist now. He could tell himself that maybe she was still having trouble standing; he could also think that she wanted *him* close. He decided to believe that.

"I didn't even think it was loaded. I was going to rush in there and bash him over the head, but I thought I should try the gun first."

He closed his eyes and thanked Heavenly Father she hadn't done that. "Addie, you'd have died."

Her eyes filled with tears again. "But he was going to pounce on you!"

What a woman, he told himself, amazed at her courage or foolhardiness or whatever it was that made a little greenhorn like Addie ferocious enough to take on a mountain lion. Maybe, just maybe, she still liked him a little.

He kissed her cheek. "I loaded the shotgun yesterday morning."

"You might have told me," she accused, giving him The Look, which pleased him more than he could say, because she sounded so wifely again.

"Yeah, I might have." He looked around, wondering just who might have heard that shotgun blast. "We're going to get out of the area as soon as we can. No telling who that gunshot may have alerted. There might be other deserters around, or an army over the horizon, and we don't need that."

She nodded, businesslike. She ripped off a section of her petticoat and went to the river, returning to wash his face, going gently around the gash on his nose, and frowning over the puncture marks in his neck. He let her, sitting on a rock in the sun, happy to be fussed over. When she finished, he went into the coop and came out with the saddlebags, blankets, potatoes, and his rifle.

When he brought up Blanco from the river, the horse shied again. "You were certainly smarter than we were last night," Ammon told the gelding, patting him into calm.

Addie was inside the coop. He peered inside, amused now to see her, hands on her hips, looking at the dangling cougar. "You know what I wish, Am?"

"That I could skin it and make you a rug?"

"That would be nice, but no. Where would we put it? I wish I had my Kodak Brownie so you could take a picture of me standing by this monstrosity. Can you imagine what my friends in Utah would think?"

Ammon shook his head, amazed. He had no plans to inform her that as cougars go, it was on the small side. Also, when he had taken a closer look while Addie was at the river, he noticed that although the claws were formidable, the cat's teeth were worn down or missing. The old gent must have just wanted a refuge from the rain, same as they did. He hoped that as the years passed, if they lived to get out of Mexico, she would tell the story to their children and the mountain lion would get bigger and bigger.

He took her by the hand. "You were going to beat that lion to death for me."

She matched him serious for serious. "I guess I was."

He kissed her forehead. "Let's *vámonos*. That's Spanglish for . . ."

"I know."

As Ammon boosted her into his saddle, he turned around to see two young boys and a woman watching them, their eyes wide. They turned and stared into the shed.

"My wife killed that cougar," he told them.

"Oh, Am!"

Ammon took the reins. Not trusting the road or even the tree line right now, not after both noisy barrels, he led Blanco into the water, which only came up to his knees. He walked down the Rio Papigochic, wanting to leave no tracks. After a short distance, he stopped and looked back. Two *paisanos* with wicked-looking machetes were approaching the chicken coop now while the little boys danced around and pointed inside.

Addie looked back too, her eyes troubled. "We don't know who is friend or foe, do we?"

"We don't. That's why we can't trust anyone." *Except each other*, he thought. *Trust me always, Addie.* He looked into her eyes and felt the gentleness of her gaze in a way that made him swallow and look away, suddenly shy around this woman he knew pretty well. She looked like she was thinking that exact thing.

He continued down the river another mile, hunting

for a good place to hide and finding nothing. They were losing their tree cover as they left the sheltering mountains. He knew the Rio Papigochic would continue its leisurely journey across open land better traveled by the light of the moon. He looked ahead and saw what he dreaded—a cloud of dust that had to be someone's army, heading south as they were. He didn't know what to do. *Please, God*, he prayed.

"That's an army, isn't it?" Addie asked.

"I'm afraid it is." He looked behind them, wondering if they should go back. As he stood there in the river, he noticed an ox pulling a two-wheeled cart that had probably never known the silence of greased wheels. An old man walked alongside the beast, keeping pace. He appeared to be singing, but who could tell, with the noise from the wheels? The wheels had caught his attention for another reason; they were bright red, and the wagon bed was blue. Ammon knew that cart.

He let his breath out. "We're going up on the bank now," he told his wife. "Hang on. I'll help you off, and I want you to just stay here with Blanco in the shade of the trees."

She nodded and gripped the pommel, her face serious, unable to hide the fright in her eyes. In a moment Blanco stood on the bank, shaking himself. Addie held out her arms to Ammon and he lifted her down. "Just stay here." He touched the frown between her eyes, knowing how much she did not want to be left alone.

Taking his time—this was Mexico, where only criminals hurried—he walked in the tree line paralleling the road and prayed he was right. With a deep breath, he stepped out from the protection of the trees as the cart made its slow way toward him. He nearly went to his knees in gratitude at the sight of a familiar face, a round one with a white beard that he used to think was Mexico's San Nicolas. He raised his arm and waved.

The old man spoke to his ox and the cart stopped. He peered closer with eyes that Ammon knew were growing milky, then walked toward Ammon, keeping his staff in front of him. A few more feet, and then he laughed, put down the staff, and raised his arm too. If Heavenly Father hadn't sent Pablo Salinas to them, Ammon decided he didn't know much about Heavenly Father.

"Hello, my son! I have not seen you in a while. I was afraid the armies ran you out of our country!"

"Not me! As you say, it is my country too." Ammon grasped the old man's extended hand, then found himself in a warm *abrazo*. Pablo Salinas smelled of wood smoke and old age and wet wool.

Pablo Salinas stepped back and took a good look, shaking his head. "Are you injured, my son?" he asked, the concern in his voice warming Ammon even more.

"No, no. This is a mountain lion's blood. My woman killed it."

Pablo took another step back in surprise, his eyes as wide as a child's. "I have come from Ildefonso—I know, I know, a grandiose name for such a poor village—and what do I hear but a story of a dead mountain lion in a chicken coop. Your woman did *that*?"

"She did. She wanted to save my useless hide."

They laughed together, husbands.

"Where is this magnificent woman?" Pablo asked, looking around.

While the old man leaned against the big wheel and the ox stood patiently, Ammon told him what had happened. "So you see, my friend, we are in need of a place to hide today. We travel at night, and we are trying to get to San Pedro."

"Better you should go the other way," Pablo warned, reminding Ammon of Joselito, who had the same advice.

"I know. This woman of mine made a promise to help another woman, and she will keep her word."

Pablo nodded. Ammon knew that he had a woman much like Addie, the conscientious kind. He chuckled when Pablo shook his head.

"Señor 'Ancock, why do men like us marry women like that?"

It was a good question. They looked at each other with understanding.

"We dare not travel any more today, not with an army so close. Pablo, I throw myself on your mercy," Ammon said. It sounded more elegant in Spanish than English, and hopefully contained just a hint of the desperation Ammon felt. He had a lot of faith in the Spanish language.

Pablo looked away and thought a long moment, perhaps weighing the rules of friendship against his own safety. Ammon looked away too, so he would not appear to be pleading. Even in dangerous times, men had to be brave.

Pablo looked back. He touched Ammon's arm. "We will find a place for you and a woman who kills mountain lions. A little boy said she used her bare hands! Follow me. We will cross this river and take a safer way to my home."

Addie's eyes were big with fright as the two of them walked toward her in the sheltering trees. As they came closer, the killer of mountain lions dropped the rock in her hand.

He introduced them, and Pablo bowed in that effortless way of Mexican men who like the ladies. "I've known Señor Salinas for years," Ammon told her as Pablo nudged his ox into the river.

"He's so poor. You couldn't possibly ever have freighted for him," Addie said as Ammon steadied her in front of him in the saddle.

"No. I helped him once with a load of corn, after a wheel came off his cart." He smiled when she leaned against him. "To hear him tell it, it was pouring rain, and there were Apaches circling his cart and wolves nipping at his ox. Mexicans do like to work over a good tale and make it better."

She chuckled. "You really did freight his corn?"

"I did, all the way to Namiquipa. He swears I got him a better price because he came in such style. We had the wheel fixed and I returned him to his ox and cart."

She nodded. When she spoke again, her voice was serious. "Will we be putting him in danger?"

"Probably. He has a broken-down barn, and we will sleep there. We'll take turns keeping watch."

"No mountain lions, please!"

The sun had passed its zenith when they arrived at Casa Salinas, an adobe structure that had probably seen better days a century ago but which appeared to be standing upright out of sheer habit. They were greeted by a genial dog not much younger than his owner, and a little woman almost as tall as she was round. With an exclamation of delight as though she had been waiting for him for years, she grabbed Ammon and shook him from side to side, which made Addie laugh.

"Addie, this is Maria Salinas, Pablo's better half." He leaned closer. "She'll grab you too."

"I want to be grabbed," his kind wife said. Maria put her hands on Addie's shoulders, looked in her eyes, said, *"Pobrecita,"* burst into tears, and hugged Addie to her generous bosom.

When Addie was tight in the circle of her arms, Maria glared at Ammon. "You don't feed her enough," she declared. With Addie firm in her grip, Maria turned and walked her into the little house that stood up from force of habit, crooning to her. The genial dog followed after giving Ammon a reproachful look too.

I'm in heaven, Ammon thought. He looked at Pablo. "Can you find a good place for this horse of mine while I get the yoke off your ox?"

The biggest meal of the day came in the middle of the afternoon—tortillas and beans, with just a hint of pork from an elderly rind that Maria must have used many times. Old or young, the food was delicious. Addie ate wholeheartedly, unaware that the three of them were watching her: Ammon out of gratitude that she had a meal; Maria as determined as a mother hawk; and Pablo pleased to help his friend, *el gringo* Señor 'Ancock.

One tender moment came when Maria asked Ammon, "Where is your child?"

Addie looked at him to translate, as he had translated all the conversation around the small table. He had to tell her. "The last time I saw these two dears, you had just told me you were expecting," he whispered, afraid to look in her eyes. "They were delighted at our good news."

She nodded, her face composed. "Tell them we have known sorrow," she whispered back.

He told them, then held his breath with the beauty of the moment as Maria took Addie's hand and kissed it. "We leave it in God's hands," she said.

Touched, Ammon started to translate, but Addie shook her head. "I understand what she said. *Gracias*," she told Maria and pressed Maria's hand against her cheek.

Maria and Pablo nodded as Ammon told them of their need to sleep now and then ride when it was darker, to avoid the army. "If you will just let us sleep in that shelter behind your house . . ."

Maria shook her head, her expression mutinous. "We *have* a bedchamber."

"We must, my dear," Ammon told her. "We could never put you in danger by sleeping in your house."

She shook her head again, her lips in a pout that would have made him laugh, except that his heart wanted to break with her kindness to him and his woman who had killed the enormous mountain lion. *I love these people*, he thought, *my countrymen*.

"Please, señora," he began, but Maria wasn't listening.

Discussion over, Maria took Addie's hand and led her into the other room in the house.

Pablo grinned and watched them go. "My friend, if you want to sleep with your woman you had better do as Maria says."

"Pablo, I can't take your—"

The old man's hand caressed his shoulder. "Maria and I will watch while you sleep." He shrugged elaborately. "And if you want to do something besides sleep, we are both hard of hearing."

"Pablo, I—"

"Eh?" he asked, cupping his hand behind his ear.

After Maria left the little room, giving him a militant look that would probably have frightened General Salazar into silence, Ammon joined Addie in the small space and closed the door.

"She's impossible to argue with," he said. "Addie, if you'd rather I slept somewhere else . . ."

"For heaven's sake, Am, what have we been doing this past week? Don't be silly. Just because it's an actual bed with clean sheets . . ." His wife the lion killer pulled back the sheet.

He shed his outer clothes, including his fox stole, the one Joselito was certain contained magical powers. "Why in the world am I still wearing this?" he asked out loud.

Addie laughed. "Because that Indian would be disappointed if you didn't! Besides, I think it becomes you."

"Knothead."

He had expected the mattress to be noisy corn husks, but he sank and sank into feathers. "My goodness, Addie, this is magnificent. I would never have guessed."

He straightened out his arm and she came close, resting her head on his chest. The sun went behind clouds, darkening the room. He wanted it to rain again and thought he heard thunder. He raised up on one elbow, alert. It was artillery, not thunder.

Addie, bless her, pressed her hand against his chest and he lay down again. "There's nothing we can do about what is going on out there," she said, her voice as serene as he remembered from their best days together. "I believe we have to leave this in God's hands too."

He nodded and closed his eyes, worn out and ragged, but he had to talk. "Addie, what would you have named our baby?"

He said it softly, not knowing what she would say, so uncertain, even though he had wondered. She was silent a long while, and then he felt his arm grow damp where her head rested. He pulled her closer. When she spoke, her voice was almost too soft to hear.

"I would have wanted you to name our baby, if it were a boy. Maybe after our fathers."

"I thought about that," he told her. "David Thomas or Thomas David?"

She nodded, silent. "I wanted Betsy for a daughter. Just Betsy."

"Do we know any Betsys?"

"Do we need to?"

He chuckled. "Nope. I would have liked Betsy too.

Betsy Hancock. That's good, because when she married, she wouldn't have too many names . . ." What was he *saying*? "Addie, I am so sorry."

She nodded again. "All I wanted was for you to be with me, and you weren't. I went a little crazy."

She was baring her heart, exposing so much pain that she shuddered with it. He held her closer, both arms around her now.

"I was freighting logs in the Sierra Madres," he began. "You know the contract, because I remember that before I left you said it would make our fortune. The loggers were shorthanded, so I was helping. Some help! One of the logs rolled on my leg. You could hear the crack all over camp."

She said something inarticulate, which he took as consent to continue. "I . . . I don't remember anything after that. The doctor told me later that two days passed before he got there. The bone was sticking out. He didn't know why infection didn't set in."

"Heavens," she murmured.

"He actually had some chloroform, so he put me out so he could set it and stitch me up. I started home as soon as I could, but it was two weeks."

No need for her to know how he cried from the pain, wailing out loud to the empty forest as he gave his horses their head and let them take him home to García. "All I wanted to do was get home to you, because I knew you would make it better," he concluded simply. "Addie, as God is my witness, I had no idea."

"I know you didn't," she said finally. "Papa told me

he sent a telegram, but since the war began, telegraph service is so poor."

No need for you to know that your father forgot, he told himself. *I can leave that one alone.*

"That's quite a scar on your calf. I . . . I noticed it at the river."

He smiled, relieved. He knew that tone of voice. "Ah-ha. So you *were* admiring my manly physique!"

"Guilty as charged," she said, amused. She sighed then, and it turned into a barely masked sob. "Too guilty."

"Guilty of what? Being human? Feeling sad?"

"I wanted to call you back. I wasn't brave enough. Too proud, too upset—I can't explain it."

"I should have tried harder," he said, remembering all the letters he had sent. Any fool could put a stamp on a letter. "I should have planted myself on Grandma Sada's side porch and stayed there until you felt like seeing me."

"You had a business to run."

Heavens above, she was excusing him. "You should have been more important to me." Ammon raised up on his elbow again. "Addie, I've made a hash of this rescue. We're going to find that doctor's wife, toss the money at her, and run for the border." He sighed. "Except . . ." He just couldn't say it.

She knew. God bless her heart, she knew. "Except you just can't quite leave Mexico, can you?"

"I'm not sure I can." He sat up. Addie rested her head on his lap and his fingers twined in her hair. "Sit up and look at me."

She did as he said, her face just as serious, her eyes boring into his.

"I want you safe, so you're leaving this country." He put his fingers gently on her lips when she tried to speak. "My turn! We both have to do some heavy thinking. The middle of a war is no time to make a snap decision and eternity is a long while." He touched his forehead to hers. "Your turn."

Addie lay down, pillowing her head on him again. "I'm afraid, and I'm lonely, and I'm weary of being afraid and lonely. I'll do what you say, Ammon, because you're right. The Mexican Revolution is no time to solve our problems."

He nodded and slid down beside her. "Agreed." He closed his eyes, weary in his heart. "Go to sleep. We have to ride tonight."

"You weren't listening," Addie the lion killer said. "I said I'm afraid and I'm lonely. I'll probably be afraid until I cross the border, but I don't have to be lonely right now, do I?" Tentative at first, she ran her hand up his leg, pausing on his scar but not for long.

He was no dunce. Besides, Pablo had assured him that he and Maria were hard of hearing.

$\mathcal{F}$OURTEEN

$\mathcal{T}$HEY WERE FOUR days at Casa Salinas, because the war refused to move, or maybe because the bed was soft and Pablo and Maria the perfect hosts. By silent consent, they took turns sleeping and watching. Pablo moved Blanco into an arroyo farther back from the river, along with his valuable pig and two goats. Once while Ammon and Addie hid under the bed, a detachment of *federales* stalked through the house, eventually liberating the not-so-valuable pig and slashing the feather bed. The rooster's indignation at losing his harem ended when the rooster, silenced, joined the trio headed for the stewpot.

"He's a scrawny rooster," Ammon said, as the four of them surveyed the feathers from the bed fluttering around the house like soft snow. "Why are you so serene about this, my friend?"

Pablo only shrugged. "Rulers have been stealing from the poor since the time of Moctezuma." He nudged Ammon. "Besides, I have more hens and another rooster in an arroyo just beyond your smart horse and my *cerdo gordito*."

Although the killer of the largest cougar ever shot in Chihuahua watched her husband anxiously, Ammon and Pablo made their own reconnaissance on the second day of battle. He laughed when she made him wear the fox stole over his serape.

"Your woman worries too much," Pablo said, when they were out of sight of Casa Salinas. "Is she with child again? They get that way when they are broody."

Heavens, I don't think so, Ammon thought and felt his face grow warm. "She likes to worry," he said, which didn't satisfy him at all.

Pablo just shook his head. "When you two are married as long as me and my woman, she'll shove you out the door!"

All good humor ended as they came closer to the sound of heavy artillery. They stopped at the crossroads that led to Encarnación, the town under fire. To the west was the great Rancho Guadalquivir, owned by a wealthy man who lived in the state of Sonora. Ammon had hauled grain to Guadalquivir only one month ago; he doubted he would haul there again, since he stared, shocked to see four American cowboys hanging on the elaborate crosspiece of the ranch's *entrada*. He came forward slowly, looking around, wondering if he knew them. Attached to each man's chest with a spike was a placard announcing "Americano."

"Do you know them, Señor 'Ancock?"

Even after several days in the sun and frequent visits by buzzards, he did. "I know their boots. Pablo, let us cut them down."

The old man shook his head. "We dare not. One side or the other would take offense and all around here would suffer a similar fate." Pablo crossed himself. "Do you see why I want you to take your woman and ride to the border?"

"I see all too well."

They topped the next rise and flattened out in the lee of the hill to watch the fight in the distance, the shelling loud enough to make Ammon's ears hurt. He glanced at Pablo, who was shaking his head as he watched the carnage.

"Do they do this in the United States?" the old man asked.

"They did fifty years ago, and many died."

"Was it worth all that death?"

"I doubt it."

They retraced their steps.

He tried not to look so concerned when Addie met him at the gate with the genial dog who had taken a shine to her. She saw right through him, so he told her about the dead American cowboys. She turned away and took a deep breath.

"And you want to stay in Mexico?" she asked quietly, then returned to the house ahead of him.

Pablo whistled through his teeth. "I don't know what she said, but you will probably be sleeping in the other room tonight, my friend."

"We're riding tonight, so it doesn't matter." He looked at Pablo. "How can I get her out of this country *now*?" he asked in English, knowing his friend had no answer in either language.

Unhappy with himself, Ammon went in the tiny kitchen, no more than a lean-to on the adobe house, where he couldn't even stand upright. Addie tried to smile at him. Maria held out a plate of misshapen tortillas.

"Your wife made these," she announced. "If she stays with me a few more days, she will be an expert. Try one."

He did, after Maria shook a little precious sugar and cinnamon on it and rolled it up. "*Buen sabor*," he said.

Addie's smile was genuine, reminding him all over again how eager she was for his approval, even in the worst of times. "You mean it?"

"I do." It *was* tasty. He put his arm around her shoulder and led her into the backyard. "Pablo thinks the fight will end soon. Let me take the money to the woman in San Pedro. I know I can convince Pablo to take you the other way toward the border."

She looked at him a long time, as if he wasn't measuring up and she didn't want to disappoint him with that knowledge.

"*¿Qué es*, Addie?" he asked finally.

"You trust someone besides yourself to get me to the border?"

It was a simple question, but it told him worlds about her. The only answer he could give was the truthful one, the frightening one.

"No, I do not," he said. "You're riding with me."

She rested her forehead against his chest, and his arms went around her.

After two days of silence in the distance that meant both victory and loss, they left Casa Salinas. Maria cried and Pablo crossed himself again and insisted on putting the sign of the cross on their foreheads with ash.

"Between that and my fox fur stole, I think we're covered," Ammon joked to his wife as they walked to the arroyo where Blanco, patient horse, had been stashed.

"Not yet." Addie stopped when they were out of view of the house.

He knew what she meant. They knelt together and took turns praying for their safety. It touched his heart when Addie included Pablo and Maria Salinas, the two boy-soldiers, Serena Camacho, whom she had never met, Joselito, the poor people in Encarnación where the fight was, and the doctor's wife, whoever she was.

"Are they getting under your skin too, honey?" he asked her when she finished and just stayed on her knees, as though there were others to pray for, in the whole immensity of Chihuahua, but she didn't know their names. All she could do was nod.

Pablo had found a cork for the canteen that lacked one, and both were full now. Maria and Addie had slapped out tortillas and cooked them on the griddle until Ammon had to protest that Blanco would be overloaded. She still insisted on a pot of beans that Addie balanced on her lap.

As a parting gift, Addie took Grandma Sada's ring from the chain around her neck and gave it to Maria, who protested and backed away, but accepted it finally, as she cried some more.

They rode in silence, Addie wrapped in a better *rebozo* that Maria insisted on giving her to replace the shawl from Grandma's attic. She shivered in the cool evening air, a plain enough invitation for him to tighten his grip around her.

The valley in front of them was silent and empty. Through the day, he and Pablo had watched the dust cloud of a moving army heading east, traveling fast. He did not understand what it meant. Was the army pursuing? Being pursued? He kept looking over his shoulder to the west, wondering if there were another army just over the horizon.

This uncertainty only added to the mystery he had always known about Chihuahua, a state of vast emptiness and large ranches. There were times he could ride for days and see no one. Other times, he could top a rise and find himself in the middle of a herd of cattle and cowboys everywhere, occasionally a buffalo, relic from an earlier age. Now it was armies everywhere—or nowhere. An army was the last thing he wanted now.

When they came to the four corners, where the Guadalquivir gates still sprouted their tragic crop of dead men, Ammon pressed his hand gently against his wife's head, forcing her face into his chest. He sang to her when she started to cry.

"Addie, it's not too late to return to Casa Salinas and Pablo," he whispered when she was silent. "He'll get you to the border."

She shook her head, so quiet, and they continued toward the scene of the battle.

The name may have been grandiose, but Encarnación was just a village, typical of the vastness of Chihuahua. Nothing moved now. He pushed Addie's face against his chest again as he rode down a side street and came to a flapping circle of vultures, ripping and gulping. They didn't even fly away as Blanco shied and whinnied.

Ammon looked closer in the moonlight, repulsed but curious. When it dawned on him that the creatures couldn't fly because they were too gorged on dead men's flesh, he looked away too.

There were no standing buildings. From coop to city hall, every structure had been pounded to rubble by what he suspected was General Salazar's rebel army, fighting the *federales* of el presidente Madero, whose powers were weakening.

He rode through the silent plaza in such despair that he swore when he saw the tile fountain blown into shards. The flagpole had been sliced in half and the tri-colored flag of Mexico drooped down to the gravel.

From the depths of his serape, where she had turned her face, Addie thumped him. "Am, you promised me you wouldn't use language like that!"

Trust his wife to keep him civilized in the middle of chaos. What was it about women? "I know, and I'm sorry," he told her. "I just remember this village as a lovely place with a wonderful fountain. The people were always so kind to me. I used to take a siesta under the trees in the plaza."

"Maybe you'd better close your eyes too."

"Wish I could."

He turned Blanco toward the flag. The gelding picked his way carefully through the rubble. Ammon took out his knife and cut the cords tying the flag to the pole. He pressed the flag to his face—a shell had ripped through the eagle and snake—then tucked it in his saddlebag. Someday, maybe if he lived long enough, and Addie still tolerated him, he could get her to mend it. They could fly it from their own rancho's flagpole or maybe over his business in Pearson. He looked around at all the destruction and death, wishing such a future were even possible. Right now, he wouldn't have wagered a *centavo* on it.

"Mexico is breaking my heart," he whispered to his wife, and she kissed his neck.

He couldn't leave the smoldering, silent village fast enough, vowing to skirt around all such places in the future. They rode for an hour, Addie sitting up again. After days of being hobbled for safety in Pablo's arroyo, Blanco wanted to move faster, but Ammon held him reined in. He knew his lively horse wasn't accustomed to a slow and steady pace, but slow and steady should see them to San Pedro by dawn.

He smiled to himself when they came to a series of low rises and falls in the land that always made him wonder if this was what the ocean was like—wave after wave. He knew this stretch of road had lulled him to sleep more than once. Good thing his freighting team was smarter than he was. A shake of the harness by his lead horse was usually enough to keep him alert. Still, he felt his eyes growing heavy at the undulating sameness.

Sleep vanished after midnight when they topped yet another rise and blundered into the rear of an army. Without a word, he pushed Addie's face against his chest again. "Put your *rebozo* over your head," he whispered, his eyes on the *soldados*, who were looking back at them in what he hoped was only curiosity. Or not. He heard clicks as Mausers were taken off safety, sending goose-flesh marching down his spine in ranks like soldiers.

To turn back meant death. He willed himself calm and said a silent prayer that was a jumble of Spanish and English, relying on the Lord's linguistic abilities to turn it into good sense and as sincere a petition as he had ever asked of Deity before.

Keep riding, he told himself. "Addie, pretend to sleep. Don't show your face," he whispered, his lips barely moving.

"*Hola, hermanos. ¿Qué pasa?*" Might as well brazen it out and speak first.

The soldier closest to him smiled and rested his Mauser in his lap again. Good thing Addie's Spanish was practically nonexistent. She wouldn't have enjoyed that much profanity at once, as the soldier went through his salty version of the battle that had raged in the village of ghosts behind them. Ammon nodded and threw in a comment only when the narrative lagged, which wasn't often. The soldier seemed to think he had destroyed Encarnación by himself and didn't require much commentary.

Ammon listened, his arms tight around Addie, who shivered with fear. If the man was even telling half the truth, the battle had unfolded as he and Pablo had thought, watching it from a distant hill. Salazar's forces had blasted away at a village loyal to Madero and sent the *federales* fleeing east toward Namiquipa, where the guerrillas were heading now.

"But you know how it is," the soldier concluded, with a great yawn. "We will follow and some of the *federales* will join our ranks. They always do."

Obviously trying to keep himself awake, the *soldado* leaned so close to Ammon that he could smell the onions on his breath. "And what have we here?" he asked, poking Addie.

"*Hermano, ten cuidado,*" Ammon chided, deciding to become the greatest actor since Edwin Booth had toured the West. "*Mi mujer está embarazada.*"

The soldier laughed and moved away, joining his *compadres* again. He repeated what Ammon had said, and they all laughed that sleepy laugh of men too long in the saddle, trying to stay awake.

He watched them move along so easily, men accustomed to the saddle like he was. Most were *mestizos*, the mixture of Indian and Spaniard that made Mexico what it was. Here and there, he saw Indians riding bareback, some with guns and some with bows and arrows. And there were the *soldaderas*, some with children. Dogs trotted along too.

The urge to bolt and run was so strong that Ammon could barely restrain himself. For the longest hour of his life, he rode beside the rebels, laughing and joking as Addie shook in fear and burrowed into him like a frightened animal. He whispered to her once, "Is this *mi mujer* who killed the biggest cougar ever seen in Chihuahua?" which earned him a pinch in a sore place. At least she quit shivering.

As the column moved slowly in a direction he wanted to avoid, he gradually slowed down Blanco until they had fallen back to the even more sleepy rear. After another careful fifteen minutes, they were alone in a valley of undulating slopes again. He reined in Blanco, his eyes on an Indian on horseback who watched a moment, then continued with the army.

"You can sit up," he said in English.

She did, looking at him with old eyes. He kissed her forehead, and her eyes softened, to his relief.

"I've never been so frightened," she said.

"That's two of us."

"What did you tell that awful man after he poked me?"

He chuckled. "I told him you were expecting. Must've worked."

She nodded, not even batting an eye. "Where are they going? I hope not to San Pedro."

"He said they're heading to Namiquipa, where the bulk of Salazar's bandits are, just a jump behind the *federales*. Apparently Encarnación was a *federal* stronghold." He sighed. "No longer. They wiped it off the map."

"Will they attack San Pedro too?" she asked.

"No. Apparently it belongs to Salazar already."

Addie had that distant look in her eyes again, the look he hated to see on a woman's face, especially his wife's. Maybe he could distract her.

"Do you know the doctor's name?"

"Menendez. He even bowed and introduced himself, after he kicked those men down the stairs."

"His wife's name?" Maybe he was trying to distract himself. It wasn't working, as he thought of the bruises on Addie's arms.

She gave him a wry smile. "All he said was Señora Menendez. I'm to take the money he stole from your privy to a *panadería* near the plaza. I don't even know what that is."

"It's a bakery. If the soldiers haven't stolen everything but the mixing bowls, we'll buy some *pan dulces* and beat it for the border once we're done. You're under no obligation to do anything else, are you?"

Addie shook her head. "He told me to give it to . . ." She looked at him. "He did say her name! 'Give it to Graciela and tell her to take the train to El Paso at once.' Could that be *our* Graciela?"

"Maybe. I had heard a secondhand rumor that she married a doctor from Chihuahua, and there aren't many doctors in this state."

"But one involved in the revolution?" Addie asked, skeptical. "Surely she married a wealthy man who would have nothing to do with a rebel cause. You might be mistaken."

"I might be. You remember Graciela, don't you?"

Addie nodded, that patient smile on her face again, the one that made her always seem wiser than her years. "I already told you I did! All you boys in the eleventh grade were in love with her that term she spent at Juárez Stake Academy."

"That we were," he agreed. He was thinking out loud then. "I wonder—well, we know the doctor is with Salazar's insurgents and San Pedro belongs to Salazar. What does he look like?"

"He's tall, for a Mexican, and his English is good. I was frightened and I don't remember any more than that. Why does it matter?"

"I'm starting to wonder if he fixed my busted leg."

"Well, what did *your* doctor look like?" she asked so patiently as though he were deficient.

He rubbed her head the way he used to when she teased him. She just grinned at him.

"I was almost out of my mind with pain. I do remember he spoke English, but as soon as he knew I spoke Spanish, that's the language we used." He gave what he knew was a put-upon, theatrical sigh. "And we know he prefers privies for peeing and doesn't mind stealing money."

Addie patted his chest. "Am, he told me explicitly that she was to use the money to get out of Mexico. If this is *your* Graciela, he wants her to be safe." She said something low in her throat. "I was so frightened by those other men. I suppose he didn't think I was listening."

This time, he pushed her head against his chest gently, keeping his hand on the side of her head, liking the familiar feeling of her hair. "Go to sleep, Addie. After all, you're *embarazada* and need your rest."

She pinched him again in that sore place and laughed.

They arrived in San Pedro as the sun was rising over the eastern mountains. It wasn't far from where the roads split toward San Pedro one way and Namiquipa the other, but Ammon had taken his time, dismounting and walking to the top of each rise before motioning Addie forward on Blanco. He vowed never to be so careless again.

The directions the doctor had given Addie to the *panadería* were rudimentary, at best, but he knew the town. He easily supplemented her directions, which made her lean down from her perch on Blanco and pat the top of his sombrero to get his attention. He looked up at his pretty wife, pretty despite dirt on her face, tangled hair that would have sent her into mild hysteria a few years ago, and mud streaked on her skirt.

"What is it, my lovely little thing?" he asked in Spanish.

She blushed, which made him wonder just how much Spanish she really knew. "Nothing much, Am," she replied, her voice gruff. "I used to wonder why you wanted to do something as hard and dirty as freighting for a living, but my goodness, you know every little town in Chihuahua, don't you?"

"Almost. Could be it's paying off."

He looked at her, until she looked away in that touching sort of shyness he remembered from their earliest days of marriage, when they were still dazed and getting used to the whole business of loving each other.

"Thanks, Am," was all she said, but it suddenly meant more to him than any freighting contract.

"Here we are," he said two blocks later and helped Addie down. She winced from so many hours in the saddle. She bent down and then stretched and peered into the window.

"I think I see a light in the back."

He nodded and led Blanco to the rear of the adobe and wood building, breathing in the fragrance of *pan dulce*, every Mexican's favorite breakfast, his included. He knocked, just a soft tap, as uncertainty flooded him. He wondered if the time would ever come again when he could knock on a door, or just answer one, without gnawing doubt.

From the flour on his soiled apron to the dough clinging to his hands, the man who answered the door could only be a *panadero*, and an overworked one, at that. He rolled his eyes and started to close the door. "We open at seven."

"We're not here for bread," Ammon said as he put his foot in the door. "Please, we have some money for the wife of a doctor."

The *panadero* opened the door wide and ushered them in, after a careful look behind them in the alley. Ammon tied Blanco's reins to an iron ring by the door and closed it quickly. Maybe he had misunderstood the *soldados* who had told him this was a Salazar town. Why the concern?

And what was it about Mexican women of a certain age? Like Pablo's *mujer*, this wife of a baker he didn't know had already sat Addie down and was handing her *pan dulce* carved like a flower and coated with pink sugar. There was also no misunderstanding the critical look the woman flashed his way, as though wondering how a *tonto* as old as he was could possibly mistreat a woman so badly that she had no time to wash her face or put on a clean dress. And trust Addie to suddenly look so sad and helpless, and not the mighty hunter who had stalked and killed a man-eating mountain lion. Not a word had been exchanged, but the whole thing made him smile. Pa had joked once that women were a separate species, and Ammon had to agree.

"My wife is in good hands," Ammon said to the baker, who brushed the little pills of dough from his fingers. "You have a fine woman."

The baker beamed at the compliment. He perched himself on a stool, obviously ready to indulge in that Mexican pleasure of spooling out a whole morning, if necessary, making sociable chat and eventually working around to the reason for the visit. Ammon hated to disappoint him because he had come to enjoy leisurely conversation too, more evidence to him that he was more Mexican than American.

"Señor, it is this way—my wife was under an obligation to give some money to the wife of a doctor, and this was the address. Is there such a woman under your roof?"

The baker nodded, his eyes wary now. "And . . . and what is she to do with this money?"

"She is to use it to leave Mexico."

There was no mistaking the enormous relief that filled the baker's whole face, as if he had won a lottery, found a silver mine, and been declared chef to the pope all at the same time. The baker reached for Ammon's hand and pumped it up and down.

"This is music to my ears!" the man declared, tears in his eyes. "Soon?"

"Probably," Ammon said, wary now. "Our only instructions were to give her the money. *When* she leaves is her busin . . ."

"Wife! Wife!" the baker shouted. "The Empress of Siam is going to leave us!"

Ammon stared as the man and his hefty woman grabbed each other like children and started to dance. Addie stared too, open-mouthed. Giving the dancing couple a wide berth, she edged around the kitchen until Ammon had his hand on her waist.

"Maybe you should get the money and leave it on the table," she whispered. "I'll hang onto Blanco. Are you sure *panadería* means bakery? This is a lunatic asylum."

By unspoken consent, they both edged toward the door. Ammon was turning the knob when the baker clamped his hand—strong from kneading dough—on Ammon's shoulder. He held his breath, but the baker just gave him a friendly shake that made him wince.

"Bring in the money. The Empress is still asleep upstairs. She never rises before nine o'clock." The man clapped his hands. "You have made me a happy man!"

FIFTEEN

THE EMPRESS OF Siam did turn out to be Graciela Andrade, but not quite the Graciela he remembered from Juárez Stake Academy. Her eyes full of fire, this Graciela stomped down the stairs, ready to scour the *peones* who had dared to make so much noise and wake her up before nine in the morning. She was dressed in a robe that might have been impressive once. Like most of Mexico, Graciela Menendez Andrade, physician's wife, had fallen on hard times.

Ammon understood why the baker called her the Empress of Siam. Under the protection of his *English in Our Modern World* textbook in the eleventh grade, he used to take sneak peeks at her lovely eyes, tilted in a way reminiscent of Oriental potentates. He also understood why the baker was so eager to see the back of her, and soon. In the fractured Spanglish his Academy friends all spoke to the irritation of their teachers, his best friend had called Graciela Andrade a "complicated *chica*."

"D'you think she'll recognize us?" he whispered to Addie as Graciela stood at the turn of the landing.

"You, maybe," his wife whispered back. "You and

your friends were all silly over her. She never noticed me. I was younger and quiet."

"And that's one of the many reasons why I married you," he said in her ear. "Plus you kill cougars."

Addie laughed out loud, which made Graciela turn and stare because she preferred to be the center of attention, and she wasn't, just then.

"Hola, Graciela," Ammon said.

Graciela looked and looked again, her haughty expression softening. She swallowed several times and came down the stairs slowly. She looked from Ammon to Addie and back to Ammon, her hand to her throat.

"You married Addie Finch?" she said in English, still staring at them both.

"Smartest thing I ever did," Ammon replied promptly, which made Addie lean closer until their shoulders touched.

"Did you come to rescue me?" Graciela asked, her eyes suddenly hopeful, the disdain gone.

"Not really," Addie told her. "Your husband saved my . . . saved my life in Colonia García. He gave me some money for you to use in getting out of Mexico. That is why we are here." She smiled. "We're having enough trouble rescuing ourselves."

"And then we're hotfooting it to the border. I'll go get the money." Ammon looked at the baker. "Maybe you would let my wife and me sleep here today and then leave tonight?"

The baker opened his mouth to speak, but Graciela began to cry, her hands in her hair, not tugging too hard, as far as Ammon could tell, but just enough to make the baker's wife start wringing her hands. *Simple soul*, he thought, half amused. *She's just playing you.*

"You're just going to leave me here?" Graciela asked, through her tears.

"You're welcome to come along with Addie and me," Ammon said. "We travel at night and do a lot of walking. Let me get that money. You can take the train and be in El Paso in two days. At least right now, it's all Salazar country. *You* couldn't be safer; us, not so much."

The room got quiet, Graciela discarding her fake tears as quickly as she had adopted them. The baker and his wife looked at each other. Addie edged closer to him, and Ammon felt his stomach start to roam about his insides.

"Graciela, what's wrong with your husband's plan?"

Trust Addie to get right to the meat of the situation. While he was trying to calm his own fears, she had gone to Graciela, touching her arm lightly. "Tell us. We have to know."

It was softly spoken, simply said, and Graciela did not hesitate. "My husband"—she spit the word out—"has abandoned General Salazar and General Orozco and sides with General Huerta now."

And this is Salazar's town, Ammon thought, shocked. He glanced at Addie, who seemed more perplexed than worried.

"But your husband saved me, and General Salazar was in the room too," Addie said. "Two or three weeks ago, that's all."

Graciela's words were bitter. "Since then, he has

changed his mind. Oh, it chafes me! He leaves me in this . . . this wretched little town, living in a bakery . . ."

Addie increased the pressure of her hand on Graciela's arm, but her voice was no louder. Ammon watched them, grateful their conversation could only be in English because he could not imagine what the baker and his wife were thinking.

Addie must have had the same thought as she exchanged a worried look with him. She stood a little taller then and interrupted Graciela, who had switched to Spanish. "Graciela, not another word in Spanish. You owe these kind people that courtesy." She leaned closer, her voice kind but firm. "In fact, I think you should just burst into tears about now, and let Ammon do the talking. If you have to complain, do it in English."

To Ammon's amazement, she did precisely that, collapsing into Addie's welcoming arms, sobbing her misery about the perfidy of husbands, her lumpy bed, and the fact that there was no glycerin and rose water anywhere in town for her skin, which was turning into leather.

"Addie, take her upstairs," he whispered. "What in the world is the matter with her?"

Addie gave the weeping Graciela a push toward the stairs again. "You know she's not used to this sort of life, Am," she whispered in his ear.

"You're an angel. Have I told you that recently?"

She smiled and shook her head. When she looked directly in his eyes, he saw something more this time: He saw a confident woman. "I can manage her." Her cheeks bloomed with color then. "I know what it is like to go a little bit crazy." She followed Graciela upstairs, looking back once to give him such a glance.

My goodness, life is full of surprises, he told himself as he turned back to the baker and his wife. "I will have her off your hands by nightfall," he promised. "You are loyal to General Salazar?"

"We are," the baker said, drawing himself up.

"Then I can only applaud your great courtesy to the wife of someone now disaffected from your cause," Ammon said simply.

"We have honor. The doctor left her under our roof, and we could not just turn her out."

"Although we have been tempted," the baker's wife added. Without a word, she turned to the table where *pan dulces* were cooling on a rack and handed one to Ammon.

He gave her enough money for several. "For my wife, when she comes down."

"Your wife is a saint," the baker said.

"Why, yes, she is," Ammon agreed. "And do you know, she saved my life by Rio Papigochic by killing a mountain lion."

The baker's wife gasped, her eyes like saucers. "We have heard that story! How she wounded the lion, then killed it with her bare hands!"

"*Claro*," Ammon said, perjuring himself without a qualm. "She can handle Graciela."

"And you too, eh?" the baker said, a twinkle in his eye.

Ammon felt his face flame. "Even me," he said solemnly, then laughed, which made the baker and his wife beam at him as though he were a long lost son.

Once they knew he was taking the Empress of Siam off their hands and understood he was the husband of the lion killer whose fame was spreading, negotiations went smoothly, requiring none of the lengthy diplomacy he was prepared to expend to keep Addie safe. With the crook of his finger, the baker led him into the alley, showing him the stable across the way, the one with the door nearly hidden, where he kept the two old geriatrics that pulled his baker's wagon. The horses were as generous as their master, moving over to make room for Blanco, sharing their grain.

In a further burst of generosity—he could see the regime of the Empress of Siam coming to a welcome conclusion—the baker even agreed to let Graciela take one of the old nags. When Addie came downstairs, assuring them that Graciela had cried herself back to sleep, the baker's wife sat her down and gave her more pan dulce with powdered sugar, washed down with goat's milk. Addie ate until she had to raise both hands in protest.

While she was eating, the baker's wife bustled around in the room over the kitchen, coming down to announce that the sheets were clean and there was even water for a bath. Addie took the woman's hands in hers and kissed them, a gesture so full of humility, and so exactly right that Ammon felt the last bit of callus burn away from his heart.

A pleasant glow replaced the callus a few minutes later when he washed his wife's bare back, got in a kiss or two, and received the same treatment after she dried off. He decided he wasn't as tired as previously thought, which seemed to dovetail with Addie's plans too. When they woke much later, the shadows had changed. Now was the time for strategic planning, rendered more enjoyable by his wife in his arms.

"We'll just take Graciela along with us and head for the border. Depending on where the armies are, we might aim for the North Western Railway, just beyond Dublán," he told her. "You know, take the railroad in style. At this point, we're about the same distance from the railroad as we are from the mountains."

"Will you come out with us?"

He wanted to lie, but he couldn't. "I'm not sure, Addie. Just not sure yet. I still want you out, because it's not safe." He kissed her bare shoulder. "Okay?"

"I'll think about it," she said after a long silence. "Maybe you're right," she said later in a quieter voice. And then, "We could probably use the five hundred dollars."

But man proposes and God disposes; in this case, Graciela dug in her heels and refused to go along with the plan. Even in her self-absorption, Graciela seemed to know that tears and tantrums wouldn't work now. She became the young woman he remembered from Juárez Stake Academy, sitting so still—reminiscent of Addie— but with an intensity burning inside that neither of them had any proof against.

"All I want to do—what I *must* do—is return to my home on the San Diego Ranch." She raised her hand when Ammon opened his mouth to object. "I know you mean well, but I fear for my parents."

"They might be in the United States," Addie said.

"When did you last see them?" Ammon asked.

Graciela smiled at him, her eyes lively now with the memory. "The last time I saw you! We were visiting Rancho Chavez in early summer. You were hauling grain and dusty. I wanted to offer you cool water, but Señora Chavez and my mother made me sit down again." She looked away, her lips trembling. "My mother."

"I remember."

"Do you . . . could they still be there? I have heard nothing."

I hope to goodness they are not, he thought, distressed, remembering the stables. He glanced at Addie, who exchanged his worried look for hers.

"You know something," Graciela said simply.

"I went to Hacienda Chavez three weeks ago. It was burned."

His words hung in the air like a bad odor. Graciela looked away and Addie took her hand. Both of them looked at him, and he knew they were going to Rancho San Diego, whether he wanted to or not. All he said was, "I'm having the hardest time rescuing anyone."

They left when twilight started to work its magic in the plaza of San Pedro, that time of night when, in better days, the young men and young ladies began to walk around, observing each other in that coy Hispanic way. Ammon always enjoyed this gentle part of life in Mexico before the revolution, when nightingales sang and someone usually strummed a guitar with varying degrees of expertise.

It was different now. The plaza made him sad, with

too many flags and men with *bandoleras* and Mausers. He had no idea where the young girls had gone.

Graciela had not been pleased with the baker's poor excuse for a horse. He had found an equally antique saddle, generous now that the Empress was on her way, and saddled the rickety horse. Graciela looked around and frowned, then sighed. *Ah, the beginning of wisdom*, Ammon thought hopefully, careful not to smile.

Trust Addie to make everything right. And to think he had feared she knew nothing of Mexico; how wrong he had been. After the baker's wife, tears in her eyes, had stuffed Blanco's saddlebags with more tortillas and *pan dulce*, she insisted on giving Addie a cheesecloth bag full of *queso fresco*.

"*Gracias, mi madre*," Addie said. Of course it wasn't right or proper, except that it was. Ammon held his breath at the loveliness of his *mujer* kneeling in front of the baker's wife while she traced a sign of the cross on Addie's forehead.

Addie rose so gracefully, so serene, and backed up to him, holding up her necklace, the one she loved so well. Silently, he worked the stubborn clasp and handed it to her. "I'll get you another one someday," he whispered.

"No need," she said so softly. "You're all I want."

She took her wedding ring off the chain, then touched the pretty locket one more time before she handed it to the baker, gesturing for him to do the honors. With tears in his eyes, he put it around his wife's plump neck. Now it was his turn to work the stubborn clasp.

Addie handed her wedding ring to Ammon. "Put it

214

on my finger, like you did in the St. George Temple," she said, her eyes so kind. "I won't take it off again."

He did as she said, then hoped the baker and his wife would not mind their lack of propriety as he gathered Addie close. He shouldn't have worried. The kind couple had turned away modestly.

They traveled in silence that night, away from the Salazar stronghold of San Pedro. Graciela objected to dismounting to rest their horses, but Addie convinced her it was best if she wanted to make it home to her parents' house. She and Graciela walked together, talking to each other, Addie soothing, Graciela complaining, until they were both silent. They saw nothing and only heard coyotes tuning up on distant hills.

Luck found them at first light along a river he couldn't remember, in the ruins of a town he had forgotten, blasted to pieces like Encarnación. The church still had a partial roof, so Ammon left the women to clear away broken glass and evidence of wandering animals while he led the horses to water and sheltering trees.

When he returned, Graciela had already wrapped herself in a shawl, facing toward the wall, somehow looking like a portrait of indignation. "She's angry at us. She'd like to blame us for this, but she can't quite figure out how," Addie said, amused. She stood on tiptoe to speak in his ear. "She wouldn't be much fun on a picnic, would she?"

Ammon chuckled. Trust Addie to make the best of the situation. In a dark corner somewhere, she had found a cast-off chasuble, much troubled by mice. Shaken out and rolled up, it made a passable pillow. Before they slept, he asked her, "Whose turn is it to pray?"

She looked at him, a question in her eyes, which softened when she understood he was thinking back through two years of sorrow about to be forgotten forever. "Well, let's see. If I remember, you usually liked to say the prayer before you left on one of your freighting trips. And I said it when you returned."

"That's what I thought. My turn." Her soft "Amen," when he finished made him finally understand, at the advanced age of twenty-six, just exactly what a tender mercy was.

The day was overcast and then rainy, which meant the three of them ended up sitting with their backs against cold adobe, where part of the roof remained to keep off some of the rain. Ammon found a dry enough corner where Addie sat and shivered between his legs while he thumbed through Alma, looking for the end of Old Ammon the Nephite's missionary journey in the land of his enemies.

"Addie, it says here that Ammon and his brothers were fourteen years away from home." He showed her the passage. "All we have to do is get Graciela home and get two train tickets like civilized people. If what those *soldados* told us was right, the army is down near Namiquipa, and we're heading north. I think we can do it."

Wet but not so miserable, they waited until the rain stopped and enough moon came out to show them the way, since this wasn't a route he ordinarily took when he teamed. The road was too narrow, and he didn't remember any villages. After midnight, they crossed what he hoped was Rio San Miguel. He knew the San Miguel joined with the Piedras Verdes to create the Rio Casas Grandes, which flowed by Dublán in the far distance. It was too cloudy to tell, but he also hoped they were in the valley that he knew led to Rancho San Diego, at 150,000 acres, one of the smaller holdings belonging to Luis Terrazas.

Graciela seemed to know where they were once they started up the valley. "Hurry up!" she called, moving ahead of them. She dug her heels into her creaky old mount, who already looked like he was about to drop to his knees and crawl the rest of the way.

"Have a little patience," he called. "It's time to dismount and walk them."

There was enough moonlight to see the vast disdain on Graciela Menendez Andrade's face. Ammon shook his head and helped Addie dismount. "She'll feel a bit different when that nag flops over and cocks up his toes."

He sighed with weariness when Graciela disappeared over the next rise. He knew Addie was as tired as he was, but she just chuckled and bumped his shoulder with hers.

"What do you think Evangeline would say if she could—"

He stopped her, suddenly alert, when shots sounded where Graciela had disappeared. He peered into the gloom, his hand on Addie's arm.

"What should we . . ."

Ammon never thought the baker's horse could move that fast, but he galloped toward them now. Graciela rode hunched over, her hair streaming behind her.

". . . do?" Addie finished, her eyes wide with fright.

"Say the fastest prayer you can think of," he said and waved his arms to stop the horse.

Its eyes rolling in terror, the baker's horse stopped. Ammon jerked Graciela from the saddle just as the horse flopped over, dead. It looked like an army coming at them. Ammon closed his eyes, hoping there would be fewer *soldados* when he opened them again. No such luck; this nightmare was real.

Graciela opened her mouth to scream, but Addie clamped her hand over her mouth and gave her a shake. Addie just looked at him, and he saw all the love in her heart. *Please, Father*, he prayed. *We have to live.*

The soldiers slowed down. They had stopped firing, but they approached cautiously now, curious. Ammon willed himself to relax. Both of the women were looking at him, Graciela in terror, and Addie in utter confidence. He took heart and knew what to do.

"Let's see how well we can act," he said. "Addie, you have to keep your head down because they can't see your light eyes. I want you to cry and wail as though your heart is breaking."

She nodded, even as Graciela stared at him as though he had grown another head. He snatched up a stick and thrust it into Graciela's hands. "I want you to start beating your horse."

"He's dead," Graciela snapped.

"They don't know that! I want you to start abusing me with every curse you can think of, only for heaven's sake, don't mention my name."

"You are out of your mind," Graciela said, throwing down the stick. The riders were only the length of a plaza away now.

Before he could stop her, Addie grabbed Graciela by the hair and shook her, thrusting the stick back in her hand. "You do what he says, or I'm going to shoot you before the soldiers do!"

Bravo, Addie, Ammon thought. "Cry, Addie."

"That's easy," she told him as she burst into loud tears, wailing and flailing about as though she were possessed. Graciela stared at her a moment, then started beating the dead horse, all the while swearing at Ammon so impressively that he stared in amazement.

"Your turn, Blanco," he whispered as the soldiers came closer. He clapped his hands three times as though in frustration, and Blanco lurched into a limp. Addie clung to the horse and sobbed, her face turned into his mane, delivering a creditable performance as a woman desperate to save her lame horse. John Barrymore would have been impressed.

Ammon took a deep breath and turned to face the soldiers, grateful down to his toenails they were not *federales*, who would have shot him without a qualm and done whatever they wanted with his eternal companion and the Empress of Siam. They could have been the guerillas of Victoriano Huerta, Pascual Orozco, Ines Salazar, or any of a dozen men who had anointed themselves rebel leaders. They looked like he did, irregular soldiers in a nasty war. Now he had to convince them they were brothers. He touched his fox fur stole for luck.

He picked up another stick and shook it at Graciela, then bowed to the men. "Thank you for chasing back my worthless sister-in-law!"

Graciela shoved him and screamed invectives at him worthy of a sheep shearer. She pounded him and scraped his face with her fingernails while he tried to ward her off, all the while shouting, "And now she has ridden her horse to death and my nag is lame. And my woman, *ay de mí*! Dry your tears, woman!"

Addie cried louder, adding a little touch of hysteria as she clung to Blanco. Ammon looked at the soldiers surrounding them and shrugged. "What do you do with women?" he asked, hands out.

He held his breath, hoping, and there it was. One of the soldiers—probably a married man—started to laugh, and then another. Soon they were all laughing as the women carried on. Ammon put his hands over his ears, relieved to see one of the soldiers crossing a leg over the saddle, while others sheathed their rifles. Others stretched in that way of relaxed riders, not men bent on murder any more. Someone rolled a *cigarillo*.

One of them rode forward, plucked the stick from Graciela, and gave her a swift stroke to the legs, as though she were a child. She glared, and he backed away as she spit at him. He laughed and threw the stick away. "We could shoot the noisy one, and your sister-in-law, and maybe that poor white lump of dog meat. Just say which ones, or all three."

Ammon shook his head. "I'm taking my sister-in-law the witch to my brother. Let him deal with her."

He reached for Addie, who pulled away and kept up her tears, leaning into Blanco. "And this one is mine for keeps. I'll chastise her later."

The leader nudged his horse close to Graciela. "You do what he says, witch. Suppose you had run into *federales*?"

Ammon held his breath as the man took his pistol from its holster. *Please no*, he prayed, as the soldier pointed the Colt at Graciela, then raised it in the air and fired. "*¡Viva la revolución!*" he shouted, then spurred his horse past them. The others laughed and followed. Soon even the faint hoofbeats faded away, and they were alone in the immensity of Chihuahua.

Ammon's legs wouldn't hold him, so he sat down on the ground. He clapped his hands three times and Blanco perked up, stepping away from the dead horse. In another moment, he was cropping grass. Addie blew her nose on her dress and wiped her eyes. Ammon held out his hand to her, but she shook her head and walked to Graciela, standing so alone with slumping shoulders, her expression impassive.

"Look at me, Graciela," Addie commanded.

The other woman looked, then looked away.

"I meant every word I said," Addie said, her face close to Graciela's. "I'll shoot you if you ride ahead or ever argue with Ammon. I killed a cougar, and you'd be easier!"

Graciela turned away, a lonely figure. Ammon watched as Addie let out a big breath and walked to Graciela. In a moment, her arms were around her, holding her in a tight embrace, the best illustration he had ever seen of "reproving betimes with sharpness," and all that followed.

When he thought he could stand up without making a fool of himself, Ammon walked to the dead horse. *And now we've ridden a horse to death just like the guerillas*, he thought in sorrow. He looked north, wishing with all his heart that he could clap his hands three times and have the US border materialize in front of them. And here they were, going toward to a ranch that might not look any better now than Hacienda Chavez with its dead occupants.

"Well, *mujeres*, we'd better start walking," he said. "Addie, you're a woman in a million."

SIXTEEN

THEY TOOK TURNS walking and riding all night, coming to each rise fearful, but they might have been the only persons in all of Chihuahua now. By unspoken consent, no one wanted to stop as morning came and rain pelted them. There was no shelter in sight, but Ammon and Graciela knew where they were. Ammon also knew Addie would walk beside him without question.

"I just want to go home," Graciela said quietly to him, when he boosted Addie onto Blanco for her turn. "I don't know what I will do about my husband." She touched his arm and spoke softly, probably so Addie couldn't overhear. "I envy you, Ammon 'Ancock. You and Addie have never had hard words, have you? I want to murder Paco Menendez."

He looked at Addie, who was looking back at him, the smile on her face serene, but tinged with genuine humor. He knew she had heard Graciela. "What d'you think, Addie?"

"I've been inclined to murder Ammon," she said, so matter-of-fact that Ammon had to look away because he wanted to laugh. "It passed. Maybe not as soon as it should have, but it passed. Don't give up on the doctor yet." She gave that low laugh he liked so well, and when he turned back, she was looking at him, serious now. "Chances are, he hasn't given up on you."

Addie nudged Blanco ahead, a signal to Ammon that his wife wanted to be alone with her thoughts, but hopefully not her misgivings. He had always respected her quiet moments because they were part of what made her so lovely to him. Graciela watched her go. "I spoke out of turn," she said, sounding remarkably humble for the Empress of Siam.

They were all so tired. He sauntered along more slowly with Graciela, not bothering to avoid the puddling water because it would have taken more effort than he possessed. He told her about the great sorrow of their lives, and the rift it caused because they were both too proud to bend. Graciela listened, her eyes troubled. "You know you'd rather keep her here. You still want to get her to the border?"

"Even more," he told her. "Addie is so precious to me that I cannot endanger her further. Our country is not a safe country." He nudged Graciela's shoulder. "Addie's right. Don't give up on your doctor, even if he did change sides. It's not written anywhere that doctors are geniuses any more than freight haulers are."

Graciela laughed. They walked quietly then until the three of them walked in single file across the expanse of what he knew was the San Diego Ranch. In their solitude, they might have been on the moon, but they each seemed to need their solitude right then.

It is my revolution too, Ammon told himself. He

looked ahead to his wife, whose head nodded forward as if she slept. *How do you see it, my love?*

The rain let up in mid-morning as they trudged on, taking turns on Blanco, with no complaints from Graciela, who seemed to have learned something from last night's terror. He hoped the lesson would last. She was riding now, so he walked beside his wife, holding her hand.

He knew the San Diego land because he had freighted grain, hides, lumber, and even a grand piano like his mother's to Graciela's father, who ran the ranch for Señor Terraza. He watched Graciela, waiting for that moment when she would probably rise up in the stirrups when she saw the main house, with its pinkish stucco covering adobe bricks, the three delicate arches at the entrance, and ornate tracery carved from volcanic rock.

There it was. Graciela rose in her stirrups, leaning forward, her smile so happy. He pointed out the *hacienda* to Addie. By chance, he had been freighting grain to San Diego that early morning in March last year when Francisco Madero gathered his eight hundred insurgents there in preparation to attack Casas Grandes, where old dictator Porfirio Díaz's federal troops were garrisoned. No one had known it at the time, but it was almost the opening shot of the revolution, right in his lap.

Ammon squinted to see a few horses and riders in that same plaza in front of the elegant but understated mansion. It didn't appear to be usual ranch business, but nothing had been the same anywhere in Mexico since Madero and his troops left here for Casas Grandes and destiny.

"You ever go to the *hacienda*?" he asked Addie.

"I tagged along with Evangeline once, when she visited Graciela's older sister. I spent the day in the kitchen eating *dulces*." Addie shaded her eyes with a hand to her forehead. "I hope Graciela's parents are here. It doesn't look too busy, though, does it?"

She spoke too soon. Ammon stopped, tugging on Addie's hand, when a line of soldiers on horseback seemed to materialize around the corner of the *hacienda*. Almost as if they were in formation, another line swung out from the other corner.

"Pray, Addie," he said.

Ahead of them Graciela had pulled back on Blanco's reins. She looked back at Ammon, confusion in her eyes. "My parents are here," she said calmly as though the statement would suddenly change things that were going wrong before their eyes.

When Ammon and Addie joined her, walking no faster than before, Graciela dismounted. She came around Blanco and touched Addie's shotgun that Ammon had jury-rigged next to his own rifle in its scabbard.

"Don't even think it, Graciela," he ordered. "They'll blow us to dust."

She took her hand away as though the shotgun stock burned and walked beside them in their own pathetic formation, a man and two women and one tired horse against more troops than he had seen since he and Addie rode at midnight with guerillas. Addie pressed her lips tight together, her head high.

"I'm sorry I forced you to take me home," Graciela

whispered. "Once . . . once we see my parents, they'll straighten out everything."

Ammon said nothing. He had a good idea where her parents were, and it wasn't on the San Diego Ranch. He managed a smile when Addie put her hand under his shirt and hung onto his belt.

"Getting saucy, Mrs. 'Ancock?" he tried to tease.

"I'm not letting go of you," she replied, gripping him tighter. "Who are they?"

He shook his head. He had no idea, except that they weren't *federales*. Their own trip across Chihuahua had turned up few government soldiers, and he wondered if Madero was even still in power. These were more men dressed like him, from sombreros to *bandoleras* to dirty clothes. No one had a fox fur stole, though. He thought about pointing that out to Addie, but one look at her face told him that wouldn't earn him any husband points.

Because they couldn't do anything else, they walked steadily toward the troops, who parted their lines so they could pass, then closed behind them. No one said a word; the only sound was the horses. The only action came from the nearest soldier, who plucked the shotgun and the rifle from Blanco and tossed them to two other riders. Moving his hand slowly to avoid alarm, Ammon took his *bandolera* from around his neck and dropped it in the dirt as he walked.

Silent, watchful, the troops escorted Ammon and his little army directly to the front steps of Hacienda San Diego. There was one thing to be said for revolution: this was the first time he had ever gone right to the front door. Graciela's father had told him years ago to go around to the adobe office next to the stables and not to bother anyone in the big house.

He glanced at Graciela, feeling suddenly sorry for the Empress of Siam. Her face was already a mask of sorrow, as though she knew that whoever opened the door would not be Don Marco Andrade or his lovely wife, Luisa. Those days were over, and Graciela knew it now, as the revolution came home to roost in her heart. He reached around Addie and touched her shoulder.

The door opened, and there stood General José Inés Salazar himself, not Ammon's choice for a gracious host, since he was the man who drove the Mormons out of the colonies. Startled, he looked into Salazar's smiling face and remembered something his father had told him years ago when his sisters had ganged up on him. Pa had stretched a friendly arm across his shoulders, pulled him close, and whispered. "Son, you need to work with what you have here, and it happens to be sisters."

And you just happen to be General Salazar, he thought even as he hung back, uncertain.

God bless Addie. Maybe she had learned the same lesson better than he had. He watched as she squared her shoulders, removed her death grip from the back of his britches, and took the two steps onto the porch in her usual light-stepping fashion. She held her hand out to the general. It shook, but she didn't back down. Ammon held his breath.

"General Salazar, it seems that I am still in your debt and need your help."

If surprise was a tactic, the general became a victim. Startled in turn, he grasped the hand she held out to

228

him, and then he recognized her. He pulled her closer, but it was a gentle tug because Hispanic men could be so courtly.

"I remember you," he said in excellent English. "Colonia García?"

Addie nodded. "I thought you might remember. I owe you and Doctor Menendez my life." With her free hand, she gestured to Ammon. "This is my husband. He rescued me after you did. I keep getting rescued."

Still holding her hand, General Salazar threw back his head and laughed. Ammon glanced around at the soldiers, dismounted now, crowded so close to them in front of the *hacienda*. No one else was laughing. He watched, afraid, until something seemed to change. Whatever tension, whatever threat had followed them up the shallow steps, vanished when the general laughed. Everyone seemed to relax, all because his wife was the funniest human in Chihuahua right then. Her cheerful statement was so ludicrous that Ammon had to smile.

Ammon felt the tension leave his shoulders. *We can do this*, he thought. Addie was looking at him now as though she expected him to say something intelligent.

"General, it seems I am not half so good at rescuing my wife as you are." Maybe that was the right touch—appeal to the general's vanity.

To Ammon's chagrin, Graciela stormed up the front steps. "Where are my parents?" she demanded and broke the web of charm Addie had so artfully spun.

Salazar released Addie's hand, but to Ammon's relief, moved her gently behind him as though to protect her. The general stared at Graciela until he recognized her too. He gave her a long look, as though measuring her. Graciela stood still, her face troubled. She glanced at Ammon for something—reassurance?—and all he could do was shake his head slightly.

Salazar took her hand too, but it wasn't a gentle grip. He pulled her close and stared into her face. "I know you," he said finally, biting off his words, his eyes grim. "Your worthless husband is now my enemy. He rides with General Huerta, the Jackal." He gave her a shake for good measure, his face even closer to hers. "Are you a traitor, as well?"

Ammon knew what Graciela would do next, and she didn't fail him. She burst into tears, which made half of the soldiers crowded on the porch take a step back. Salazar was made of sterner stuff. He didn't step back, and his expression grew thunderous. This was the man President Junius Romney had said he feared more than any other rebel leader because he was so changeable. "Mark me, brethren, tread lightly around this one," he had told the Juárez elders quorum only a week before Salazar's demands had sent the women and children fleeing across the border. Ammon looked at Addie, watched her swallow down her fright and tease out courage of her own from somewhere down deep.

"General, let me help you," Addie said, her voice quiet but firm. She took Graciela's other arm and General Salazar released her. "Are you a traitor?" he shouted again, so loud that Ammon flinched. "Are you?"

Both of Addie's arms circled Graciela as she cried louder. Ammon watched as his wife whispered something in her ear that reduced the noise to a manageable level. She held Graciela tight, smoothing back her hair, treating her like the child she was in a crisis.

"She's so young, General, and she wants her mother," Addie said, turning all her trust on the man that not one Mormon in any of the colonies trusted. It was a look so kind and gentle that Ammon knew—hoped—even Salazar couldn't resist.

He couldn't. "Take her to the kitchen," he snapped.

Addie nodded. She hesitated, then put her hand on the general's arm. "Sir, do you know where her mother is?" she whispered.

Ammon held his breath. The general threw up his hands, exasperated. "On the moon? Jupiter? In a ditch?"

"General, please," Addie said. "She's so young . . ."

"Hacienda Chavez!" he shouted. "Get her out of my sight!"

Ammon turned his head, sick as he thought of the bodies in the stables. *How on earth are you staying so calm?* he asked himself, amazed at his wife. Addie smiled her thanks, unperturbed. Ammon looked at her grip on Graciela's fingers, which was turning them white. Graciela obviously got the message, because she stopped crying.

"She's no younger than you are!" Salazar declared. He shook his head, his expression dazed, as though he wondered why women even existed. He glared at Ammon. "Where does such a woman come from?" His expression changed again, and he laughed, a rueful sound now. "Is she always so sensible, your wife?"

"Most generally," Ammon said in Spanish, switching to the language where he knew the general was more comfortable. "Still, I try not to cross her."

Salazar chuckled, his rage forgotten. Maybe he had a wife too.

"Of course, you may have heard rumors from Ildefonso near the Rio Papigochic of a woman who killed three mountain lions," he said, testing the waters.

Salazar's eyes widened. "We have all heard of that woman." He looked at the two women. "*Your* woman?"

"She saved my life," Ammon said simply. "We were surrounded and she saved my life."

"And now you are my prisoners. What do you think of that?" Salazar asked.

He heard a sound and looked around to see the soldiers going through Blanco's saddlebags, pulling out the Mexican flag he had rescued from the broken standard in Encarnación. The Book of Mormon came next, to be thumbed, ruffled, and tossed on the ground. Next came the smelly canvas bag Dr. Menendez had stolen from his privy. Ammon watched as the soldier opened it. No money. What on earth had Graciela done with it?

Addie surprised him again. Releasing her punishing grip on Graciela, she walked down the shallow steps again into the circle of mounted men. She picked up the Book of Mormon, lying there in the dust. Elaborately, she brushed it off, handed the book to Ammon, and returned to Graciela.

"It's just a book," Salazar told her, sounding faintly apologetic.

"It means a great deal more to us, General," she said kindly. "To the kitchen, you say?" She drew herself up proudly. "I learned how to make tortillas after Am rescued me."

Salazar laughed again, genuinely amused. He nodded to Addie as she started down the dim corridor to the kitchen, Graciela tight in her grip. As Ammon watched them, Graciela tried to pull away, maybe to run. Addie grabbed her hair and yanked on it until the other woman slowed down.

Salazar gestured for the *soldado* to bring him the canvas bag. He held it at arm's length, looking at the two Hs, then at Ammon. "Your company?"

Ammon nodded. "I've hauled for you and your *patrón*, General Pascual Orozco," he reminded the general. "Also for your enemies, as you well know. We were told to be neutral."

"You Mormons were also told, on pain of death, to leave my country," Salazar reminded him.

"I had to find my wife," Ammon said. He glanced at his Book of Mormon in his hand and thought of Old Ammon the Nephite, a prisoner before King Lamoni. If it worked for Old Ammon . . .

"General, how can I serve you?" he asked, which made Salazar laugh until he wheezed. The soldiers looked at each other, uneasy, wondering about a *gringo* in ragged clothes with two helpless women who seemed to think he had something to offer. "I am serious. Think about it for a while, if you please. If there is something I can do for you, I will."

Salazar was silent. He gestured for Ammon to follow him, closing the door behind them.

"My horse . . ."

". . . will be taken care of," Salazar assured him. "*Tonto*, let me think."

He waved Ammon away, and Ammon started down the hall after his wife. He could smell beans and tortillas far ahead and he wanted some. He was passing an open door when Addie called to him from inside. He stopped and looked in, appalled by what he saw.

A man lay on a blood-soaked chaise longue, the kind that privileged women reclined on in women's magazines. Ammon had never seen a real chaise longue, because colony women never had that much time on their hands. The man was moaning and picking at the equally soaked sheet that covered his bare body. Graciela, her eyes wide and terrified, had flattened herself against the wall. Addie knelt by the man, her hand to his forehead.

"Am, he's burning up. And there's all this blood. I don't know what to do, but I'm going to try." She glared at Graciela. "*You* go to the kitchen. Bring me water in a basin, towels, and something to drink." Graciela couldn't leave fast enough.

Am knelt beside her, and she took his arm. "He's in agony! Just bless him to die soon," she whispered. "You did that for Serena's brother."

He kissed her forehead and looked closer at the wounded man. "I know him," he said. The man winced at his words, so he lowered his voice even further. "He is Pedro Ochoa, the general's second-in-command. He ranches near here, or used to."

"Yes, he did," said Salazar from the doorway. "What are you doing?"

"I'm going to wipe his body with cool water,

because he is burning up," Addie said, keeping her voice low. "I'll need a clean sheet to cover him, and another pillow or two to prop him up so he can breathe easier." She spoke decisively, tucking away her fear in some quiet place out of reach. "He was shot through the lungs, wasn't he?"

Salazar nodded, coming closer. "At Encarnación. We have no doctor." He tapped the top of Addie's head to make her look up. "Can you help him?"

"Not beyond making him a little more comfortable," she said. "I will do everything I can for him. I pledge this to you on my honor."

Salazar nodded. "Are all Mormon women so useful?" he asked Ammon.

"All the ones I know."

"Perhaps I should not have been so hasty . . ." He stopped, frowned, then gave Ammon that searching look that had skewered Graciela so neatly on the porch. "Let's see how badly you want to serve me."

"Only ask it."

He was standing with Salazar now, as Addie continued to press her hand against the wounded man's head, doing nothing more than touching him and easing her fingers through his tangled hair. She performed no useful service beyond letting him know that someone cared enough to touch him, and Ammon knew she was perfectly right.

Salazar switched to Spanish. "I know where that worthless Dr. Menendez is. I am going to send you to bring him here."

Ammon nodded. "I can do that. I'll start right now."

"I'm not done yet! When he is back here, and after he treats Pedro, you'll kill him for me."

Ammon cried out, and Addie looked at him in alarm. "It's all right, Addie," he said, as his heart plummeted into his boots. He looked at the general. *You are a cold-hearted man*, he thought. "I can't bring Dr. Menendez back here and then kill him," he said.

Salazar's face split in a grin that Pa used to call a gallows smile. "Then tell me, Mormon, which of the women will die first? Or would you rather I just turned them over to my soldiers? That is your choice."

"No!"

"On second thought, I'll keep your wife for myself. She's charming."

Think, Ammon, he told himself. Addie was watching him now, her eyes anxious, and he wondered again how much Spanish she knew. It became so clear to him that everything in his life had distilled right down to this moment. He closed his eyes, not in fear now, because he was beyond that at last. The dead soldiers under the tablecloth, Serena sitting beside her dying brother, the rebel army at midnight, Addie's pain in her miscarriage, his own grief—it was nothing compared to this moment. *Please, Father, I haven't time to think this through*, he prayed silently. *I'm doing my best. Maybe that's all anyone does.*

As he stood so silently in agony, it was as though someone stood behind him, speaking in a voice so quiet that he strained to hear it over the heavy breathing of the wounded man. *Give it all away.*

I have nothing left to give, he thought. *I doubt he wants Blanco and he can't have Addie.*

All of it.

Salazar was pressing him back into a corner, both hands on his shoulders, as Addie started to rise, fire in her eyes. *Please God*, he prayed once more as he watched Addie look around for something to use as a weapon.

Then he understood, as sure as if the Lord God Almighty had given him—one of His denser mortals—a slap. "Stop, Addie," he said, and Salazar looked around in surprise as she came at him with a stool. "It's all right, Addie," Ammon said as he grabbed the stool before it landed on Salazar. "I can fight this battle." He looked at Salazar, whose eyes were wide. "I would have to wish you good luck if you took on my wife, General." He smiled, calm again. "General, I have a much, much better idea. Shall we talk it over in another room before my wife murders you? She killed three cougars, remember? Let's go in another room, shall we? It's safer somewhere else right now."

SEVENTEEN

SALAZAR DIDN'T ARGUE. With a stern look at Addie, who had returned to Pedro Ochoa's side, the general gestured to the door. His face inscrutable now, he stalked down the hall toward the kitchen, brushing past Graciela with her pan of water almost as if he didn't see her. He stopped before a closed door, slammed it open, and stabbed his finger inside. Ammon followed, feeling better than he had in days, even though he smelled bad and wanted tortillas and beans, even Addie's misshapen ones.

"Sit down."

Ammon sat.

"This had better be good."

"It's wonderful, General."

They sat at a small table in what might have been a card room at one time, a place for gentlemen to go after dinner and smoke. He knew Luiz Terrazas was a fine shot, and the walls testified to his prowess. Ammon looked around at the stuffed heads.

"No pumas. My woman is a better shot," he said, then looked Salazar in the eyes. "How costly was your battle at Encarnación? Besides Pedro Ochoa, I mean."

They stared at each other. Salazar blinked.

"It took a lot of ammunition to blast out the *federales*," Salazar said at last, almost as if admitting it meant pulling the words from his throat with pincers. "And we lost guns. *Ay de mi!*" He pounded the table with his fist. "These *indios* and *peones* who come to fight know nothing about aiming carefully and firing. And at the first sign of trouble, they throw away their rifles and run, even though the battle is not lost! How can anyone win a war with such troops?"

"Easy enough, if you have more rifles and ammunition. General, I have a lot of money."

"You?" Salazar said, his contempt undisguised. "Your woman is in rags and your boots are about to fall off your feet. I don't believe you."

Ammon started to rise, thinking of all the bargains he had made with Mexicans who wanted him to haul freight on their terms, not his. He knew Salazar would stop him. He did.

"Sit," the general said wearily. "Tell me your fable of fabulous wealth, rivaled only by Coronado, I am certain."

"I'll do better than that. I'll take you to it. It's not far, just in Pearson."

Salazar's expression changed. The skepticism vanished and was replaced by the cunning look that Ammon always knew came next in negotiations with Hispanics. "Why should I believe a word you say?"

Ammon leaned toward the general, getting closer than an American would let him get, because *gringos* backed off. "I never joke about money," Ammon said, giving each syllable all the weight such a subject needed.

"Ahhh." Salazar leaned back now, the cunning replaced with understanding. "How much?"

"Enough to buy many Mausers and shot and shell." He shrugged. "I have heard that The Jackal has the ear of the American ambassador who happens to be in El Paso, so just go to Douglas instead." He chuckled. "Would you be surprised to know there is a gun runner in Douglas who had me freight Mausers to Pancho Villa? Just mention my name."

They looked at each other, appraising, measuring, like fighting cocks before the match began. Ammon went for the kill. He leaned back in his chair and stared at the ceiling. "It must be hard for you to get any backing now, if The Jackal has the ear of that fat man in the White House."

"Nearly impossible!"

"Well, then . . ." was all Ammon said, and sat back to wait. *Take your time*, he thought. *King Lamoni thought for a whole hour. I can wait that long if Old Ammon did.*

Apparently the general needed weapons more than King Lamoni needed answers. "Very well, and what do you want in exchange?"

"Not much. Once I give you the money, I'll find your worthless doctor. You will put the women on the train to El Paso."

He had to give the general credit; Salazar wasn't through yet. "Ah, yes, the women. I could kill you right now and tell your wife to take me to the money."

Ammon leaned forward again, which forced General Salazar to lean forward too. They hunched over the table like conspirators. "General! Do you seriously think I would ever tell a woman such a secret, especially a wife?"

They laughed together.

"I put the women on the train, and you will still bring back my doctor? Why?"

It was easy to be serious because he knew the desperately wounded man in the next room. "I happen to like Colonel Ochoa, General," Ammon said. "I want him to live too, and go home to his wife, Ramona, and their sons. I will bring back the doctor, but when Menendez has done all he can for your colonel, you will put him on a train to El Paso too."

Salazar digested that. "What about you?"

"I don't care what you do with me, General. I really don't." Ammon spread out his hands, a man with no guile or secrets, as he gave it all away.

"In Pearson, you say?" the general asked, after a long pause. It was the kind of pause that would have reduced an American to biting his nails, but not a Mexican like Ammon.

"I'll take you there after I have some beans and tortillas. Could I borrow a horse? Mine is tired, and I want to ride him tomorrow for the doctor."

"You will ride for Carrizal tonight, because Colonel Ochoa is dear to me."

"Carrizal? That's not too far. I will ride tonight, and the women will go on the train as soon as possible. I would also like a safe conduct pass for both of them and for me, as I ride to Carrizal."

"You shall have it." The look in the general's eyes was proud then. "Not that you need a safe conduct pass in all of Chihuahua. *I* own it."

And for how long, you pompous idiot? Ammon asked himself. He held out his hand to the general. "On your honor, señor," he said as he always said to seal a negotiation.

Salazar shook his hand, and Ammon felt all the terror in the universe drain from his body. His woman was safe; nothing else mattered. He had the word of honor from a man he did not trust, the man President Romney feared. *I am working with what I have, Pa*, he thought.

While Salazar called to a man to arrange the horses, Ammon walked down the hall to the kitchen. Pia Sanchez still presided over the cooking stove as she had in better times, when he could always be sure of a good meal after a freighting job for Señor Andrade. As she filled a bowl with meaty chunks of pork and chilies, she scolded him for being so thin and dirty, and for dragging his pretty wife all over Chihuahua. She thrust it into his hands, much as she had always done, irritated because he was a man.

He asked for another bowl for the pretty wife he had dragged all over Chihuahua and carried it down the hall to her, where she devoured it almost as fast as he ate his meal. When he finished, he took her hands and told her where he was going with General Salazar. He looked for terror in her eyes, but he saw none this time. Obviously Addie had learned how to work with what she had too. Maybe marrying him in the first place was proof of that.

"When I get back from Pearson, I will ride for Carrizal and Dr. Menendez. You show Pia Sanchez what to do for the colonel here, and get on the train to El Paso with Graciela as soon as Salazar lets you. And he will. He gave me his word of honor." He looked around. "Where is she?"

"In her old room, crying. She may be a problem. She is still convinced her parents will come for her." She searched his face, worried. "Am, you said something about Hacienda Chavez . . ."

He rubbed his cheek against hers, unable to speak for a moment. "Get her on the train. I don't care how, but get her on the train."

She nodded, her eyes on the colonel now. She had wiped him clean, bandaged his chest, and propped him up so he could breathe easier. He appeared no better, but he was not soaked in blood. "He whispers for Ramona," Addie told him, her voice low.

"His wife. You'd like her." He gestured to her and she was in the circle of his arms in a moment, her head resting against his chest.

"Why is revolution so hard?"

"Everyone wants a little power, and then a little more," he told her, speaking into her hair. "People like us, like Serena Camacho, like the Salinas family—we just hang on and hope to be standing when the hot winds die down." He looked at the colonel again. "I'll give him a blessing that he stay alive long enough for Dr. Menendez."

Without a word, Addie knelt by the bed as he placed his hands gently on the colonel's head, asking the Lord to bless this man. "But in all things, Lord, Thy will," he concluded, then kissed the colonel's forehead. "He liked to ride along with me when I freighted around Chuichupa. He could tell the best stories."

Ammon and General Salazar left for Pearson in early afternoon, accompanied by ten *soldados* bristling with weapons. "I have ordered them to kill you if you do anything strange," Salazar said.

"I won't even blow my nose," he assured the general. *Just let the privy be standing*, he prayed silently, then wondered how many ridiculous petitions Heavenly Father listened to each day, on average.

The privy was standing, and so was his stable and wagon barn. The corral was full of sheep now, and a family was squatting in the quarters he had added on two years ago, when he left Addie and García in such despair. As they watched, a small boy came out of the privy, hitching up his pants. When the boy saw them, he ran into the corral, scattering sheep. The soldiers laughed and shot off their *pistolas*, which earned Salazar's disgust.

"No wonder I have no ammunition," he groused, after giving his troops a filthy look. "Now where?"

Ammon pointed. "There."

"You're joking," Salazar said, and Ammon saw the telltale signs of anger blotch the general's neck and forehead.

"I told you I never joke about money," Ammon reminded him as he dismounted.

The privy was a mess, which made the general reluctant to come closer than a few feet from the open door. The family had been using it, to Ammon's surprise, but seemed not to understand the need to add any lime. All the better, Ammon decided. Even the crown jewels of

England and Scotland combined would have been safe in his reeking privy. Pilots in aeroplanes droning high over-head could probably smell the *necesario* of Señor 'Ancock.

Blue bottle flies hummed everywhere in the privy. The younger members of the current household had missed a few times, so he stepped carefully. A hand-kerchief to his nostrils, General Salazar leaned into the privy, then leaned out even faster.

Good. The lid to the second hole remained nailed in place. He took out his knife and pried it up. Perfect. When he reached his hand inside, Salazar gasped. Ammon grinned and ran his hand along the boards. His grin widened as he felt the strong box.

"*Aquí está*," he said.

"You drop it, you'll go diving after it," Salazar said, then stepped out of Ammon's line of sight.

Quickly, he set the box on the floor, then reached inside again, groping against the back of the vault. He smiled as his fingers touched the tarred rope. He closed the hole and tapped the nails back in place. When he carried the strong box outside, tucked under his arm so no one could see it, Salazar backed away, shaking his head.

"General, you cannot deny it is a good place. Hold it while I mount, please."

Ammon wished he could have had Addie's Kodak Brownie to snap a picture of the reluctance on General Salazar's face as he held the stinking strong box. He made Salazar hold it again when he dismounted in front of the North Western Railway depot. "I want to find out when the next train leaves," he said and went inside before Salazar could say anything.

All the stationmaster could do was shrug his shoulders and say, "It will be here sometime, señor, if no rebels have cut the line. *Ojalá*," he added, helpful if vague. He glanced out the door then and saw General Salazar. He gulped. "It will be here this evening, on the dot." The dot of what, he did not say.

As he started to leave, Ammon noticed a familiar face, one of the clerks from the lumber company, sitting on a bench, looking dejected. "I've been waiting a day, Ammon," he said ruefully. "Just trying to get out of this country."

Ammon looked out the window, where General Salazar sat, his frown deepening, not a patient man. "Tell me, John, is there anyone at Colonia Juárez?"

"One or two men. Not everyone left when your leaders said to."

When they turned the bend and headed closer to the river again, Salazar signaled for his troopers to ride ahead. For a terrifying moment, Ammon wondered if the general planned to shoot him. *He gave his word of honor* warred with, *this is revolution*, until all he could do was close his eyes and pray.

"Open the box," Salazar demanded, his hand nowhere near his sidearm.

Ammon did as he said. He looked down on hard-earned money, freighting in the furnace of summer and the icy grip of winter, always in danger from one faction or other. Greenbacks, pesos, francs even, paper money, and coins. He glanced at the general, hoping it was enough, and was rewarded with General Salazar's look of enormous satisfaction.

"Your arms dealer is in Douglas, Arizona?" Salazar asked.

"Pablo Rincón, and he's not *my* arms dealer," Ammon protested with a laugh. "I do know he has no love for General Huerta."

"Very well." The general closed the lid. "I am taking my troops that way, anyway. We'll just leave sooner."

"And the women?"

"On tonight's train. I still expect the doctor, may boils smite his worthless hide."

"I gave you my word, General."

Dusk came earlier now. It had been several weeks since Ammon had seen a calendar, but he reckoned it was the middle of September when even Mexico began to recover from the heat.

Addie and Graciela were both in the kitchen, his wife gamely slapping out her less-than-perfect tortillas. The Empress of Siam just stood against the back wall, unable to do much of anything because she was gentry cut loose in a land in revolt against people just like her. All her life she had been waited on by servants who now carried guns and weren't particularly concerned with her well-being.

The light in Addie's eyes when she saw him took the tired right out of his bones, even as his body cried out for sleep. He sat at the kitchen table and ate the beans and tortillas Addie put before him. Even more than food, he relished the way her hand rested on his shoulder. She ran her thumb across the back of his neck, a gesture soothing and edgy at the same time.

He closed his eyes when he finished eating and pillowed his head on his arms for a few minutes before General Salazar strode into the kitchen and shook him awake. "Your horse is saddled and here is your safe conduct pass," the general said. "Tomás and Joaquin will ride with you. They insisted on safe conduct passes too, like silly women! My soldiers! You will ruin me, Mormon. If you do anything other than snatch the doctor and bring him back here, they will shoot you. Go now."

Ammon hung back. "A moment, *por favor*, with my wife," he requested. Salazar shrugged and walked away, calling to his next in command, his mind already on a thousand other details.

Ammon took Addie's hand and walked her out of the *hacienda* at the ornate front entrance. "Salazar will take the two of you to the train depot in Pearson," he said, his arm twined through hers. "Keep your eyes down and stay close to Graciela. It's usually about five hours to El Paso, but who knows? Addie, I love you."

She turned to him and rested her head against his chest, her arms tight around him. "I'd rather wait here for you to return."

He held her off from him and looked into her eyes, then pulled her close again. "Chihuahua is a powder keg. Get Graciela . . ."

"I know, I know," she grumbled, impatient with him. "Get that silly woman on the train!"

He kissed her hair. "When you get to El Paso, have

someone direct you to the lumberyard. My folks will be there, and your father will have five hundred dollars for—"

"I don't want it!" she insisted, her voice fierce.

"Then give it to Graciela," he said, patient with her. "Which reminds me: where is the money that was in the canvas bag?"

She managed a slight smile and patted the front of her dress. "I'll give that to Graciela. Who knows what the doctor will do or where her parents are?"

He hesitated, and she saw his indecision. She took his hand and pressed it to her lips.

"You know where they are, don't you?" she asked quietly.

Holding her close, he told her about the horse barn at Hacienda Chavez, and the bodies jumbled together. "I thought at first they were stable boys, but no. I suppose the soldiers left the women there when they finished with them," he whispered.

Addie gasped, her hand to her mouth. "Are you certain?"

He nodded. "As near as I can be. Graciela's mother had such long blonde hair. Remember?" He pressed his forehead to Addie's. "Don't say anything to Graciela. I don't know . . . maybe her father escaped." He sighed. "She'll need money; give her all you can."

"I'll tell her, once we're on the train," Addie told him, her voice low. "She has to know."

They had walked to the horse corral where two mounted *soldados* waited, Blanco between them. He stood there, Addie pressed so close to him. He hesitated again, but she knew him.

"You're not coming out, once you finish here," she said. It was no question.

He hated to tell her. The firm way she had pressed her lips together told him she wasn't going to make it easy for him. "No. This is my home. I'm going to Colonia Juárez and see who is there. Addie, I never planned to go back. I was just going to rescue you, apologize for being a fool two years ago, and get you on the train."

"We still have a problem, then, but it's a different one," she told him, her voice unsteady now. "I love you too." She looked away. "I think there's more, but it can wait." She took his hand. "When will I see you again?"

"Revolutions don't last forever."

"Our marriage does, Am." She kissed him and clung to him, letting him lift her off her feet and hold her close. "Our war is over," she whispered into his ear, then made him set her down. "*Vayas con Dios.*" She gave him a long look, then turned around decisively and started back to the *hacienda*. She was just a small woman trapped in a nasty war, a *soldadera americana* who had killed three mountain lions and driven off wolves, if he could believe Salazar's troops and their breathless account this afternoon on the way back from Pearson.

As he watched, she stopped, then bent over suddenly as though someone had cut her in two. She rested her hands on her knees, head down, and wailed. He closed his eyes and put his hands to his ears.

When she was silent, she did not look back, but continued on her decisive way. He mounted Blanco and tugged on his reins to point him east to Carrizal.

EIGHTEEN

To LISTEN TO Tomás and Joaquin tell it, kidnapping el médico Menendez would be a simple matter, on the order of a stroll through the plaza in Chihuahua City, without the mariachi bands and young lovers. To Ammon's astonishment, they were almost right.

They arrived in Carrizal on the evening of the second day, slowed by autumn rain that turned into torrents sweeping across the parched desert landscape in waves, and making riding difficult. They were alone in Chihuahua's immensity, the smart people of the state obviously staying indoors.

Conversation was sparse, Ammon unsure if he was a prisoner, a *compadre*, or a nuisance taking Tomás and Joaquin away from their own campfire. For the most part, they ignored him until the dawn of the second day when they huddled in a dry wash, and Joaquin tried to start a fire. Tomás was offering all manner of useless advice when Ammon heard the sound he dreaded.

"*Hermanos*, we have to get out of this *arroyo*," he said, grabbing Blanco's reins and starting up the slope. He whistled up the other horses, which started after Blanco up the side of the dry wash.

The *soldados'* blank looks told him all he needed to know about their familiarity with rain in the desert. When he had talked at all, Tomás had told Ammon he was from the mountains of Durango and despised the desert.

Joaquin must have thought he was trying to escape, because he snatched his rifle and started firing at Ammon, who flattened himself against the slope. To Ammon's relief, Joaquin couldn't shoot any better than most of Salazar's troops; Addie was a better shot. Before he could reload, the soldier turned and gaped at the approaching wall of dirty water, dropped his rifle—no wonder Salazar needed money for weapons—and sprinted for higher ground.

Weeping and calling on whatever saints they could think of who looked after fools, the two soldiers held out their hands to Ammon, who had reached the top of the *arroyo*. Mounting Blanco, he unlimbered his rope and threw a fine loop over Tomás, struggling farther below. Blanco towed him to safety, and then it was Joaquin's turn.

When both men were seated on the desert floor as the noisy flood rushed by below them, Joaquin dusted off his filthy jacket. "*I am a corporal; you should have rescued me first,*" he said, glaring at Ammon.

Spare me from fools, Ammon thought. He pointed out in his most polite Spanish that Tomás had been farther down the slope and therefore in more immediate danger, even if he was a lowly private. Joaquin rubbed his chin, thought it through, and nodded.

At least they were on the east side of the impromptu

river. Joaquin and Tomás indulged in a lengthy debate about the difficulty of returning after the doctor was in their possession since there was no bridge in sight. Trying not to smile, Ammon explained that the river would be gone soon, soaking into parched desert soil. Their expressions told him they did not believe a word of it, but since he had saved their lives, the soldiers were not inclined to argue.

They *were* inclined to answer some of Ammon's questions as they rode steadily toward Carrizal, a pretty little town he knew well, where he liked to stop on his way to Rancho Gloriosa, another of Luiz Terrazas's holdings.

"Tell me, Joaquin, why it is that you all seem to know where *el médico* is, but no one has bothered him since he has changed sides? General Salazar is not a man to suffer fools gladly. I am surprised he left Menendez alone."

The two soldiers looked at each other and both shrugged. Amused, Ammon watched Joaquin's eyes, seeing the hesitation and confusion. "What is the problem with the doctor?" he asked finally.

"Do you know him?" Tomás asked in turn.

"Not really. Not as a friend, anyway."

"He is a lot of trouble," Tomás said.

"He stole money from me," Ammon said.

Joaquin nodded sympathetically. "You see what we mean."

He didn't, and it was Joaquin's turn to observe his own confusion. The corporal must have decided he owed more explanation to the man who had saved his life, even if he was rescued after a lowly private. "It is this way, señor. The doctor is a lot of noise and bother."

"I think I understand now," Ammon replied. "He is the Emperor of Siam."

The soldiers exchanged blank looks again and ignored him once more until they stopped for a hasty meal in a village so small there was no church or plaza. The owner of the only *cantina* in town shuttered his windows hastily as the three of them rode by.

Joaquin dismounted and banged on the door, demanding entrance. The man inside declared on the bones of his late wife that he would never open the door to rascals who never paid even one *cuartilla* for a meal, but only left a worthless paper chit. Ammon took his turn, sliding a coin under the door, which opened almost immediately.

How many favors must I owe these simpletons? Ammon asked himself as they ate. The owner gave him a much larger bowl of *posole* than the other two, which Ammon generously shared because he wanted more answers.

"Tell me, my friends," he began as they left the village. "If Doctor Menendez has gone over to Victoriano Huerta's army, are we riding into a Huerta stronghold?"

Both men laughed. "No one wants Carrizal, señor," Joaquin said when he had control of himself again. He gestured grandly. "This is all the possession of General Salazar and his *jefe*, General Orozco."

"Then tell me, Joaquin, why were you so careful to get yourselves safe conduct passes?" Ammon asked. "Do you need them?"

Joaquin merely shrugged. "One can never be too careful."

It was food for thought, followed by the strongest urge to bid both men *adiós*, turn back, and hightail it to Pearson or Colonia Juárez. "I promised General Salazar and I owe it to Colonel Ochoa," he muttered to himself in English, even as he wondered if he really *was* the fool that Joaquin and Tomás thought.

As they approached Carrizal at dusk, they were surveyed at close quarters by guerillas belonging to the camp of Pascual Orozco. They, along with Salazar's bandits, had terrorized Colonia Dublán and Colonia Juárez. He rode easily with them, listening as they boasted of skirmishes with the *federales*, as Madero's power continued to dribble away. He thought suddenly of Serena Camacho in Santa Clarita, wondering if she was still alive, and of the small people of Mexico who wanted land and peace. Maybe he should meet Addie in El Paso and start over there. He didn't want to wait for the revolution to end because he had an uneasy feeling that it was just beginning.

Carrizal was as quiet as he remembered it, just a small town with kind people and good cheese. When she knew he was freighting toward Carrizal, Addie always reminded him to get *queso* for her. Again he had a strong urge to leave, but there was Joaquin, finger to his lips as they rode down a deserted side street and dismounted by an adobe house like all the other houses.

Speaking softly, Joaquin sent Ammon to guard the back door—with what, he wanted to ask—while they went in the front. He listened to a brief scuffle inside, but no shouting came and no weapons fired. Maybe Joaquin and Tomás were more skillful than he gave them credit for. When he came around to the front, the *soldados* had neatly trussed and gagged a tall gentleman wearing a good suit, his hair slicked back. *Dr. Menendez, I presume?* Ammon wanted to ask but resisted.

The doctor stood quietly on the dark street and looked as contemptuous as a man can, with a gag in his mouth and his arms pinned back. "Señor Menendez? We're taking you back to Rancho San Diego, where your former comrade, Colonel Ochoa, lies wounded," Ammon said, pulling down the gag, which wasn't tight to begin with. "After you have tended him, General Salazar has promised you will be put on the train to El Paso."

Menendez stared at him. "I know you," he said after a long look.

"I think you fixed my leg in that logging camp two years ago."

"Ah! The compound fracture," he said.

"My wife and your wife are probably in El Paso now. That was also part of the agreement," Ammon continued. "And you stole money from my privy."

Menendez smiled at that. He sketched a courtly bow that ended in a muffled protest when Ammon put the gag back in his mouth and tightened it. Joaquin and Tomás picked him up and threw him onto what was probably his own horse, retrieved from a stable by the back door.

He tried to speak. Ammon pulled down the gag again.

"My medicine bag. In the front room," he said. Ammon replaced the gag.

The black bag was right inside the door, next to a satchel neatly packed and ready to go. Ammon frowned. Was Dr. Menendez *expecting* them? He stared at the bag until Joaquin called for him to hurry up. He picked up the medical bag and left the satchel.

They mounted and moved down the street at the same slow pace, the better not to attract attention in this little town neither side wanted. "Joaquin, he had a bag already packed, just inside the door," Ammon said as they left town, heading west.

Joaquin nodded and glared at the doctor, who struggled to stay in his saddle with his hands behind his back. "We must have snatched him just before someone else did."

"He didn't struggle too much."

"Just enough," Joaquin replied with another of his elaborate shrugs. "You know General Salazar does not want us to injure the doctor's valuable hands."

They rode all night, passing easily through other Salazar and Orozco troops, who laughed at Menendez. Joaquin stayed close to his prisoner while Tomás dozed in the saddle, leaving Ammon the odd man out. He rode ahead of the others, chiding himself for his misgivings and miserable because when he returned to Rancho San Diego, Addie would be gone.

He knew it was what he wanted, the reason he had come to Mexico. Despite their private pain, she was still his wife when he set out from El Paso, and he felt honor-bound to get her to a safe place. He hadn't really counted on falling in love with her all over again, which made him think he hadn't fallen out of love in the first place. Now she would be safe, and her father would probably whisk her away to Utah. Maybe he could visit her at Christmastime, but then they would have to begin all over again. How many times could they do that before it was just too hard?

First things first, he told himself as they came to the dry wash that had turned into a river only a day ago. Sure enough, it was dry again. He looked back at the doctor, who rode so close to Joaquin, the gag down around his neck now. They seemed to be deep in conversation, even arguing, which puzzled Ammon. Earlier, Dr. Menendez had objected to beans and tortillas in that little village, reminding Ammon of Graciela and her superior airs. Ammon had plunked down his own money again to get the man a plate of eggs and chorizo, which made Tomás pout.

Ammon rode ahead of the trio, wanting to put miles between them and their monumental silliness. He was tired of company that wasn't Addie, with her good nature and her self-confidence that had bloomed the farther they had ventured into Mexico. He wanted her with all his heart in all those ways that a man wants his wife, but especially because she made him happy.

That was it, then, he decided as dusk approached and they neared the great valley of the San Diego Ranch. He would give up his own dreams and get on that train with the doctor. Eventually he might get used to life in the United States.

They had never really left the land of undulating hills, but the hills seemed more pronounced now as they approached the foothills of the Sierra Madre. They had passed several patrols of Salazar's men, who glanced at their safe conduct papers and waved them on, intent on their search for Huerta's men, or Villa's troops, or Zapata's guerillas. And now they spoke of Venustiano Carranza, another contender for power. Each faction picked at the barely breathing carcass of Mexico, and Ammon was tired of it all.

He glanced behind, realizing how far ahead of the others he had traveled, nourishing his own black mood, and decided to wait. He knew they were close to the ranch, because just ahead were the railroad tracks of the North Western that had carried away all the women and children from the colonies, and Addie and Graciela by now.

He remembered that Joaquin's horse had shied away from the tracks on the way to Carrizal, so he rose in his stirrups to remind the corporal. He watched in stupefied amazement as Joaquin took out his pistol and shot Tomás between the eyes.

"*Viva Huerta!*" Joaquin shouted, and the doctor laughed.

Ammon stared, unable to say anything. He reached for his rifle, forgetting his scabbard was empty. Joaquin rode toward him, his pistol still out, with Dr. Menendez right behind, his hands untied now and gripping his reins, a smile on his face.

"No, wait," Ammon said, raising his hands to protect his face as Joaquin stopped and aimed at his forehead.

Nothing. Ammon put his hands down in time to watch the corporal clutch at an arrow between his eyes, then fall to the earth like a sack of wet meal. His eyes wide with fright, the doctor had raised his hands and was staring over Ammon's shoulder. He turned around too but saw nothing.

He looked again, as dusk played its own trick on him. The land seemed to open up to reveal a single Indian. He looked closer and clutched at his saddle horn.

"Joselito?" he quavered, barely believing his eyes.

"At your service, señor," the Tarahumara said. "What should I do with this other one?"

The doctor started to cry, which made Joselito snort in disgust. Menendez made a half-hearted attempt to flee until Ammon roped him and yanked him from the saddle. Menendez sat on the ground and sobbed as his horse, moving faster without a rider, quickly became a distant memory.

"Oh, stop it," he said to Menendez as he dismounted. "You're still alive."

The doctor sobbed until his nose ran, then checked his pockets for a handkerchief. "Use your sleeve," Ammon said.

"I could never!"

"Heaven help us, Joselito."

The Indian toed the dead man. Ammon flinched when he yanked out the arrow, wiped it on the doctor's sleeve, then put it in his quiver again. Menendez had gone deathly pale. He stared at his gory sleeve, then held his arm out to Ammon, as if expecting him to make it better. Ammon just shook his head.

Joselito squatted by the doctor and Ammon joined him. "Why on earth are you here?" he asked.

The Indian sighed, and it was a great, put-upon sigh. "My woman said I had to follow you."

"Why?"

"Pardon me, señor, she said you were a special kind of fool and I had to keep an eye on you, even after García."

"Has she been talking to *my* wife?" Both men chuckled. "Let us parlay in a moment," he said, and the Indian nodded.

Menendez stared at them both, as though they had lost all reason. "What about *me?*"

Ammon turned to look at him, regarding him in silence as he put it all together. "Now I understand why Joaquin was so insistent on safe conduct *tarjetas*. Where were you two really headed? Obviously Tómas wasn't in on your grand scheme."

"El Paso," the doctor said, his voice sulky now. "We are at the railroad right now, right through the middle of Salazar's country. General Huerta seems to think I can assist him in negotiating with your ambassador to Mexico."

"Not mine," Ammon said mildly. "You were just going to use that safe conduct pass all through Chihuahua?"

"We nearly did."

"True." Ammon looked toward the other dead man.

"Poor, dumb Tomás." *And poor, dumb me*, he thought. *Joselito's wife is right.*

Dr. Menendez watched him expectantly, as though he was certain of a favor. "Nothing has changed. I told you yesterday I am to take you to Rancho San Diego, because Colonel Ochoa is badly wounded. Once you have done all you can for him, you are to get on the train to El Paso. Your wife is already there."

"You know Salazar will never let me leave San Diego alive."

Ammon looked at the pitiful man on the ground in front of him. He was probably right. Depending on his mood, Salazar could be kind or cruel, but it was unlikely he would forgive a traitor, even if he did promise.

"Doctor, you're not very good at this revolution business," he began.

Menendez started to cry again.

"If it's any consolation, neither am I." Ammon sighed. "But you did save my life in that logging camp and I am in your debt. Take Joaquin's horse and get out of here."

The doctor stared at him, then got to his feet, his eyes on Joselito and his bow and arrow. He took a few steps. When the Indian did nothing, he took a few more steps. He started running then and grabbed the reins to Joaquin's horse.

"Make sure you have your safe conduct pass," Ammon called after him. "And good luck to you if you find Graciela!" He started to laugh, flopping back on the ground, tired right down to his toenails, but glad he had not sent a man to his death. He looked over at Joselito. "Did you follow me all the way from García?"

"Oh, no. I wasn't going to follow you at all, but my woman . . ." He shook his head. "They can make life so miserable."

Or wonderful, Ammon thought. He raised up on one elbow to regard the man who was probably his best friend in Mexico, considering. "I gave you all my cattle. Why does she think I am a fool?"

Joselito touched the fox fur stole around Ammon's neck. "It was this. You told me it was a valuable totem and it would bring me luck."

"Yeah, I did. Um, it will."

"I believed you, señor, until my sister saw it," Joselito said, not disguising the reproach in his voice. "She laughed at me, at Joselito!"

"Your sister? I don't understand."

"Before the troubles started, she was a servant on Rancho Medina, washing the ladies' clothes. When the soldiers turned on each other, she ran back to the mountains."

"Wise of her."

Joselito touched the fox fur again. "She told me rich women, not warriors, wear these and the eyes are glass."

I owe this man an apology, Ammon thought, embarrassed and wondering how to begin. "Joselito, it was like this . . ."

The Indian gave Ammon a little slap, as he probably slapped his children to get their attention. "My woman started to cry and wail! She is certain you do not know your totem is worthless, and she is grateful for the cattle.

She wanted me to follow you and keep you safe, because a fox fur with glass eyes won't. I am sorry to tell you that, but it is true."

"Thank you, Joselito," Ammon said, touched. "How did you pick up our trail?"

Even sitting there on the ground, Joselito seemed to draw himself up. "I am Tarahumara," he reminded Ammon, with some dignity. He laughed then, a low chuckle so infectious that Ammon smiled. "I wasn't doing too well until I came to the Rio Papigochic and heard such a tale."

"The three pumas and wolves, and what have you?" Ammon asked.

Joselito nodded. "The villagers said it was your woman. Señor, *she* is your totem."

Ammon knew he couldn't speak without crying, so he waited. He didn't want the Indian to think he was as big a ninny as Dr. Menendez. "You followed us on foot from Papigochic?"

The Indian grinned. "Not always on foot. I rode with that midnight army. You were easy to track after that, you and your woman who brings you good luck."

"I believe you're right," he said finally. "Your woman is right too. I'm an idiot, because I sent my totem away to El Paso."

Joselito sucked in his breath. "You had better keep wearing the fox fur, señor, because you *are* a fool."

NINETEEN

AMMON THOUGHT ABOUT imitating Dr. Menendez and making his own run for the border, except that his parents had raised him better. He had given his word to General Salazar, and he had to return to Rancho San Diego. He tried to explain such nobility to Joselito, but the Indian muttered something in his own language better left untranslated.

"No wonder my woman sent me to watch you," he did say in Spanish finally.

"It's my journey now, Joselito," Ammon replied. He held out his hand, then touched the Indian's fingertips. "Thank you for saving my life."

Joselito nodded as though saving lives was something he did every day. He touched Ammon in turn. "Thank you for feeding my people."

Ammon just nodded. A month ago, he would have mourned the loss of the Hancock herd. "Do this for me, my friend, if you can: Keep a bull and two cows in that box canyon. Maybe the herd will grow again."

"Will you return to García?"

"I don't think so."

Joselito's expression was kindly, concerned even. "Where *will* you go, señor?"

"Not sure about that either."

The concern grew on the Indian's face. "Will I see you again?"

"That might depend on whether General Salazar is in a good mood," Ammon told him.

"I can ride in with you."

I never knew I had such friends until I returned to rescue my wife, Ammon thought. *Who was rescued?* When he could speak, he had both hands on Joselito's shoulders. "It would be even more dangerous for you than me, my friend." He didn't care now that tears streamed down his cheeks. He wasn't even certain why he was crying. Maybe it was for friendship, for Addie in El Paso now, for his possibly short future. *"Adiós.* If I live, we will probably meet again. Let us leave it at that."

Joselito nodded and pulled the fox stole from around Ammon's neck, tossing it into the darkness. "You have another powerful totem," he said kindly.

"More powerful than my wife?"

"Perhaps. Several times, I watched you and your woman kneel. I don't know what you were doing, but you're still alive. When we meet again, you will tell me more."

Ammon nodded, thinking of Old Ammon the Nephite, who was probably smiling down on his namesake. *I will teach you more, my friend*, he thought. *It is a pledge.*

Ammon mounted Blanco and rode into the darkness. A mile later, he stopped and listened. To his relief, he heard nothing. Joselito would not survive a moment on Rancho San Diego, not with the Indians of the mountains always and everlastingly fair game for either side and all factions.

Blanco was tired, so Ammon did not push the gelding. As he rode, he composed plausible excuses for Dr. Menendez's nonattendance, each sounding more ridiculous than the one before. He decided that the truth was best, something his mother and Sister Coates, his Primary teacher, would have approved of. "I let him go because he didn't deserve to die, even if he is a spoiled, silly man, much like his wife," he said out loud, which made Blanco prick up his ears.

If he was still alive after that admission to the mercurial Salazar, he could explain the dead bodies of two *soldados* on their way to becoming a buzzard banquet. He hated to think how many bones would litter Mexican soil before the revolution ended. Of what importance were two more? And if he joined the boneyard, three?

As he rode in cautiously, Ammon expected to see more activity around the *hacienda*. Hadn't Joaquin said there was a battalion leaving to fight in Sonora? Had the troops already left? Could he be so lucky?

Two *soldados* sat on the porch as he rode to the *hacienda's* shallow steps. One of them lifted his hand in greeting, while the other slumbered on. He tied Blanco to the hitching rail and opened the front door.

"*¿Hay alguien?* Anyone?" he asked, thinking two languages were better than one.

Feeling like the intruder he was, Ammon walked down the corridor, pausing to look in the room where he had last seen Colonel Ochoa so near death. The room had been tidied and the bed remade, with no evidence of the suffering of a good man. *Que lástima*, he told himself, and closed the door quietly.

The next door was open and he heard someone humming inside. The stuffed heads on the walls glared at him. A man was seated at the table, putting down cards in a row. He smiled the welcome of someone bored with his own company and eager for a diversion, even if it was only one dirty gringo.

Cautious, Ammon made himself known to the soldier minus one leg, the stump of which was propped on another chair.

"Corporal Acosta, *a su servicio*," the card player said. "I would get up, but . . ." He dealt himself another row of cards, putting back one he did not like.

He needed no urging to talk. Ammon's question of "Where is everybody?" turned into a lengthy discourse on an amazing discovery of money to buy arms and ammunition and the need to saddle up and head to Sonora after a munitions dealer. The corporal politely reminded Ammon there was a war on.

"The general is gone?" Ammon asked, hardly believing his good fortune.

"Poof, like a hot wind," Acosta said. He pointed to himself proudly. "*I* am in charge of the San Diego Ranch. Who would have thought such a thing could happen? Would that my mamá were here to see me! She used to sew for the Andrade family." He spit on Luisa Andrade's exquisite Persian rug.

It seemed too easy to Ammon, especially since he had prepared the entire truth and many details for the man who wasn't there. "I was supposed to bring a doctor for Colonel Ochoa."

The corporal's face fell. "*¡Pobre coronel!* He did not live a day after you left." He looked closer at Ammon, not sure of his identity. Ammon knew that all gringos looked alike to Mexicans. "One of the women sat with him and cried and cried over him. Such a gentle lady."

"She has a soft heart." Tired, and not wanting to think about that soft heart, Ammon sat down at the card table. He had to know. "Tell me, Corporal, did General Salazar do as he said he would, and get the women on the train?"

The soldier's expressive face collapsed again; this was clearly not a good subject, which made Ammon sit up straight. "He tried to do that. I wasn't there"—he patted his excuse—"but my cousin said it was not a pretty sight." He chuckled. "He said one of them got on the train so quietly and calmly. The other one? Oh, no! She fought and scratched and bit and refused to leave." He leaned closer and whispered, even though the room was deserted. "My cousin said she even kicked the general in the shins."

Ammon closed his eyes, wondering into what ditch Graciela's remains had been tossed. "What did the general do?"

"He tried to reason with her, but by all the saints, there was no reasoning with that one."

He paused, triumphant in conveying his message, and laid down another row of cards. It took all of Ammon's willpower not to grab the corporal and shake him. "Did they ever get her on the train?"

"Oh, yes," Acosta said with some relish.

"That's a relief. There were people waiting for them in El Paso."

"*¡Pues, no, señor!* What did she do but crawl out the window on the other side! The general gave up and brought her back." He slapped down more cards, not so pleased now. "She is in the kitchen, burning beans and scorching tortillas and we wish she would go away."

"No one . . . no one hurt her, did they?" Ammon asked, thinking Dr. Menendez might want to take his chances with the Empress of Siam again, provided he quit politics and returned to medicine.

The corporal stared at Ammon, eyes wide with fear. "Señor! There is no one in all of Chihuahua brave enough to molest the woman who killed three cougars and—"

Ammon leaped to his feet and ran down the hall to the kitchen, calling Addie's name. She turned around at the cooking range, wooden spoon in hand, her face joyful. He scooped her up and kissed her with such a smack that Pia Sanchez, sitting at the table, covered her face with her hands and shuddered.

He knew how reticent Mexicans were about affection in public, but he didn't care, and neither did *la mujer feroz*, who was crying now and trying to gather him close. Or maybe he was crying, because he knew no one could ever love Addie Hancock as much as he did. Their war was over.

After a serious demonstration of affection that made Pia Sanchez cluck her tongue, Ammon remembered he was in the kitchen of Rancho San Diego and not his own half-burned house in García. Pia glared and handed him a dishtowel. "Blow your nose, señor, and behave yourself," she declared, and stomped from the kitchen.

He blew his nose. "I was just kissing my wife," he called after the cook. "Thoroughly." He sat down and held out his arms for Addie, who had returned to the bean pot to give it one more half-hearted stir. She sat on his lap, minus the wooden spoon.

"I was going to get on the train. I really was," she told him, her face muffled in his dirty shirt. "Am, you stink."

"I know," he replied, his voice as tender as if she had told him he was her prince and favorite plaything. "What possessed you?"

"I could not make myself put one more mile between us," she told him simply. "If you try to put me on the train again, the same thing will happen. This is my country too, and you are most definitely my husband."

He had no rebuttal, no antidote. They were in this together, no matter how long the revolution lasted or whatever happened to them. Still, he hoped she understood the magnitude of their challenge. "It's not going to be easy, *mi amor*," he began.

She kissed him to shut him up. "I gave Graciela the money her husband stole from you and told her to look up your father in the lumberyard." She patted his shirt. "He's more likely to help her than my father. After she left, I wrote a letter to my father, telling him to give Graciela the five hundred dollars." She made a wry face. "I guess we're broke. Dare we return to García?"

Ammon shook his head. "It's not going to be safe

there anytime soon, if ever. If you're willing, do this—write your father and ask him to deed us his ranch in Colonia Juárez. A clerk from the lumber company told me not everyone left. We'll go there in the morning and see if it's a rumor or the truth."

"I'm willing. I can talk Pia out of some bedding, and maybe a pot or two. We're *really* broke," she emphasized again.

Ammon provided his own emphasis for a few minutes, guaranteed to keep Pia out of the kitchen. When he finished, Addie was rosy with whisker burn.

"We *can't* live on love," she said, sounding like a wife again, which made him so happy that his scalp tingled.

"We can try, but it might not come to that."

Addie cuddled close. "I suppose you'll tell me about a magic privy in Pearson."

"As a matter of fact . . . ," he started, and laughed when she thumped him. He looked around the empty room and whispered anyway. "When I built that privy, I built two vaults, instead of just one underneath both holes."

"Ammon, you are a sly dog," she said. "What did you do?"

"I told General Salazar I never joke about money, and I don't. What he didn't know is that when I stashed the strong box, I also hung a tarred rope from the back of that unused vault. I attached another cloth bag, also tarred black so you can't see it unless you stare down into the hole, and who in the world does that, except little boys? I always look at the back wall, myself. *Ay!*" he said when she thumped him again. "We're not rolling in wealth, by any means, but there is a little more capital, uh, underground."

It was Addie's turn to giggle, so he wondered if she really understood how dangerous life with Ammon Hancock was going to be. He tried to tell her how hard it would be to remain neutral and not object when both sides and all factions stole cattle, grain, and chickens from them. She didn't seem to be listening, though, and he asked her why.

"I agree with you, Am, that it won't be easy, but let's try this: Name our ranch *El Rancho de los Tres Pumas.* Pia told me that there is even a song about me now." She frowned. "What's that word?"

"*El corrido*," he said.

"That's it! Everyone in Salazar's army is singing it. In a bunch of verses, the woman of Ammon 'Ancock kills cougars, drives out wolves, and cures *el cólera*." She folded her hands in her lap, becoming once again the serene and restful woman he loved, married, lost, and kept loving. "Any day now, there will be a verse about raising the dead, I am certain, even though poor Colonel Ochoa is dead. The song will keep us safe enough, Am, and that's all I want for us and our children."

"We'll have children," he assured her.

"Hold that thought," she told him, her face rosy again, and not from whisker burn. "I'm . . . I'm pretty much as regular as clockwork, and I'm a week late. The Salinas' feather bed was awfully fine. Remember?"

How could he forget? He held her a little more gently. "Addie, was this the worst rescue ever?"

"Probably," she told him, unconcerned. She sniffed the air. "The beans are burning."

He shrugged. "Let 'um burn. It'll just be another verse in *el corrido*, where the woman turns burned beans into *pollo en mole*."

She looked at him with some dignity. "You are not taking this *corrido* seriously."

"*Al contrario, chiquita*," he told her, cuddling her close. "You are right. It might save our lives."

For just a moment, she became the uncertain woman again, afraid he could never forgive her. As he watched her expression with all the love in his heart, he saw her smile grow and her face become a mirror of his own love.

"*Who* rescued whom?" she asked.

"Well, I rescued you. Didn't I?"

Addie just smiled.

$\mathscr{E}$PILOGUE

$\mathscr{A}$MMON AND ADDIE walked Blanco to Colonia Juárez the next day, the horse laden with bedding and pots and one chair, because Pia liked Addie. He wasn't aware of it until they passed Pearson—he resisted the urge to check the privy—but Joselito had been paralleling them in the shelter of the trees. Ammon beckoned to him, but the Indian just shook his head. By the time they arrived in Colonia Juárez, he was gone, fading back into the mountains that Ammon knew he would always miss, but which were not safe because of their isolation.

They came into Juárez fearing the worst and thinking of García, but the tree-shaded town straddling the Rio Piedras Verdes was nearly untouched by the turmoil that had sent the colonists fleeing for safety. The clerk from the lumber company had been right—several of Juárez's more contrarian occupants had never left. For a month, they and a handful of Mexican friends had patrolled the deserted streets and kept looting to a minimum.

The Hancocks spent a welcome night under a colony roof, listening to the stories of rebels riding through town and being met by a *federal* force that had taken control of Pearson and drove away the guerillas.

"It's not much protection and who knows how long it will last," their host said that night after Addie had fallen asleep, exhausted and leaning against her husband, but unwilling to go to bed until he came too.

While Addie slept, Brother McDonald told Ammon he had just missed seeing Bishop Bentley and some families that had come back briefly, then left again, driven out by Enrique Portillo and his faction.

"It won't be safe for your wife," he warned.

"I'm staying, and she won't leave me," was his quiet reply.

They moved into a house in Juárez belonging to friends because her father's ranch between Juárez and Dublán seemed a little too far away for safety. When Addie fretted that their friends might not appreciate squatters in their house, Ammon just kissed her. She thumped him when he suggested that she put a note in another canning jar.

By the time ten families returned four months later in January, Addie was showing and wearing Mother Hubbards she had "borrowed" from another house. He thought she might be shy about being seen in her interesting condition, but Addie was hungry for the society of women, who clucked over her and glared at him for keeping her in Mexico.

"She wouldn't leave," he insisted. They didn't believe him until Addie assured them, in her quiet way, that she had created an awful scene when General Salazar himself had tried to get her on the train. "I don't know what got into me," she said so sweetly, but Ammon knew.

They really didn't believe her until the day General Salazar himself rode through Colonia Juárez after spending several months in a hospital in El Paso, recovering from wounds suffered in the Battle of San Joaquin in Sonora. The residents had been wary, but Addie welcomed him into their borrowed house. In all the colonies, Ammon's wife was the only person who ever trusted the general who changed moods so fast. She blushed when the general suggested naming the expected child after him, if it was a boy, but when Betsy came in June, someone unknown left a christening dress on the doorstep.

When more families returned, Ammon and Addie moved onto the Finch Ranch, renamed Rancho de los Tres Pumas. The *corrido* with its many verses singing of the brave woman who killed three lions, drove out wolves, cured cholera, and raised the dead kept them safe, as Addie predicted. The little song of the revolution isn't sung any more, except in remote, mountainous areas where Indians still live.

The fortunes of war spared no one. After Madero's assassination in 1913, General Victoriano Huerta, The Jackal, seized power, declaring himself president of Mexico. His brief and unhappy regime unleashed more factions that raided through the colonies, stealing horses, food, and whatever appeared useful. More colonists left for a short time, but Ammon and Addie were never among them.

The cruelest blow was the loss of Blanco, swept away with other colony horses by followers of Venustiano Carranza, who had sent The Jackal into exile in 1914. For months, Ammon waited for his clever horse to come home and went about tight-lipped. Addie made her own trip to the privy in Pearson and took out enough money to buy him another Arabian, just a colt, but beautiful. He knew better than to argue with the woman who killed three mountain lions, but took the colt to Joselito for safety and came back smiling. When the raids began to die down, the horse became his favorite mount at Tres Pumas.

Joselito visited the ranch several times a year. He listened to what both Hancocks had to tell him about the Book of Mormon, but he remained too skeptical. Two of his sons were not so skeptical. Neither was his daughter, who married one of the Hancock boys and was sealed to him in the Mesa Temple in 1940.

A better businessman than a stockman, Ammon changed Hancock Haulage's name to Tres Pumas, and got his horse and team back from the US Army. After a visit to the privy in 1914, he bought two more wagons and teams, one of which he had to surrender to Pancho Villa or die by firing squad. Two years later when General John Pershing and his expeditionary force went on their fruitless pursuit of Villa, the firm of Tres Pumas and Son (only two years old, but Ammon was optimistic, as always) hauled for the US Army in Mexico and gradually mechanized. By 1920, a fleet of Tres Pumas trucks traveled the gradually improving roads of Chihuahua.

Thomas Finch had been happy to deed over his ranch to his daughter. He never returned to the colony, like others who created new lives in the United States. Ammon's parents put down roots in Springville, Utah, their resettlement made possible by the five hundred dollar down payment Ma extracted from Thomas Finch in return for her son's rescue of his daughter. Finch grudgingly gave the other five hundred dollars to a Mexican woman and her husband, a doctor, who were last seen quarreling with each other on the westbound train from El Paso to Los Angeles.

Addie settled into life on her ranch with her usual serenity, keeping her fears to herself when Ammon freighted for one side or the other, and logging lots of hours on her knees when he was gone. She discovered a certain talent for stock raising after Joselito brought down a portion of the herd hidden in the box canyon in the distant Sierra Madres. Ammon wasn't surprised at her ability. He knew she could do anything she set her mind to. She never became really comfortable with Spanish, though, but her husband and children were good natured about translating.

With the election of General Álvaro Obregón in 1920, after Carranza's assassination, the ten-year revolution tapered off. Life in Colonia Dublán and Colonia Juárez became more stable. On one of his freighting trips west, Ammon stopped in Santa Clarita and asked about Serena Camacho. No one had anything to tell him. Hacienda Chavez had been divided into small farms, as the revolution originally intended; he had to be content that maybe somewhere, Serena *la soldadera* had found her own piece of land.

His greatest joy in life remained Addie Hancock, the woman he loved, married, lost, sort of rescued, and loved again. When he came home from freighting trips, she always seemed to hear his truck and was usually standing on the porch, hand shading her eyes, watching for him. Even when he was gone, she always remembered to run the Mexican flag up the pole by the house and take it down at night.

She had patched the flag he saved from the broken staff in Encarnación, reattaching the snake to the eagle, smoothing the fabric, and sometimes just sitting with it in her lap, remembering desperate days and the kindness of strangers. When the flag wore out and had to be replaced, she kept it in the cedar chest at the foot of their bed, next to the christening dress General Salazar had left for Betsy. When she learned of the general's death by ambush in 1917, she mourned him in her quiet way, even though no one else in the colonies did.

Ammon understood, sitting with her on the porch steps long after the children were sleeping, his arm around her. He could have composed more verses for his wife's *corrido*, verses honoring the brave woman who climbed the steps at Hacienda San Diego and held out her hand to General Salazar, probably saving all their lives; the woman who picked up his Book of Mormon from the dust; the woman who sat with Colonel Ochoa until that good man died.

His woman.

ABOUT THE AUTHOR

Photo by Marie Bryner-Bowles, Bryner Photography

CARLA KELLY is a veteran of the New York and international publishing world. The author of more than thirty novels and novellas for Donald I. Fine Co., Signet, and Harlequin, Carla is the recipient of two Rita Awards (think Oscars for romance writing) from Romance Writers of America and two Spur Awards (think Oscars for western fiction) from Western Writers of America. She is also a recipient of Whitney Awards for *Borrowed Light* and *My Loving Vigil Keeping*.

Recently, she's been writing Regency romances (think *Pride and Prejudice*) set in the Royal Navy's Channel Fleet during the Napoleonic Wars between England and France. She comes by her love of the ocean from her childhood as a Navy brat.

ABOUT THE AUTHOR

Carla's history background makes her no stranger to footnote work, either. During her National Park Service days at the Fort Union Trading Post National Historic Site, Carla edited Friedrich Kurz's fur trade journal. She recently completed a short history of Fort Buford, where Sitting Bull surrendered in 1881.

Following the "dumb luck" principle that has guided their lives, the Kellys recently moved to Wellington, Utah, from North Dakota and couldn't be happier in their new location. In her spare time, Carla volunteers at the Western Mining and Railroad Museum in Helper, Utah. She likes to visit her five children, who live here and there around the United States. Her favorite place in Utah is Manti, located after a drive on the scenic byway through Huntington Canyon.

And why is she so happy these days? Carla doesn't have to write in laundry rooms and furnace rooms now, because she has an actual office.